AN EYE FOR AN EYE—THREE TIMES OVER

Charles Wheeler was a cattle dealer who paid in gold on his trading trips. But his last trip cost him more than gold—the high price was his son's life.

Wheeler blamed himself when he came home and found his little boy lying lifeless in the stable, his squirrel rifle in his limp hand. The three horses were gone, and the gold cached away in the kitchen was missing.

There was only one course of action left as Wheeler saw it. The horses' tracks were clear; they led to three of the despicable Simmons Gang and the notorious outlaw hideout of Sandy Bend.

One lonely intent man set out, riding the shadow land between law and outlaw, following the dangerous borders of justice and blood vengeance.

Outrage at Bearskin Forks

by MERLE CONSTINER

ACE BOOKS

A Division of Charter Communications Inc.
1120 Avenue of the Americas
New York, N.Y. 10036

I

THE FIRST THING Charles Wheeler noticed when he returned to Bearskin Forks, his native town, that night was that they had put a new window in the back of the jailhouse. He came into town from the rear, his horse breasting its way through the saddle-high bottom sage, because that was the shortest route to home and Seth. In the milky light of the Texas moon, he could see that this window was made of woven metal strips instead of spindly bars. It looked twice as strong, twice as good as the old one.

Wheeler was a small man with furrowed cheeks and very pale hazel eyes. He was thirty-two, medium prosperous, but so unconscious of the clothes he wore that he always seemed a little seedy. His livelihood was buying, selling, trading, and shipping cattle. He knew cows and was respected as a fair dealer.

This time he had been gone three weeks, back in the old Llano Estacado country, looking over some yearlings for Wyoming. That was his skill. Picking them up where they had too many, and putting them where they didn't have enough.

His people had been old settlers hereabouts and some Wheeler or other had lived in the area since those long ago Comanche raids. Just below the forks of a creek flowing to the Colorado River a few miles east, a settlement of a few cabins and a store had built up into a thriving cattletown. Hardly anyone added the Forks to its name these days: most called it Bearskin. It was thirty miles away from the county seat, Alice, almost as large as Alice in population, but was tucked away in an isolated pocket of hills and brush.

Wheeler walked his horse down Main Street. The town was dark, sleeping. He turned from Main into Elm, toward home.

The house was dark, as he had expected it to be, for the hour was later than Seth's bedtime. It was a nice house, a little fancier than its neighbors; since Seth's mother had died, Wheeler had done everything he could to bolster the boy's lost sense of security. He adored his ten-year-old son, and the timid child, getting his bearings again, was beginning to show again his old faith in his father.

Inside the stable at the rear of the backyard, Wheeler dismounted, struck a friction match, and lit a lantern.

Seth, in his skimpy little nightgown, lay on the rough planks of the floor in a pool of blood. His new squirrel rifle showed from half under his body.

Wheeler knew that his son was not only dead, but long dead.

He dropped to his knees and felt in vain for a pulse in the boy's wrist.

It was then the great blankness came over Wheeler. When his mind cleared, he was still kneeling and the gray light of predawn suffused the stable. His horse stood patiently beside him.

Wheeler stood up stiffly, and looked around him. There were four stalls. One for Cindy, the mare he had ridden in, one each for a bay, a roan, and a little pony-footed calico, Honeybee. Honeybee, now, or until now, had been Seth's pet, and his wife's favorite mount. Now the stalls were empty. All three were gone.

He looked at the wall. There had been three saddles

hanging there: Wheeler's best, his second best, and Seth's.

He left the stable, circled the house, and entered by the front door.

There was a newelpost in the front hall, with Seth's hat on it. Wheeler climbed the carpeted stairs and searched the bedrooms, one by one. Nothing. He descended the stairs and looked over the parlor, shuttered, never used, stuffy. Nothing. Nothing unusual either in the formal, never-used dining room.

He entered the kitchen. The kitchen had really been their home.

The hearthstone by the fireplace had been pried up and laid aside. The bricklined cavity beneath it was empty. This had been Wheeler's hiding place. In the center of the room was his strongbox, smashed and gaping; the five thousand dollars in double eagles were gone.

Much of Wheeler's back country dickering had to be in cash, in gold. He kept a reserve store in the house under the hearthstone. So it would be handy. He did this because he thought it would be a bad thing for him to draw gold from the bank just before he set out on one of his lonely excursions.

By this habit, he decided coldly, he had killed his son.

He went out into the bursting red sunup of the sleeping prairie town.

He headed for the law.

The sheriff over at Alice had appointed a local resident in Bearskin, a man named Mart Tandy, as an on-the-spot deputy. He had done this for two reasons. First: Bearskin—with its larger than normal share of county violence—was hard to get to in a hurry, and a local man on hand would be a big advantage. And second: if the sheriff himself never laid eyes on Bearskin—that hell-hole part of the county—again, he would be perfectly happy. Wheeler knew both of these men. Sheriff Markham, at Alice, was the better executive, but Deputy Tandy, when you came right down to it, was meaner. In the first place, he didn't seem to like to talk at all; he had been raised in a hard, suspicious school. If someone stopped him on the street, he hardly spoke at all. He just stared at the person's stomach just about where the navel should be, blank-eyed, but pretty wicked.

Tandy lived in a little log cabin faced with unpainted cottonwood boards, at the far end of town. Wheeler knocked on the lonely timber door. And there was Tandy, in the open doorway. It was almost as though he slept standing just inside. He was a sinewy man, with bushy black hair, and a broken nose. He was always wound tight as a spring.

He held a .44 in his hand, and had on pants. He *did* sleep in pants, ready to go.

Wheeler said expressionlessly, "They've killed Seth, and robbed me."

Tandy said nothing. He produced a shirt, and stepped outside, buttoning it.

After Tandy had gazed at the dead boy on the stable floor, expressionlessly, and had listened, seemingly without hearing, to Wheeler's account of the stolen horses and saddles and money, he inspected the inside of the house. He then accompanied Wheeler to the undertaker's home, and stood by while Wheeler made arrangements. It was only when all this had been done that Tandy said, "Mr. Wheeler, come with me."

8

In the alley behind Main Street, the merchants of Bearskin had a hitching lot and meeting place for their rural customers and their families come to town for trading. It was deserted at this hour. Here Tandy and Wheeler sat side by side on a crude bench. Tandy brought out a little bundle of sticky black Mexican cigars, lit one, and offered the bundle to Wheeler. Wheeler shook his head.

"The thing is," Tandy said at last, "I know who did it, but I can't prove it."

When Wheeler could speak, he said, "That's all I want to know, who."

"Did you ever hear of three Waco drifters knowed as the Simmons brothers?"

"No."

Tandy drew slowly on his cigar. "They was in town a short time back. I hear they was asking about you, was it true you sometimes paid off in gold."

"A lot of dealers pay in gold. Any rancher would know that."

"But these fellers ain't ranchers," said Tandy. "Fact is, only one of them is even named Simmons. Oakley, Oakley Simmons. The other two is Childress McGinn and Hibbard Leffingwell, the last knowed mainly as Snake Leffingwell."

"What do they do? Where will I find them?"

"Where you'll find them, nobody knows. What they do, everybody knows. They travel, murder, maim, loot, burn, they do whatever the whim gits into them to do."

A sweatbee lit on Tandy's knee. Tandy watched it light, watched it fly away. "I should have shot 'em, all three," he said mildly.

"When?" said Wheeler.

"When I picked them up," said Tandy. "I picked them

up, put them in jail, and they broke out. That's why the new window. They cost the county a new jailhouse window."

"You mean you arrested them? What for?"

Tandy said, "I told them I was arresting them because they was undesirable to the town. Between you and me, I arrested them out o' curiosity. I thought they'd buck, and I wanted to see if Snake Leffingwell was as fast with his gun as he was blowed up to be. But they come docile."

After a pause, Wheeler said, "And they came to town just for my money?"

"Who knows?" said Tandy. "I'd say yes, probably, likely. Your house, if they'd heard about it, musta made them drool. A ten-year-old boy is a heap safer to go up agin than a bank."

While Wheeler thought this over, visualizing it, Tandy said, "They probably went for the stable first, saddling the horses for a quick getaway, and Seth heard 'em, and run out, and got himself killed."

When he could control his voice, Wheeler said, "Describe them for me."

"No," said Tandy slowly. "And you stay out of it. This is my affair."

Wheeler made no retort to this. He got wordlessly to his feet.

Later, about ten o'clock, Seth was buried in the churchyard. There was no one present but Wheeler, and Tandy, and the minister.

And Seth.

II

WHEELER WENT BACK to the house on Elm Street, and locked up.

This could never be his home again, he knew. It was packed with phantoms and memories: all unbearable. He began upstairs, locking windows, bolting shutters, leaving everything as it was at the moment, leaving his bed made, as it was, waiting for him to come home from the Llano Estacado country, leaving Seth's bed mussed, as Seth had left it to scurry out to the stable. Finally, on the front doorstep, he locked the front door, and there he stood, with the baling wire key ring in his hand. What to do with them? He was going to be away from Bearskin, likely for a long time.

Then suddenly, out of nowhere, the image of old Judge Venable came into his mind.

When Wheeler was a young sprout, Judge Venable, Bearskin Forks' Justice of Peace, was his father's closest friend. In their day they had fought bandidos and Comanches together, broken new ground together, and had eventually retired more or less together to town. Wheeler had spent many an hour on the Venable back porch, making kites, or straightening fishhooks, with Tabby, Tabitha, the Judge's daughter, or maybe just arguing with her.

He saw the Judge infrequently now, and Tabby, since she had married that fireball young lawyer and gone with him to St. Louis, never.

The Venable small-framed house, with a double-decked veranda across its front, gleaming snowy-white, sat back on a green lawn in a cool cloud of green and gray shadow, beneath the swooping branches of an ancient grove of trees. The Judge sat in the yard in the shade of a giant elm. He was half asleep when Wheeler came up, his blue-veined hands laced across his rotund paunch, his spidery glasses askew on his rosy nose. Suddenly, excitedly, affectionately, he called, "Charley!"

Wheeler came to a stop before him.

The Judge said, "We heard about Seth."

He said no more, offered no condolences. Wheeler thought, *He's too close to me to overtalk it, to be mealy-mouthed about it.*

Wheeler handed him the keys. "To my house," he said. "I'd appreciate it if you would keep them for me. I may be gone for some time."

The old man put the keys in his lap. "Where are you going, Charley?"

"On a manhunt."

"Yes," said the old judge. "Yes."

A mist of gnats gathered in a sun mote before the old man's bleary eyes. "Can I tell you a little story?" he asked.

"Of course," said Wheeler respectfully.

"It's about a small adventure my brother and I had, back about the time you were born. My brother's family and mine lived in two cabins, side by side, up on the San Saba, if you could call it living. We had two mules. One night a couple of larcenous scum came through at night and stole them. We simply couldn't exist without those mules. Next morning, my brother and I set out to track them. He was a better tracker than I was. We separated. He found them."

The old man paused. "He found them. Both the mules and the men. The men killed him."

When Wheeler said nothing, the Judge said, "So you see, I lost both my brother and the mules."

Still Wheeler remained silent.

"Manhunt is a mighty loose term," said the Judge. "And here's something else. I never could understand how those thieves managed to murder my brother. He was the one who had right on his side, not them. He was the one who had a brilliant future ahead of him, not them. All they had was two to one against him, and superior gun skill. It doesn't seem logical."

All at once, an idea came to Wheeler. He said, "The Simmons gang broke out of jail here. Right?"

"Right," said Judge Venable.

"And before they broke out, they had to be put in."

"Correct."

"Then they must have been brought up before you when they were charged."

"I do so believe."

"I want you to tell me what each of them looks like, describe them to me in detail."

"And send you galloping off to join my brother?"

"I have no choice," said Wheeler softly. "And you have no choice but to tell me."

"If you put it that way, all right," said Judge Venable. "Oakley Simmons, the leader, is about six feet two, thin as a rail, with a stoop to his shoulders, red-haired. Childress McGinn is short, barrel-chested, with curly black hair. Snake Leffingwell looks like an average cowboy, except he's got a puffy lower lip, like he's got a quid of tobacco under it. I don't see how you'll ever know them from this feeble description."

"One way, it'll help me sure," said Wheeler. "If I catch them all together."

"Let's hope you don't."

"Let's hope I do."

As Wheeler turned to leave, the Judge said, "Tabby's back."

Wheeler came to a halt. "Is she well?"

"Not too well," said the Judge. "But well enough, I guess, all things considered. She's been through terrible days. Up in St. Louis, her husband got drunk and fell off a steamboat."

When Wheeler left the Judge, he went directly to Main Street.

He asked questions up and down Main Street. *Did anyone know anything at all about the Simmons gang, individually, or as a group. Their habits of life? Their kinfolk? Had anyone seen them in town? Had anyone seen them leave?*

He did not mention his murdered son, and the boy was not mentioned to him.

He described the stolen horses and saddles in detail. *Had they been seen? Where? With anybody?*

He visited all places of natural assembly and asked questions, in the livery stables, saloons, stores. He talked to citizens sunning themselves on sidewalk chairs and benches before the store-fronts. He interrogated loafers by the public watering trough.

The Simmons brothers were known by name, it seemed, but that was all. Nobody knew anything further, or wanted to know anything further.

People looked at Wheeler sometimes with sympathy, but mostly with fear.

Three hours of this brought him nothing at all.

He saved Louey Hackett for last. Louey, even more

14

than Deputy Tandy, was the one man in Bearskin who made it his business to know all arrivals and departures, to know every stranger and to learn as much as possible about a stranger's background. Louey ran a card room in the back of an abandoned dance hall, which he called, *The Shorthorn Social Club*. It was a pretty out-at-the-elbows congregating hole. Wheeler didn't like the place or the-man, but he had no choice. The front of the dance hall was boarded up, and only a door at the back led into the card room.

When Wheeler stepped inside, he found the room deserted at this hour. There were four or five tables, empty but for Hackett sitting at one, brazenly practicing card manipulation. Hackett was a brawny man with a meaty face and mile-deep eyes.

He put down the cards and said, "Charley, I'm sorry. What can I do?"

Wheeler knew that he meant it, and suddenly liked him.

Wheeler said, "I want to know about the Simmons brothers, so-called."

"You don't want much," said Hackett amiably.

"What do you mean?" said Wheeler.

"I mean this," said Hackett. "If I was to tell you something that would help you locate them, and there was a survivor, that survivor would come back and plug me if it was the last thing he ever did. This isn't a probability, it's a certainty. Most outlaws live for cold cash, and steer shy of the risk that comes from personal vengeance. The Simmons brothers are outlaws, their own personal style of outlaws—because they think it's fun. And vengeance would be as much fun to them as cold cash, maybe more."

"So I'm wasting my time here, too?" said Wheeler.

"I don't know anything," said Hackett. "Believe it or not, just as you choose."

Wheeler started for the door.

Behind him, Hackett said in a mild voice, "Don't lump me with the others. I'm on your side."

Wheeler closed the door behind him, and returned to Main Street.

About the first person he saw was Tabby, backing out of *Ellenby's Dry Goods*, with a stack of bundles. Even then, when it seemed her back was to him, she managed to recognize him before he really recognized her.

She was even more beautiful than he had remembered. She was in mourning, in black taffeta and a St. Louis veil, but nobody could ever put that massive braid of straw-colored hair, which gleamed down over her shoulder, in mourning.

Wheeler said, "I was sorry to hear about your husband." He couldn't quite remember his name, and was afraid to take a crack at it.

She met his eyes defiantly, ashamed that her husband had been so drunk, trying to face it out in front of him, and said, "Steamboats are dangerous."

"They sure are," said Wheeler earnestly. "Can I help you home with those packages?"

"Thank you, no," she said, smiling. "Truthfully, I think bundles are fun." Suddenly serious, she said, "You are deep in our hearts, Charles."

He made no answer.

She said, "My father and I just got back from the county seat. The news about Seth was the first thing that met us. I never knew Seth, he was born after I left, but I knew his mother and loved her."

Wheeler said nothing. She had had her tragedy, too.

"What are you going to do?" Tabby asked.

"That depends," he said.

When they had separated, and he was passing the Slater House, the town's weathered and rambling hotel, Louey Hackett came up to him at a fast walk and stopped him.

"I've been looking for you," said Hackett. "You know Jude Rawlings?"

Jude Rawlings was a small rancher, over by the Colorado River. Wheeler, wondering what was coming, said, "Slightly. I mean, by sight only. Why?"

"For a year he's owed me a debt," said Hackett. "But we won't go into that. The point is that just now he's paid that debt. He's given us what might be a little information."

"Us?"

"A few minutes ago, I was talking to him. He would talk a little different to me than he would talk to you. Right now, though, he's agreed to meet you."

"What's he got to say?"

"Maybe nothing, maybe a lot."

"Where is he?"

"Waiting for you. By the watering trough in front of the Tulip Rose Restaurant."

Jude Rawlings was an unskillful, hard-luck rancher with a perpetual complaint against the world. He dressed like a rancher, talked like a rancher, but essence-of-rancher had been left out of his makeup somehow, and, though he worked hard, things never quite jibed for him. For bad weather, sterility in calving, bad market prices, he blamed everybody, including his wife. When Wheeler approached and stood beside him, Rawlings said, "You kin turn and go away. I've changed my mind. I ain't got nothing to say to you."

After a pause, Wheeler said, "I've had a mighty bad

ten hours. I've had about all I can take. I don't believe I want any trouble from you, too."

His manner was calm, almost serene, but as he stood there in the golden sunlight there was something weary and very sinister about him.

Uneasily, Rawlings said, "What did Louey Hackett tell you?"

"Just talk," said Wheeler.

"It's likely nothing, nothing at all," said Rawlings, trying to dismiss the whole thing with a superficial chuckle. "Nothing to get excited over. But here it is."

He started by explaining that he kept a few sheep. It embarrassed him terrifically to even mention it. He kept them, he said, because his woman was fond of mutton. He kept these sheep over at a rocky end of his place, and coyotes had been getting the lambs; the whole world was against him, not only weather and humans and such, but animals, too. Coyotes.

He went out to look around and found a dry wash that was just a hive of coyote dens. He spread his poison, but as it was about sundown, he decided to spend the night and recheck in the morning to be sure he hadn't missed any. He slept that night up out of the wash, back a little on the prairie, a couple of dozen feet from the wedge of the wash. Then, just as he had told Louey Hackett a few minutes ago, a little past midnight he heard horses. They were passing him down in the wash.

"I woke up," he said, "and looked around, and went back to sleep."

"You didn't worry about this?"

"Why should I? If I couldn't see them, they couldn't see me. I try never to worry about nothing."

"But the next morning you looked into it?" said Wheeler.

"Well, naturally. Midnight travelers, on my land? I went down into the wash."

On the wash bed he had found tracks, all right. Tracks that hadn't been there before.

"How many?" asked Wheeler.

"A mess of them."

"That's no way to answer a question," said Wheeler. "How many?"

"I already told you. A mess. You're a hard man to talk to."

"Was one of them a little pony-foot, with a worn shoe on its near forefoot?"

"How should I know," said Rawlings, annoyed. "Reading sign is for Indians and little boys. I always been a heap too busy to meddle with that nonsense."

Wheeler gazed at him in amazement.

"Not coyotes," said Wheeler laconically.

"Oh, they wasn't coyotes," said Rawlings. "I can swear to that. They was wearing horseshoes, and that's good enough for me."

Wheeler said briskly, "We're going out there. Right now. I'm going to get my horse. You get yours, too, and meet me here in five minutes."

Rawlings pursed his lips in hesitation. "I can't say yes to that and I can't say no. I'll have to study it over. I ain't exactly shore I'm ready to leave town right now."

"You're ready," said Wheeler shortly. "Move!"

Rawlings moved. But Wheeler had to say this for him. He didn't dash. He just sort of seeped.

Wheeler got his horse. He got some provisions, too, and lashed them behind his saddle.

He had no idea how long he might be gone.

III

WHEN THEY REACHED IT, a couple of hours later, Wheeler saw that this end of Rawlings' ranch was pretty sorry—thin sage, thinner grass, and scattered plate rock. The dry wash itself was deep, and fairly narrow at its bed; its almost sheer sides were crumbling with channeled, eroded clay, and blotched with knots of dry grass tufts. The tracks were there, all right.

Dismounted, they examined them, Wheeler on hands and knees, Rawlings standing beside him, disdainful, skeptical, and a little scared.

The sign was poor and old, and sheep had almost obliterated it, but it was there, in faint, almost invisible traces.

There were two sets of new shoes—the bay and the roan had just been to the blacksmith—and a third set, worn in that certain way. There was no doubt about that third set. These tracks had been left by the little calico, Honeybee.

Wheeler got to his feet. Rawlings, watching his face, said, "This what you was hopin' for?"

"Yes," said Wheeler.

"Yes?" said Rawlings. The affirmative answer really frightened him. Wheeler could tell he wanted no part of the Simmonses.

Rawlings said, "Well, I'd better be getting along. My woman will be expecting me."

Almost instantly, it seemed, he was gone. This time, he didn't seep. They had come down into the wash by a side gully, and even after Rawlings had ridden up the gully and disappeared on the prairie, Wheeler could hear his frantic diminishing hoofbeats.

Wheeler, again in his saddle, started up the wash to trail his horses, but the tracks were few and far between; the bottom of the wash bed changed abruptly to loose shifting leaf rock.

One thing he knew, though: at this stretch at least, the riders had been forced to stay in the ravine, for now he came to a section with no side gullies, no avenues of exit.

Then the left side of the ravine broke away emptily to the east, in a low-pitch slope of silt and pebbles to the prairie above, and here the three horses had ascended.

For about twenty-five feet or so he got good clear impressions, and saw that they had gone up above.

There was no doubt about this. And there was no doubt about something else, too. These horses were unmounted. Riderless. Simply running loose.

The rage that came over Wheeler almost paralyzed him.

Now he knew for certain that he was up against an experienced and cunning crew.

It was a good guess that the Simmons gang had ridden his horses as far as the ravine, had then turned them loose, let them run free, and had taken off either with new mounts or on foot.

The men he was searching for could be anywhere. Now they had days, miles, headstart.

He wondered whether he should backtrack and try to trail these desperados, or continue forward, and reclaim his stolen horses.

The men, of course, were gone. He doubted seriously

if anyone now could trail them at this stage of the game. Especially when they were so careful, as he had seen, in confusing their trail.

And these horses were more than horses to him. One had belonged to his wife. All had been pets of Seth.

He picked up his reins and moved up the slope.

Almost immediately, up on the prairie, the horses scattered. They had been grazing, Wheeler knew.

He set to work patiently following them.

They scattered, but never too far from each other. Raggedly, loosely, they vaguely stayed together. Wheeler thought the roan would surely impose his personality on the others, and lead them.

Wheeler now began to concentrate on the roan's tracks only. As sundown approached, he soon saw he was right. The others would disperse, wander, and, after a bit, halfheartedly reassemble about their leader.

The sun had gone down, and the prairie was luminous in gilt afterglow, that brief interval which preceded dark, when Wheeler rode up to a big pecan tree in a small ranchyard.

A shabby rancher, his wife, and wiry little boy were sitting on kitchen chairs beneath the tree, enjoying the thin dry evening breeze before retiring. There was a small log cabin, a big log barn, and, between the barn and cabin, joined to them, was a pole corral. On one of the corral posts was Seth's saddle.

Wheeler introduced himself to them, dismounted at their invitation, and told them the whole story. They were overcome, stunned with grief for him. He had never seen such people.

"They're in the barn, all of 'em," said the rancher. "Horses and saddles, and the horses is in better shape than when they wandered in. Some had long brier scratches, and I doctored 'em. We been using 'em. What do I owe you for their use?"

"What do I owe you for their care and keep?" asked Wheeler.

"Hah!" said the woman. "Just try and pay us something."

"I don't have my bills of sale to prove ownership," said Wheeler. "I left town in a hurry."

"I never went much for writin'," said the rancher. "I'm afraid us here goes mainly by the looks of a man."

"That's a bad practice," said Wheeler sternly.

"I know," said the man sadly. "But it's a habit I cain't seem to get out of. This-here's my boy, Griffin. Griffin Darnley. We're the Tennessee Darnleys. Would you care for Griffin to help you take 'em back, in the morning, after we've fed you and slept you?"

Wheeler fixed his eyes on the little boy and stared.

After a pretty long period, the woman said, "What's so interestin' about Griffin? You cain't seem to take yore eyes off him."

"Sh-h-h!" said Mr. Darnley. "The gentleman ain't a-studyin' Griffin. He means no offense. He's just thinking over some problem."

And Wheeler was indeed thinking over a problem, and had come to a conclusion.

Huntsville was the answer. Up at Huntsville, the state penitentiary, they might very well have information on Simmons and McGinn and Leffingwell. According to his figuring at his present bearings, Huntsville, up in Walker County, must be about one hundred and fifty miles generally northeast, by a little east.

To Mr. Darnley, Wheeler said, "How do I get to Huntsville?"

"Gracious, son," said Mr. Darnley. "I ain't never even heard of it."

"You mean Bearskin?" said Mrs. Darnley. "Is that another name for Bearskin?"

"No, it isn't," said Wheeler politely. "But it should be."

"He's already told us he come from Bearskin," said Mr. Darnley, kindly reproving his wife. "He'd shorely know how to git back to where he come from."

"Griffin here," said Wheeler, pointing to the boy. "Does he know the way to Bearskin?"

"I sure do," said the boy. "That's where I lay in my stock of hoarhound candy."

"When you git it," said his papa.

"When I git it," said the boy.

Wheeler said, "Thank you for your offer of hospitality, but I'm moving against time and must be getting on. Now, I'd appreciate it if in the next few days Griffin would take my horses and saddles into Bearskin and leave them in the care of a Judge Venable." He produced a five dollar gold piece.

"Of course, the boy'll do it," said Mr. Darnley. "And put your money away. The Darnleys have never got around to working on that principle."

Wheeler said, "In my estimation, there's nothing lower than a father who will take hoarhound candy away from a growing boy!"

Darnley grinned. His gums and teeth were yellow from home-ground snuff. He said, "Take it, Griffin. Thank you, Mr. Wheeler. I have a feelin' you'll always be welcome here. And when I say welcome, I mean just that and no questions asked."

That night, Wheeler put Cindy, his mare, on a long picket and slept by a spring, about nine miles northeast of the Darnley cabin.

Next morning, he waded her across the water pans and shallow rapids of the Colorado at Cherry Point Ford, and reached the opposite bank about nine. The side he had just left had been high prairie, well above all danger from the river's overflow, but here the bank was low, with barren gravelly ridges. All fords, at all times, had been dangerous. In the old days they had been favorite spots for Indian ambushes. Now they were notorious as bandit and outlaw rendezvous.

Beyond the low gravel ridges was a narrow strip of pebbly bottom land, then a mat of wild grapevines, with red grapes as big as the ball of his thumb, and then came an outer lip of massive pine timber. Wheeler was glad to get into the timber, out of sight. Glad to leave the ford behind him.

The pine continued around him for days, and he learned to love it. The forest of resinous masts around him, the filtered sunlight, the silence, the cushion of deep needles, muting Cindy's hooves. The pine stopped eventually, like the slice of a knife. He passed through chaparral. He crossed vast tablelands of sage. He skirted mesquite thickets. The people he contacted, and asked questions of, were mighty few and far between. But finally he found that he was well into Walker County. He should have guessed it, for he was in green rolling hills now. Like Virginia hills, he'd always heard them compared to.

The molten, blistering sun announced midmorning from a glaring sky, when he rode down the street at Huntsville.

This was a very old town, much older even than Bearskin, for the great Sam Houston had spent his declining years on his front porch here.

The penitentiary was on a narrow road in a small hollow, with its own little graveyard across the road from it. At the corner of the prison road, which T'd into the public road, was a shed of squared logs, partly covered with crêpe myrtle, an oak chair with a raw-hide bottom by its doorpost, now empty. Wheeler passed it, took the prison road to the long, squat gray building behind it. At the prison gate, he dismounted, and hitched Cindy to a ringbolt in the wall.

In five minutes, he was in the warden's office. Because he was without official standing, it took him another five minutes to talk the warden into believing him and trusting him.

It was a bleak gray office, and the warden was a bleak gray man. Wheeler sat across from the warden's desk and told his story and made his requests.

The warden said, "So you want any information, any information at all about each and every member of the Simmons gang?"

"If you please," said Wheeler.

"This is very irregular," said the warden, smiling faintly. "How do I know that actually you're not a friend or relative, trying to aid and abet someway?"

"Well, I'm not," said Wheeler, trying not to lose his temper.

"Did you say you're a U.S. Deputy Marshal?"

"I certainly said nothing of the kind. I said I am an independent cattle dealer."

"That's what I thought you said. That you're a U.S. Deputy Marshal. In that case, I'll be glad to co-operate."

He called an assistant, gave an order to him when he entered the room, and they waited in silence until the assistant returned. He carried a large folder labeled:

SIMMONS GANG. Placing it before Wheeler, he departed.

Before Wheeler touched it, he said, "I'd like to ask you two questions. Were they here with you for a while?"

"For a while."

"For what?" said Wheeler.

"Murder."

"Why did you ever release them?"

"We didn't release them. They killed a guard and broke. In fact we have a dead-or-alive out on them, on each of them. It was Leffingwell who engineered the break. In fact, he claims no prison in the world can hold him."

Wheeler opened the folder and took out a sheaf of papers. He read the pages carefully, one by one, making brief notes. When he had finished the dossier, his notes read:

SIMMONS GANG:

Simmons, Oakley, leader.

His record is a lengthy one, ranging in and out a dozen jails, including everything from rape, through mayhem, to paymaster robbery.

Description:

Height: six-three

Hair: sticky red

Weight: 133 lbs.

General Comment: Hunched shoulders, tubercular appearance.

Remarks:

All these men state they are from Waco. In fact, none of them is from Waco. Simmons is from the Wind River country, Wyoming; Leffingwell from the Cherokee country in the Public Land Strip; and McGinn from Alice, county seat of Linton County.

Their backgrounds are very indistinct.

Each of these men is extremely dangerous.

The warden watched Wheeler lay aside the Oakley Simmons records. He said, "They are nearer animals—beasts—than any humans I ever laid eyes on."

McGinn, Childress, second man in charge

This man has the worst record of the three, and is thought to be insane. (Wheeler did not bother to itemize the shocking crimes.)

Description:

Height: five-one

Hair: jet black, very curly and tangled

Weight: 140 lbs. Very big chest.

General Comment:

There must be special caution with Childress McGinn. This man, sane or insane, has been frequently acknowledged to have a greater intellect than many of his adversaries. He is certainly the most savage and bloodthirsty of the three.

Preparing to continue, Wheeler glanced into the folder. It was empty. "Where is the Leffingwell information?" he asked. "Don't you have anything on Hibbard Snake Leffingwell?"

"The Leffingwell file is in another cabinet," said the warden. "I don't think you're interested in that."

"Why not?"

"It's closed. Leffingwell is dead."

"Dead?"

"I received a telegram to that effect two days ago," said the warden.

"How did he die?" asked Wheeler.

"He was killed in a gunfight, resisting arrest, by a deputy sheriff named Tandy."

"Tandy! Tell me about it."

"I don't know anything about it," said the warden. "I just received this telegram from Tandy, saying to close him out. Just what I've told you, and nothing else."

Things were moving fast. Wheeler said, "When did they kill your guard and get away from here?"

"A month ago."

"We had them in jail at Bearskin a couple of weeks ago," said Wheeler.

"My Gawd!" said the warden.

"And they broke out there, too."

"That would be Oakley Simmons. He says no jail can hold him. What were they in for?"

"As undesirables."

"Well, they're certainly that," said the warden dryly.

"What I don't understand," said Wheeler, "is this: Why hadn't Tandy been told they were red-hot? Why hadn't a dodger gone out on them?"

"A dodger did go out on them, of course," said the warden. "But it probably went to Alice, instead of Bearskin, because Alice is the county seat. How often does Tandy get up to Alice?"

"Not often," said Wheeler. "They say he loathes and despises it."

Wheeler thanked the warden and left. In twenty

minutes, he was on his return to Bearskin, backtracking the route by which he had come. Alice was his big goal now, but first he wanted a little talk with Judge Venable.

IV

It was about five o'clock in the afternoon, days later, when he came out of the pine forest and saw before him the Colorado River and Cherry Point Ford.

His mare breasted her way through the tangle of wild grape vines, crossed the low gravel ridges, and splashed through the shallow rapids and water pan pools to the farther bank.

Here, an apron of flat chalky pebbles came down to the river's edge. Behind this beach, sharp time-splintered limestone shards, with rocky rubble at their bases, showed the entry to the winding passage that led up to the high prairie to the west. The setting sun hit this stony scarp from behind and laid shadows of the shattered rocks across the pebble, almost to the water.

Abruptly, one of these shadows altered. One instant, it was the silhouette of a sharp rocky peak, and the next it seemed to expand, somehow, to inflate, losing its sharpness.

Wheeler threw himself from his saddle crouched tightly behind a boulder, and a rifle shot slammed out, spewing gravel by his bootheel.

Someone in front of him, high at the Prairie's edge, had hoped to kill him. Had hoped, and failed, and furiously touched off his gun at a poor second choice.

Wheeler, sixgun in hand, waited. His attacker must do one of three things: retreat, wait for another try, or advance and flush Wheeler out.

Wheeler waited a cramped half hour behind his boulder. Down on the beach, the protuberance had withdrawn from the rock shadow, and the shadow was again clean and sharp.

Though he was certain the man had gone, yet he waited another half hour. The danger now was mutual, to attacker as well as victim. The sneak attack had failed; the sneak had gone out of the punch, and the victim had been warned. For another thing, before long it would be dark, and all men are equal in the dark.

The man, bushwhacking, had wanted an advantage, and had lost it.

Wheeler got cautiously to his feet. There was no sign of life along the top of the scarp.

The man had lost his advantage. But would it make any difference to him? He had tried it once, he could try it again—another time, somewhere else, where it would be safer.

Wheeler made a search of the terrain. First, he located the perch from which the man had shot—but this had been a very cunning man, sign-wise, and no tracks whatever had been left. Deciding it would be useless, to search for sign of a hidden campfire, from such a careful man, he returned to the beach.

He was convinced, though, that somewhere there would be a relic of a campfire.

This hadn't been a chance traveler, who, passing by, and having nothing better to do, had taken a potshot at him. This, he felt in his bones, was a man who had waited here for him. Waited days, maybe as many as five days.

And this man's name, he was also convinced, was either Childress McGinn, or Oakley Simmons.

Something, maybe it was instinct, kept insisting the name was Childress McGinn.

The word had got out somehow, likely through Darnley, that Wheeler was Huntsville bound.

And now the Simmons gang had turned. They—at least one of them, McGinn probably—had declared hidden war on him.

Well, that was just as good. That was the way he wanted it.

Now that things had begun to tighten so drastically and surprisingly, now that the gang had suddenly begun to show signs of strain, Wheeler ate his supper— a can of pink salmon and four crackers—standing on the beach by his mare's neck. He mounted immediately afterward and continued his ride without camp or rest.

He rode throughout the night. Dark had fallen when he passed the Darnleys'. From the Darnleys' he took a shortcut across the prairie, passing Jude Rawlings' at a distance, and arrived in Bearskin, almost knocked out from exhaustion, about ten o'clock. He stabled his mare at the Magnolia House, reserved a room, and headed immediately for the Venables.

Though most of the town was already dark, its inhabitants early to bed, a light showed in Judge Venable's study window, gilding the shrubbery by the windowsill, for, as Wheeler had heard, the Judge was a late and hungry reader. Wheeler ascended to the porch, tugged at the bellpull. After a moment, Judge Venable himself, in robe and carpet slippers, spectacles and book, welcomed him and led him back into the study.

Sitting in this study again was to Wheeler like taking a return visit into his boyhood. In the old days when he had been here sometimes with Tabby, he had always been in breathless awe. Same turkey red rug, thinner now; same clumsy black furniture, battered now; same floor-to-ceiling bookshelves pleasantly smelling in musty old leather. Same enormous lamp on the table, with its shade of green and ruby stained glass, and fringe of copper beads. The Judge set out a decanter and glasses, sank into an easy chair, and got an ancient, oily pipe going. He said wryly, "Well, at least you're home."

"But not for long," said Wheeler.

"I hear you've been to Huntsville," said the Judge.

"And where did you hear that?" asked Wheeler, annoyed.

"I think it was at the barbershop," said the Judge, puffing slowly. "But it may have been at the feedstore."

"Or maybe both," said Wheeler. He first told of the attempted bushwhack at the ford, and then began at the beginning and told of his interview with the warden.

"The information on the Huntsville records," declared Wheeler, "states that Childress McGinn has ties with Alice. Could it be that they are holed up there at the county seat, only thirty miles to the north?"

"Oh, I wouldn't think so," said Judge Venable. "Would you?"

"Nevertheless, I'm going to Alice and try to run them down," said Wheeler. "I came to ask you where to start. Do you know of any McGinns there, or around there?"

The Judge pondered. Finally, he said, "None."

"None?"

"Not at the moment. There was a family of squatter McGinns, a disreputable old man and his son, who lived up the Little Oro Box Canyon a couple of miles out of town. But the old man caught gangrene from a rusty steel trap, and the boy, eighteen then, pulled out and disappeared. I hear the community was mighty glad to see him go."

"And the boy's name was Childress," said Wheeler.

"Well, yes," said the Judge reluctantly. "But get out of this thing, Charles."

"Why didn't you tell me this in the beginning?" said Wheeler angrily. "I swear, you can't even trust your best friends these days."

Tabby came quietly into the room, and took a chair just inside the door. Not exactly joining them, not intruding—away, but not too far away.

Wheeler said, "Hello, Tabby." She still looked pale, but not as pale as she had looked on the street with her bundles.

She said, "Hello, Charles. I hear you're a running man these days."

"To, not from, there's a big difference, of course," said the Judge, trying to head off any unpleasantness in the conversation.

"There's mighty little difference at all, in my opinion," she said. "A running man is a man who has thrown away everything else in life for just that. He doesn't care if his meat is raw, or if there's no food at all, or the orphanage burns, or smallpox stalks, or boys and girls take moonlight walks. All he worries about is his daily quota of running. No matter what happens, he's got to get that done."

"What's wrong with her?" asked Wheeler, in an aside to the Judge.

"I'm not sure," said the Judge. "But I think it's gastric."

Tabby got up and left the room.

After a moment or two, Wheeler rose to leave. He

35

said, "The tell me Snake Leffingwell was back in town."

"That's right," said the Judge. "He sure was."

"I wonder why he came back?"

"I doubt if he could even answer that question himself."

"What do you mean?"

"I mean," said the Judge, "that he was dead at least a couple of days before he came back. Tandy brought him back, across a packhorse."

"What happened?" asked Wheeler. "Did Tandy explain it?"

"Does Tandy ever explain anything? Both of them, the live man and the dead man, had inch thick travel-dust all over them."

"And there was no doubt it was Leffingwell?"

"No doubt whatever. I personally can testify to that. Snake Leffingwell, or rather his mortal remains. With a cluster of bullet holes about the size and color of a raspberry tart precisely over his heart."

Judge Venable walked with Wheeler to the front door. Out on the porch, he said, "The Darnley child brought around your horses, Honeybee and the others. They're out back, in the stable. They've never been in better hands. Tabby tends them and grooms them as though they were the children she never had."

Wheeler said, "Thank you," raised his hand shoulder-high in a farewell salute, and walked away into the night.

In the lobby of the Magnolia House, he stopped at the desk for his key and asked the clerk to wake him about an hour before dawn; that would be around three o'clock. He didn't say so to the clerk, but that would put him in Alice around sundown next day. He said good night, and mounted the steep stairs beside the desk, to the upper corridor.

High on the corner where the corridor turned, was a bracket and lamp, with a tin reflector behind the lamp chimney. Standing against the wall, under the lamp, was a frail little man, turtle-faced, in shabby patched denim. Beside him was a boy just like the man in miniature, looking heartbroken, holding a rumpled paper sack.

It was Mr. Darnley, of the Tennessee Darnleys, and his son, Griffin.

Darnley said, "Give the gentleman back his candy, Griffin."

The boy poked the sack at Wheeler. Wheeler locked his hands behind his back, to show he wanted no part of this, whatever it was. He said, "Oh, no, you don't. What is this all about?"

Darnley looked grim. "He brought yore horses in, like you asked. What did he do then? Why, he went to the store, bought himself a quarter's worth of hoarhound and a pair of new copper-toed brogans. When the storekeeper saw the five dollar gold piece, he asked the boy where he had got it, and the boy made a big showoff speech and told him all about you, and Huntsville, and everything."

Calmly, Wheeler said, "What was wrong with that?"

"In my mind, knowratin'-off another man's private business is jest about the sorriest thin' a feller kin do in public. The boy has to give you back the candy. He's wore his shoes, and the store probably won't take 'em back, but he'll make that up to you, too. Not in money, we seldom git our hands on any money. But in pelts. And I'm afraid they're goin' to be squirrel pelts."

Wheeler turned to the child. "What's your opinion of this?"

"Whatever Papa says," said the boy. "And I'm sorry I done it. Papa says you might have been on a secret cattle deal, f'rinstance, and didn't want no rival to know it."

Wheeler said, "Tear off a piece of that sack, son. No, I don't want the sack itself, just a piece."

He put the paper against the wall, took a pencil stub from his pocket, and wrote: *Tabby, give this boy or his father the roan and Seth's saddle. These people are the Tennessee Darnleys. Take a good look at them while you're at it. They are mighty fine people. C. W.*

"Take this paper to the Venables," said Wheeler, handing it to the father. "It makes young Griffin a present of my roan and Seth's saddle."

"Forever, for free, and for keeps?" said the boy, pop-eyed.

"Yes," said Wheeler.

"I'll have to think this over," said Darnley. "I always been a little slow about takin' charity."

"It isn't charity," said Wheeler.

"Then what is it?" said Darnley.

Wheeler said, "If you lost your little boy, wouldn't you try to make it up to other little boys?"

Darnley thought this over carefully, then nodded.

"Well, then," said Wheeler. "The roan was Seth's special pet."

They stood paralyzed. Wheeler walked to his room, and fast.

The room, Number 17, at the end of the hall, showed lamplight through its keyhole and under its doorsill. Without slowing his step, Wheeler entered. Deputy Sheriff Tandy, boots, hat, and all, was stretched out on his bed, waiting for him. "How did everyone know I was in town?" Wheeler asked. "I've scarcely got in."

"How does everyone know it's going to be a cold winter or a hot summer?" said Tandy. "Mother Nature spreads the word." He swung his boots to the floor and sat erect on the edge of the bed.

When Wheeler simply looked annoyed, Tandy amplified. "Seems like these days people are a heap interested in you. Since you've put on warpaint."

"I haven't put on warpaint," said Wheeler.

"That seems to be the general opinion."

"I'm just trying to finish unfinished business," said Wheeler.

"I've told you before," said Tandy, "and I'll tell you again. I'd take it kindly if you'd leave said business to me. And go back to your cattle dealing."

"And you came here to tell me that?"

"I came here, and waited forty minutes, to tell you exactly that," said Tandy lifelessly. "I hear you've been to Huntsville."

"Yes."

"You get to fiddling around, not knowing what you're doin'," said Tandy, "and you could mess this thing up. I'd hate to have to take you in for obstructin' justice."

"I'd dearly love to have you try," said Wheeler, getting suddenly mad.

Wheeler's anger amused Tandy. He asked almost humanly, "Did you learn anything at Huntsville?"

"Yes," said Wheeler. "Two things. I learned that one of the Simmons gang, Childress McGinn, once lived in Alice."

"I could have told you as much and spared you the trip," said Tandy. "For what it's worth. What was the other thing?"

39

"I heard you killed Snake Leffingwell while I was away."

"I won't try to deny it," said Tandy. "Ah, yes."

Wheeler studied him. Black bushy hair, old-time style, flat eyes, thin sleepy mouth. He seemed neither elated nor excited at the mention of the Leffingwell thing, scarcely interested in the subject. It seemed to be only a memory now, and hardly that.

Now, in this roundabout way, they had come to the thing which so fired Wheeler. The thing he wanted to know all about so avidly. Keeping his voice utterly bland, he asked, "How did it happen?"

"He started to draw on me first," said Tandy. "I gave him his chance again. He was overrated."

"I didn't mean that," said Wheeler. "I mean how on earth did you find him?"

"I looked for him."

"I don't get it," said Wheeler.

"I'm a deputy. That's my trade. I'm going to find the others, too."

"It couldn't have been that easy," said Wheeler.

"I asked a few questions, got a few answers, went there, and there he was."

"You still haven't told me where."

"About halfway up the hill, beyond a thicket of briers, looking the other way, keeping his eye on a trail down below in the valley, watching for such as me."

"And you tried to arrest him, and had to shoot him?" said Wheeler.

"I yelled, 'Defend yoreself,' and when he tried to draw, I shot him."

"And you called that a gunfight?" said Wheeler.

"It wasn't no strawberry festival," said Tandy softly.

"You look at it yore way, I'll look at it my way."

"Was he there alone?" asked Wheeler.

"Alone," said Tandy. "They must be scared. They had separated from each other."

"Where is this hill?" asked Wheeler.

"North."

"North of Bearskin, or north of Alice?"

"North of the Rio Grande."

"The whole United States is north of the Rio Grande."

"Then that doesn't help you much, does it?" said Tandy. "So you can throw away yore deputy's badge and leave it all to me, like I been advisin'. And if you think I'm going to tell you who or what sent me to that hill in the first place, yore wrong there, too. I don't give out information like that. Such things is trade secrets."

He got to his feet, and left the room.

Wheeler took off his shoes and put out the lamp. He hadn't expected Tandy to be exactly cooperative, but he hadn't expected him to be this noncommittal, either.

All his life he had been forced to tackle his problems alone, and he could tackle this alone, too, if he had to.

He was no better off than he had been before, but no worse off, either.

He stretched out on the bed and slept.

At three, the hotel clerk knocked on his door and awoke him.

All through the predawn night, through sunrise and the scorching day, Wheeler rode north, reaching his destination—the Oro Creek Canyon country, just three miles south of Alice—in the late afternoon, just as he had calculated. It was a route he had ridden many,

41

many times before. It was supposed to be a pike between Bearskin and Alice, but it was more like a back
country logging road, up and down through craggy
hills, a faint trail at best, overgrown, flanked constantly
by scrub timber, slashes, burnovers, briers, dusty mesquite thickets. There was a time, when he was young,
when he knew every inch of this terrain, up to the
very edge of Alice itself. There were bear here then,
and floods of deer. Now he saw nothing as he passed,
but big-eyed mule ear rabbits.

Oro Creek had made a curlicue web of canyons and
gullies and channels, and Little Box could be spotted
from some distance away by the giant cottonwood which
grew on its rim, at its dead end. There was an open
slope from the upper level to the lower, and Wheeler,
guiding his mare down the unsure shale and dry clay
clods, descended. He came out in a little pocket, surrounded on three sides by canyon walls.

He was about ten feet from the tumbledown structure which he knew must once have been the McGinn
home.

It was one of the mangiest, makeshift huts he had
ever seen.

It was roofed with a tattered canvas wagon sheet,
weighted down with boulders and its sides were weath-
erproofed with hides, some old and warped and stiff,
some so new and green that they stank in the sun and
attracted clouds of flies.

The newness of some of these hides told him that
though the place might have been once abandoned,
it was again occupied. From his saddle, in the best of
courtesy, he called, "Hello! Hello, the house!", and
wondered what sort of a visitation would appear.

A woman appeared, middle-aged, tawdry, grimy,

giving off a mixed odor of cheap rose scent and sweat. In one hand she held a little pearlhandled penknife, in the other, a half-gutted, skinned rabbit. If the hut was dregs, she was worse dregs. In almost a snarl, she said, "How did you git down here? No road leads down here."

"Mine does," said Wheeler, and waited.

She thought this over, and then said malevolently, "Well, jest turn right around and take it back out again."

Wheeler said, "Where's your man?"

"Not too far away," she said. "So watch yourself. I got a loud scream."

"I'd like to talk to him."

"If he comes and finds you, he'll talk to you, all right."

"A family once lived here named McGinn," said Wheeler. "An old man who died of gangrene and his boy, Childress. I'm looking to the boy."

"I've heered of 'em," she said. "But when we moved in, they was long gone. They was nothing here, not even scorpions."

Suddenly he realized that she was not only being hostile, which was natural to her, but that for some reason she was being cautious, too.

Staring at the repulsive rabbit, Wheeler said roughly, "I'm hungry."

"They's restaurants in a town three mile north o'here," she said spitefully. "Or maybe you jest come from there?"

"I came from the south," said Wheeler, "in a manner of speaking. And restaurants are not for me, you could say."

"Money problem?"

"No money problem. I'm just bashful at people looking at me."

She pretended not to hear. Finally, she said, "What did you want with this Childress McGinn?"

He could hardly believe his ears. She was interested.

He knew better than to say anything, anything at all.

She said, "No money problem, eh?"

"Not right at the moment," he said. "Last week, yes. And more than likely a couple of days from now. Easy come, easy go. But not at the moment."

After a long pause, she said, "Wait a minute," and disappeared inside the hut. When she returned, she had a newspaper in her cupped hands. In the center of the paper, sagging, was a mess of cold greasy baked beans, a chunk of cornbread, an inch thick slice of sowbelly, all swimming together. She put the paper on the ground, gathered up its sides and tied them with a string, making a ball out of it. She handed it to him, and he took it.

He said, "Thank you."

" 'Thank you' ain't enough," she said. "That'll be ten dollars."

Then, under her breath, she said venomously, "And don't eat it here. Get goin'. Get movin'."

He took fifty dollars from his pocket and handed it to her.

She said happily, "So much? Why, thank you!"

" 'Thank you' isn't enough," he said coldly. "I expect a favor."

Again she was wary, cautious. "What favor? I generally don't do favors."

She held the money behind her while she spoke, however.

"Feed them when they come through," he said. "Tell them it's on me. Tell them it's already paid for."

"Feed who?"

"Childress and Snake and Oakley."

"Snake won't be through," she said. "Never again. He was kilt by a man named Tandy. Who are you?"

"You know better than ask a question like that," said Wheeler, grinning.

She lowered her voice and said, "Where did you hear they was comin' through? I heard they was hidin' out at Sandy Bend."

There were hundreds of Sandy Bends in Texas. And it might not even be Texas.

He said, "If they told you that, plans might be changed."

"They didn't tell me that," she said. "I heard it from Union Pacific."

"Union Pacific who?"

"Union Pacific Pearson. The bartender in town at the Eagle Saloon. Childress' uncle."

Trying to look suspicious, Wheeler said, "Childress never said—"

She said, "The less you know, the longer you live, and the happier."

He nodded, and rode away, guiding his mare up the incline.

He didn't throw away the nauseating bundle of food until he almost reached Alice.

V

THE TOWN of Alice, Linton County seat, had a railroad, and so important was it to local ranchers and the community at large, that the townspeople believed they had built it personally, everyone chipping in, even little children and dogs, and, therefore, owned it. The railroad took out Linton County cattle but it also brought things in: drummers, and businessmen, investors, and —down under the cars, huddled on the rods—drifters.

These drifters fell roughly into three groups: full-time tramps; outlaws, big and little, on the dodge; and unemployed wandering cowboys. But all of them, including the ordinarily harmless cowboys, could be dangerous if the situation was right. That is, if the party was broke and long-time hungry.

In the center of town, bisected by the railroad tracks, was Court Square, with its two story courthouse, cupola and all, and facing the Square was a rectangle of the town's best shops and offices, most everything spick-and-span in bright paint.

About two blocks south of the Square, though, also along the railroad tracks, was a ramshackle cluster of squalid buildings, eateries, saloons, and flea bag hotels. Known as Drifters Row, this area was infested by scum, both local and scum-on-the-wing.

The cutthroat, hell-roaring kettle drum of this area was the Eagle Saloon, a brown building with black-painted windowpanes.

Wheeler had passed it many times, but had never had occasion to enter. Now, he did.

The room was blazing with lamps, to keep the management on the safe side with its precarious clientele. The room was crude, stable-like, with a long bar and tables and chairs. The only decorations were the bottles on the backbar on either side of the foggy mirror. For this establishment was not for amusement; it was for drinking purposes only—serious drinking.

The place was filled with riffraff, noisy, argumentative. There were two kinds of riffraff, Wheeler knew: harmless riffraff, simply filthy, like livery stable loafers; and a type that was filthy, but dangerous, too—malcontents that would fight anybody, at the drop of a hat, over anything, with chair legs, guns, jackknives, anything that could maim, or be made lethal. The room was more than salted with buckos of this particular breed.

At the bar a skinny, chinless young fellow in ragged clothes which had originally been cowboy but were now pretty much hobo, was trying to pawn a stag-handled bowie knife with the bartender. The bartender, a greasy, obese man with a rash of pimples around a glossy black waterfall moustache, was ignoring the cowboy, treating him like he was dirt. This man with the moustache, Wheeler was sure, must be Union Pacific Pearson, McGinn's uncle.

He pushed through the crowd, confronted him, and said, "A lady in a box canyon sent me to you."

The bartender, speaking to the ragged cowboy, said, "Go over and sit down. We'll discuss this later." The cowboy wandered away and sat alone at a table in the corner.

To Wheeler, the bartender said angrily, "That ain't no way to talk. Before strangers!"

"I'll have to decide that myself," said Wheeler. "I'm in a hurry. How do I get to Sandy Bend?"

"Why ask me?" said the barman. "I don't believe I know him."

Wheeler was suddenly faced with a problem. Was it a person, not a place? He had to make a choice. The barman could be testing him. He had to play it whole hog, right or wrong.

He said, "You know what I'm talking about. Sandy Bend is a place, not a person."

"They's lots of Sandy Bends," said the barman, half wary, half going along with it. "What was this lady's name that sent you to me?"

He hadn't the slightest idea. He said, "Oh, no, you don't. No names, please."

The barman nodded. So far, the answers seemed right to him. He said, "This is going to cost you money."

"That's okay," said Wheeler. "If it's not too much. Everything seems to cost money. I just paid ten dollars for a disgusting mess of beans and sowbelly."

"That's her regular price," said Pearson. "A man on the dodge has to learn to pay his way. We take chances too, you know."

"So I've heard," said Wheeler.

The bartender smiled at what he thought was meant as a joke, and said, "I guess you're all right. But I got to ask you one more question. What's this?" He laid a dried rabbit's foot on the bar.

"A rabbit's foot," said Wheeler.

"But which foot?" asked Pearson.

So far it seemed easy. There was only one rabbit's

48

foot that people talked about—the left hind foot. It was supposed to be lucky.

"Right!" said the bartender heartily. But a corner of his mouth sucked in, just a little, and Wheeler knew he had been tricked.

He looked at the foot again. From the arrangement of its toes he could see he had been too hasty. It was a right hind foot.

"Right hind foot, I mean," he said easily.

The barman turned his shoulder and raised a finger to a group at the bar about twelve feet away. Two men came forward and joined them.

These two men, hunch-shouldered, bull-chested, stank of filth and sweat. One had a nose which had been beaten so badly and so often that it was now entirely shapeless, the other was so drunk he could hardly stand. They smiled at Wheeler evilly, munching him with their eyes. Wheeler knew them for what they were—bullies, of the sort that fought only in pairs, and against what they considered weaker men. Wheeler's small size, they thought, made him fodder for them.

The bartender said, "If you think you can throw this man out, there'll be a glass of beer in it for each of you."

"Draw two," said the man with the shapeless nose.

"And when you got him outside," said the bartender, "you can persuade him not to come back, that's worth an extra glass a piece."

"Draw four," said the man with the shapeless nose.

This was a situation. Wheeler wanted no violence, not here, not at this time.

In a mild voice, he said, "I don't believe I want any of that. The first man that touches me, I'll gun."

"They ain't armed," said the bartender, smiling.

"I might get so excited I don't notice," said Wheeler.

"That's been took care of, too," said the barman. "Looky!"

Down the bar, three men were left in the group from which those two had detached themselves. Now these remaining three were standing, their sixguns out, staring, waiting.

This was obviously an old setup here. All the way easy, taking no chance. "And I got one, too," said the bartender, showing a big Colt.

The room became dead still.

"You're tryin' to cause a ruckus," said the bartender. "And before witnesses. So if I got to kill you, I got to, and like everyone knows, the law will be on my side."

Wheeler went expressionless. The odds were impossible. It was sure death, or a brutal crippling beating.

"Maybe you'd better hand me that gun o' your'n, right now," said Pearson, the bartender. "And be mighty careful with it. You heard me. *Hand it over!*"

The ragged cowboy said from his table, loudly and clearly, "I sure wish I could be of some help to somebody, sometime. But how kin I, with nothing but a busted ole hunting knife? I better be gittin' along to my rocky bed under the water tank and forgit the whole thing. But I kin tell you gentlemen one thing, I ain't going to sleep peaceful."

He got up, ambled with painful slowness to the door, and disappeared outside. All motion, all conversation was suspended, held midbreath, until he was gone.

The little interruption had given Wheeler three minutes more of life. It wasn't much, but it was the best this likable boy, helpless himself in this den of wolves, could do, Wheeler realized.

And any interruption was a distraction. Wheeler's gun came up and out, seeming to jump of itself, roaring and exploding as the metal of his gun muzzle came up out of the leather of its holster lip.

Because the bartender was almost on top of him and couldt't miss, because his weapon was at full cock and Wheeler knew the man would really relish killing him and rectifying what might have been a blunder on his part, it was the bartender whom Wheeler drilled. He let off one shot only, saw the skin mar between his eyes, and pivoted to do the best he could, in the short time allotted to him, on the three men down the bar.

One of them was on the floor, flat on his face, in blood.

The other two had dropped their weapons and were standing with their arms over their heads, stretched desperately high.

Deputy Tandy was standing just inside the door, his gun in his hand, held unconsciously, as though it were a tool, not a weapon. He holstered it and Wheeler went through the tables to join him. Even as he went, even with the reaction that now set into him, Wheeler could sense that the room was icy with fear. With fear of Tandy.

"Well," said Wheeler calmly. "You saved my life. And I mean just that. I didn't have the ghost of a chance."

"That's what I get paid for," said Tandy curtly.

"And just at the right split second," said Wheeler.

"That part wasn't too hard," said Tandy. "I was waiting outside the door."

"But how did you happen to be waiting outside the door?" asked Wheeler, sweating.

"I seen yore mare in Court Square. I'm gitting to know you a little by now. I figgered you was messing around, looking for trouble somewheres. I thought I'd better take a hand."

"The odds," said Wheeler, "were bad for me. They were bad for you, too."

"I didn't notice at the time. A deputy ain't paid to fill his head with foolishness, like odds."

Tandy's tone of voice implied that the conversation was closed. However, as an afterthought, he said, "Do me a favor?"

"If it's reasonable," said Wheeler, grinning.

"Go to the courthouse—"

"I was going anyway."

"Go to the courthouse and report this to the sheriff."

"Wouldn't that be your job?"

"That's my job, all right," said Tandy. "But he'll understand. He'd expect as much. Him and me can't seem to stand each other."

Tandy left the saloon.

A minute later, when Wheeler, too, went outside, there was no sign of Bearskin's deputy.

Wheeler started for the courthouse.

Over the years, Wheeler had had much business at the courthouse, naturally, and now and then a little business with the county's sheriff. Some of the sheriffs Wheeler had known in the past had been little inconspicuous men, quiet and capable, but so ordinary that he'd hardly known when they were around. But he sure as hell knew it whenever around Sheriff Markham. His very manner said he was the Boss Man.

Wheeler turned the huge brass doorknob, as big as an apple dumpling, and entered the office.

The sheriff, a dowdily dressed man, with permanently inflated cheeks which always looked as though they were on the verge of whistling secretly and mysteriously—and sometimes did—sat pompously behind his desk. He was always nice to Wheeler, but not too nice; he could never figure just how much Wheeler made a year.

Wheeler told him about the gun battle in the Eagle Saloon, making the first part hazy and vague, the second part, the fight, specific and detailed.

Gradually, as he listened, Sheriff Markham's wattles grew fiery red. Angrily, he said, "I'm glad to hear Pearson has departed our lovely town, and nobody's blaming you, o' course, but that Tandy is very hard to stomach, very hard."

"He looked mighty good to me," said Wheeler. "Standing just inside that door."

"The point is," said Sheriff Markham coldly, "that Alice is properly and fully equipped to handle its own difficulties. We don't need no outsider coming in a'trying to show us up."

"But he's your very own deputy."

"He's my very own *Bearskin* deputy. How do I know he won't get the idee to run agin me sometime? Great oaks from little acorns grow."

"I wouldn't call Tandy a little acorn," said Wheeler.

"I would," said Sheriff Markham with loathing. "A hard, mean, troublemaking little acorn."

"How are you making out on Seth's murder?" asked Wheeler.

"On that item," said the sheriff, "permit me to offer our office's heartfelt sympathy."

"How are you making out?"

"These things takes a great deal of thought and time."

"So you're getting nowhere?"

"We know who done it. The Simmons gang. And

that's a pretty start, you'll have to admit. And one of our deputies, I might add, has already tracked down and killed one of them—Snake Leffingwell."

"What would be your official opinion," said Wheeler, "if I'd set out on my own, and run down and kill the other two? Capture them if I could, but kill them if I had to?"

"My official opinion would be disapproval," said Sheriff Markham.

"You talk like Deputy Tandy," said Wheeler, not impressed.

"You mean he talks like me? I hope so. We're both law officers."

"You don't want me poaching, is that it?"

Sheriff Markham's face showed genuine shock. Aghast, he said, "That's the most terrible thing I ever heard. It sounds like a Comanche. I know, ever'body knows, they done you a grievance. But to run 'em down alone, and catch 'em, and poach 'em—it jest ain't human!"

Wheeler could stand no more of this. He left the office, and the courthouse.

The idea had been growing on Wheeler that the man he wanted to talk to was the chinless ragged cowboy tramp who had done such a good deed in the Eagle.

The man had put out a sort of message, too, when you came to think of it, as he had left. He had said he was going back to his rocky bed under the water tank.

The railroad's water tank, Wheeler knew, was in a weedy patch of land, just south of the town's limits.

Leaving his mare hitched at the public rail in Court

Square, he started through the night for the town's south edge. It was a beautiful summer's night, starry, with the skirl of tree frogs—sights and sounds he usually enjoyed so much—but now he walked stiffly alone, tense, tight-fisted.

VI

THE WATER TANK by the railroad tracks, when Wheeler came up to it, loomed like a great tomato can on stilts, black against the luminous sky. The grass surrounding it was knee-high, but under the tank, between the tank's sloping leglike supports, the grass had been wallowed down in a cozy sort of nest. Here, by groping, Wheeler located and touched the cowboy. The tramp came up to a sitting position with a jerk. *He's learned to be mighty sensitive to probing hands in the dark,* Wheeler thought dryly.

"Oh, it's you," said the tramp. How he could tell, in this dark, Wheeler wondered. Riding the rods, hitting from pillar to post, he must have had to develop a sixth sense to survive. "How did you get out of the Eagle?" the cowboy asked.

"Walked out," said Wheeler.

"Stepping over a few things in the process, I bet," said the cowboy admiringly. "They was four guns on you. You must be a wonder."

"The law walked in," said Wheeler, "and surprised them. I want to thank you for what you did, for giving me that half-second edge."

"Thanks accepted," said the cowboy. "But don't offer me any money for doin' it. A broke man will do almost anything for money. But they's one thing he won't do. He won't help a man in a hole for money. When he gets that far down the scale, he better eat rat poison and give up."

"I'm a cattle dealer," said Wheeler, "and getting along pretty well. I could use a helper, if he was the right man. You like to travel. All right. You'd do a lot of traveling. We could try it for a while. If it turned out that you could get along with me, and I could get along with you, it might work into something okay for you."

"That's work," said the cowboy. "No matter how sweet an icing you smear over it, you're offering me work. I could get along with you all right; I know, and I'm never wrong with people. But I couldn't get along with work. We've met before, and we loathe and despise each other. So jest shake my hand, and let me get back to sleep."

"One thing more," said Wheeler. "I may be wrong, way wrong, but back at the Eagle, from something you said, I got the idea you'd like me to come here under the tank and have a little chat with you."

"From your point of view, I thought mebbe."

"From my point of view? In what way?"

"I heard you ask the bartender at the Eagle how to get to Sandy Bend. Is it important that you get there?"

"Yes."

"And you wouldn't stay away, even if I so advised you?"

"No. I'll find it on my own sooner or later. You can bet on that."

"Ever heard of Two-Pine?"

"Yes," said Wheeler. Two-Pine was an old abandoned mining locale, about a hundred and fifty miles southeast of Bearskin. Decades ago, when the rush fever had swept the country, men had penetrated the miserable rocky area. It had a stream, Wheeler had heard, and was entered by a gulch and a gulch only. Wheeler had never been there. Nobody ever went there. He said, "What direction and how far from Two-Pine?"

"Get to Two-Pine, and that's it."

"That's it?"

"Two-Pine and Sandy Bend is the same thing. Sandy Bend is the outlaw trade name for it. Nobody but outlaw talking to outlaw ever calls it Sandy Bend."

After a moment, his end in sight, Wheeler said, "I'm much obliged."

"I've been studying you over," said the cowboy. "And I do believe I've got you placed. You're the cattle dealer—who everybody seems to like, the way I get it—who got his little boy killed while he was away."

"That's right," said Wheeler woodenly.

"Do you know what Sandy Bend is?"

"My father used to tell me he caught mighty big fish there in the old Indian days."

"Sandy Bend is a outlaw hangout, hideout. Live by the gun, die by the gun. Exclusively, absolutely, nothing else but outlaws. And all that goes with it. Understand?"

"I understand," said Wheeler. "Now I'll tell you something. I've got the Simmons brothers in mind."

"They're there," said the tramp. "I've never been there myself, but I hear things."

As Wheeler sat in silence, the cowboy said, "I hear the child was killed in Bearskin. That means you're from Bearskin."

"Yes."

"When are you going back?"

"Right now. I've got to get this business finished." *Running man,* Tabby had said, *get in that daily quota.* "Maybe I'll sleep a few hours in the sage," he added, embarrassed. How right she had been.

"How are you going?"

58

"By the old pike," said Wheeler, wondering.

"Know Halfway?"

In the old days, Halfway, midway between Alice and Bearskin, had been a road ranch, with a few beds and a big corral for travelers wanting a little safety in night stopovers, moving small herds of cattle or horses on a short shuttle. Times had changed, though, the country-side was not quite so wild, and Halfway had changed, too. Now it was mainly just an empty, rambling build-ing, catching a few wayfarers but subsisting more on its tiny cotton patch.

Road ranches had a bad reputation for bedbugs. Wheeler hated bedbugs. He had never stayed there.

He said, "I know it. I've passed it a thousand times."

"Well, pass it once more. Tomorrow," the cowboy said sleepily.

"Why?"

"You're looking for the Simmonses," said the cowboy. "Everyone knows that. That could mean the Simmonses know it, too. I don't want to surprise you, but did you ever think you might be a nuisance to 'em? That they might be lookin' for you, too, and first?"

"Do you know that as a fact?"

"No, I don't. It just come into my mind."

Pressing him, Wheeler said, "But why Halfway? What tie-up have they got with Halfway?"

"See?" said the cowboy, annoyed. "I tried to keep you away, and I do believe I've drove you to it."

"What tie-up does the Simmons gang have with Halfway?"

"I don't know for a fact that they's any tie-up at all," said the cowboy. "And I shorely do not wish to give you no idee I am the possessor of no such knowledge."

"Well, then?"

"But—"

"But what?"

"But now and then, here and there, when I am happily indulgin' in my earthly travels, I have met certain gentlemen different from other gentlemen, shall we say, because of nice lively professional acting gun-thumbs. And many of these certain gentlemen, when soused to the ears, which is their favorite recreation, have a kind fatherly word for this place, Halfway."

"I see," said Wheeler. He nodded in the dark, said good night, and left.

The sun next day, a ball of gaseous canary fire, was just past its zenith, when Wheeler came down the old pike and saw for the first time, really, the delapidated hostelry known as Halfway. He had heard that it had frequently changed hands in the past few years, and that its current tenants were a family named Haggerty. As Wheeler turned into its lane, he saw it looked like any other working farm, as far as its surroundings went, well tended cotton field behind a teetery, weathered barn, mule lot, small efficient corral (the old road ranch corral had long ago been taken down), and little windmill behind the barn gable. The only thing that didn't fit into the working farm picture, of course, was the house, the old hostelry, with its curled, gaping clapboards, rotting window frames, and mossy shingles. The house, and the man who leaned back in a splint-bottomed chair before it, against its door frame. He was dressed in shabby black broadcloth, like a townsman down on his luck. *Maybe,* thought Wheeler, *he's a boarder.*

Wheeler rode up, swung out of his saddle, hitched his mare to the wheel of an empty wagon nearby. He walked forward and the man in the chair—beaknosed, small slaty eyes—watched him, appraised him, tried to classify him. Wheeler said, "Is this place a hotel? I've been riding most of the night and all day."

"It used to be a hotel," the man said, dismissing his visitor with the tone of his voice. "But now it's a farmhouse. A private residence. Your nearest hotel is down at Bearskin."

"I'm looking for a Mr. Haggerty, I think the name is," said Wheeler.

"You've found him," said the man shortly. "Get it over, and get gone."

Wheeler said, "Does the name Kansas Pete mean anything to you?"

He'd made it up on the spur of the moment, and said it levelly, but it had come out so silly that it was all he could do to keep from laughing.

Haggerty mulled this over. Finally, he said, "I don't think so. Why?"

"He told me it would. I want to swap a horse."

"I don't swap horses. I raise cotton."

"Sell one, then."

Haggerty got up, came lazily forward and scrutinized Wheeler's mount by the wagon. "Not much of an animal. But maybe I could use her if the price was low enough. What do you want for her?"

"Not this one," said Wheeler. "Say some other ones."

"Ones? More than one? How many?"

"I'm not in position to say at the moment," said Wheeler.

"When did you have in mind to offer them?"

"You know how it goes. I'm not in position to say at the moment."

If he wasn't sounding like a quick-shuffle horse thief, Wheeler thought, no one could.

Haggerty relaxed. He said, "I generally stick pretty close to just farming, however—"

Wheeler knew he had him hooked.

"However," said Haggerty, suddenly razor-sharp. "It won't cost me nothing to take a look at them, will it."

"And you'll have the money ready?" asked Wheeler.

"I do all business, any kind of business, with ready money."

"And just one thing more," said Wheeler. "And this part you might not like. It might be the middle of the night when I deliver them. You might not like to buy strange horses in the middle of the night."

"Why not?" said Haggerty. "I got lanterns, haven't I?" He was greedy now, lest the deal get away from him. He said, "Come in and have a bite."

"Oh, I don't think so," said Wheeler, careful that he didn't overplay it. "I don't want to put you out."

"Well, a drink, then? To sluice out that throat. You look a little travel dusty."

"Sounds good," said Wheeler, and they went inside. They went down a dim narrow hall with creaking floorboards, past open doors, past a queasy-looking parlor with cheap black furniture and a vase of gilt that looked like a bunkhouse table, set with enamel paper artificial flowers, past a dining room with a table plates and wooden-handled tin knives and forks, and entered a closed door at the hall's end.

Now they were in a small room with a midget bar and a pair of kegs on trestles at one end of it, beer and whisky.

"You've got a nice cozy farmhouse here," said Wheeler. "Could this be your wife's sewing room?"

"I don't have no wife," said Haggerty. "I just have a few growed sons. You must have heard about this room from the man who sent you to me. They tell me it's famous among you fellers."

"And the bedrooms are upstairs?"

"What will you have? Forget the bedrooms."

"Beer, please," said Wheeler.

Haggerty filled a couple of schooners with a flourish and they sat at a little wire-legged table, sipping peacefully, slowly, batting off flies.

"This Kansas Pete," said Haggerty ruminatively. "I can't seem quite to bring him into my mind's eye. Was he short or tall?"

"Medium," said Wheeler. "That's the best way to describe everything about him, I'd say, medium. He sure thinks the sun rises and sets in this place, and in you."

"They all do," said Haggerty smugly flattered. "I'm a very friendly and toleratin' host to any feller that wants, say, to keep out of public sight when he's on the move. Who did you say some of yore other acquaintances was?"

Here it was, the opening he had been working for, and now Wheeler wasn't sure just how to handle it. He had the man maleable, receptive, but it was heads or tails, win or lose.

Placing his beer glass carefully on the wet tabletop, Wheeler said, "Right at this minute I'm trying to locate one Oakley Simmons and his sidekick, Childress McGinn."

In a sour, arid voice, Haggerty said, "The boys from Waco."

Pretending to impart a confidence, Wheeler said, "Sometimes they claim they're from Waco. But the truth is that McGinn is from up near Alice and Simmons is from Frog Butte, Wyoming. Up in the Wind River country." He made up that Frog Butte thing on the spur of the moment, and added it to give a nice touch of authenticity.

"I heard about the Wind River part," said Haggerty. "But I never knew till now just where. Well, to give you the information you're after, you can find them down at Sandy Bend."

"Sure?" asked Wheeler.

"Sure," said Haggerty. "And now that you've got your information, just haul your carcass out of my house and off of my place."

He was no longer amiable, sociable.

Wheeler looked surprised.

Haggerty said, "They been here in the past, quite a few times, and paid proper, like anybody else. But I don't want them here again, ever, and you can tell them I said so when you find them."

"That's going to make them mighty mad," said Wheeler, playing along.

"Of course it will," said Haggerty. "But what of it? I swing more power than they do, and they know it. They're lone wolves, nobody likes them. I got a mess of pretty dangerous friends, and they know that, too."

"So you don't want them here anymore," said Wheeler, as though he wanted to get the message straight.

"Them, or none of their cheap friends, and that last includes you," said Haggerty angrily. "I cater to a high class trade here, not child-killers."

Frozen, Wheeler stared at him.

"The way it come to me," said Haggerty, "they robbed a house and slaughtered a little boy down at Bearskin and stirred up a heap of trouble for all of us. Was you in on that?"

Kent.
Mild, smooth taste.
Micronite filter.

King size or
Deluxe 100's.

Kent.
For all the right reasons.

America's quality cigarette.

A PRODUCT OF
Lorillard

20 CLASS A
CIGARETTES

KENT

WITH
THE FAMOUS MICRONITE FILTER

DELUXE 100's

Unable to speak, Wheeler simply shook his head.

He walked with Wheeler out of the room, out of the house. His face deep red in indignation and fury, he watched Wheeler mount. As Wheeler rode from the farmyard, Haggerty yelled after him, "And cancel our deal about them horses!"

VII

THE WESTERN SKY was curdled with the red and magenta of sunset, and the roofs and chimneys of Bearskin were soft with the first shadows of twilight, when Wheeler returned to town. He stabled his mare at the Magnolia House, slept for an hour in a chair in the lobby, and had a beefsteak in the hotel restaurant when he awoke. He awoke a little stiff, but fully resuscitated. He walked to the Venables, asked, and got their permission to shave. He shaved in the kitchen, with lukewarm water from the still warm cast iron stove, then joined the Judge and Tabby, in the Judge's study, where they were sitting, concerned, waiting for him.

"What happened?" asked Tabby.

"Nothing much," said Wheeler, sinking into a chair. "A man wanted to buy some stolen horses from me, but changed his mind. That's about all."

He didn't tell them about the fight at the Eagle Saloon. It was about time, he decided, to spare them the harrowing details.

"Nothing," said Tabby. "Everywhere, nothing. Why don't you be sensible about this, and give up?"

"I'm just getting started," said Wheeler grimly.

"I don't like this streak in you, Charley," said Judge Venable, uncomfortably.

"It's not a streak," said Wheeler. "It's me."

"What are you going to be like when it's all over?" said Tabby.

"Dead, probably," said Wheeler.

"But that's the way you want to die," said Tabby. "So you'll die happy."

"There's nothing happy about it," said Wheeler steadily.

"I know," said Tabby, deeply contrite. "I'm sorry. I'm ashamed of myself."

"She was just trying to knock some reason into that skull of yours," said the Judge.

"I know," said Wheeler. "I understood."

Tabby studied him speculatively. "What is it, this thing that has moved into you? Is it gore? Do you want to see blood all around?"

"No," said Wheeler carefully, trying to explain it even to himself. "It's hard to put in words. It has nothing to do with blood, or revenge. It's something I've got to do. It's like when a fence comes down, you fix it. When a waterhole becomes foul, you clean it out. You worry about it, you don't brood about it, you just do it. It has to be done."

"When you bring it off, if you bring it off," said Tabby, "you won't feel happy, won't feel satiated?"

"No," said Wheeler quietly. "I'll just say, well, that's done."

Judge Venable said bitterly, "You'll just say, I got that fence fixed."

"That's about it," said Wheeler.

"What if, in the meantime, it grows on you?" asked Tabby. "And you get to think that fixing fences is the only important thing in the world, and you get to looking around for somebody else's fence to help fix? What if you turn out like Tandy?"

"We'll cross that bridge when I come to it," said Wheeler.

"You don't think that's possible?" asked Tabby.

"Of course it's possible," said Wheeler thoughtfully.

"If that time ever comes," said Tabby, "it'll be 'good-bye Charles Wheeler' from me. It'll be 'it was nice having known you.'"

"Maybe, the way you look at it," said Wheeler, "maybe I'm there already. Maybe it's good-bye right now, and I just haven't realized it?"

"Don't push me," she said, and got up and left the room.

Judge Venable said heartily, "A friend, a man back in the hills, just gave me some fine whisky he made himself. Would you like a taste?"

Wheeler didn't answer. In fact, he didn't even hear. The Judge frowned.

He went to a cabinet and came out with a quart bottle half full of whisky. He held the bottle to a lamp, shook it, and his lips moved as he counted silently to himself. "Good homemade whisky has birdshot beads," he said lightly. "And I like 'em to stay on till I count to twelve. If they're too big, or burst too soon, I don't like it. However, once I bought whisky from a man who put horse manure in it, the oil in the manure made the beads hold a little longer." He smiled but Wheeler didn't respond. He poured Wheeler a glass of whisky and handed it to him; Wheeler took it, drank it, and nodded his thanks.

The Judge took a chair facing him, leaned back, and sighed heavily.

Wheeler said, "Been down to Two-Pine fishing lately?"

"If you call thirty years ago 'lately.' Why?"

"I don't know. I thought I might go down there and try my hand."

68

"I see," said the old Judge. "I see. Well, you stay away from Two-Pine."

When Wheeler made no response, Judge Venable said, "If the rumors I hear now and then are true, it's changed its nature. It's become a sort of no-good rendezvous."

"Whatever that means," said Wheeler.

"You go there, and you'll find out. They say it's an outlaw hideout of sorts."

"Then why isn't it cleaned out?"

"For one thing, its denizens are supposed to be mainly secondraters. In the second place, it's got too efficient a signal system. A stranger shows up, and its residents simply disperse for a while and reassemble when the coast is clear."

"Years ago," said Wheeler, "I was there with my father. I remember that the countryside was hell and that the place was in a sort of pocket. I don't remember how we got in."

"The trail comes in from the north, between two storm-blasted pines on the lip of a split rock, and descends, among a forest of giant boulders to the sandy bend in the creek below. There, by the creek, is where the old mining huts used to be. I doubt if the pines are still there. Or the huts, for that matter. The outlaw camp may be anywhere."

"So I follow that trail down," said Wheeler.

"That's what you don't do," said Judge Venable lazily.

Wheeler looked at him.

"That's the obvious trail, and the one they've got so strongly fortified," said the Judge. "It's just a natural labyrinth of bushwhack traps. You go in the other way."

"What other way?"

"The old Comanche way," said the Judge. "My, what a store of useless information an old man like me picks up and takes with him to his grave."

"It's a long way from useless right now," said Wheeler. "Let's hear about it."

"You circle around to the south, until you hit the creek below the place," said the old man. "Then you follow the creek upstream. The shore dwindles to a little strip of pebbles, and after a while, big chunks of limestone begin to edge the creek. You come out between two of these rock masses, and there is the pool. The wonderful fishing pool. It's big, and surrounded by the rock masses, grown now considerably in size. Facing you is a limestone bluff behind the pool, pitted and crumbling, reaching almost to the sky, it seems, and over it, at the top, comes the little trickle of water which comes down the pocked and pitted cliff face to form the beautiful, tranquil pool at its base. You continue to follow the creek upstream."

"How?"

"It looks like you're blocked, but you aren't. You take your horse into the pool and traverse its west edge. You stay close as you can—along a narrow underwater shelf—to the rocks which flank it. That pool is deeper than the courthouse at Alice is high if your mare steps out too far."

"And then?" asked Wheeler.

"Pretty soon, to your left, you see something. The cliff face to this side has been split, forming a sort of wing, a kind of false front which you could notice from the south edge of the pool. A little path goes up from the base of this split. You ascend it. And then you come out on a flat upper level, with a sandy bend on the creek, and the remains of the old huts along it."

"And that's all?"

"And that's just the beginning. From then on, it's good-bye, dear friend."

Wheeler nodded, spoke his thanks, said good night and went out into the sweet, soft summer night.

Tabby was sitting in the dark of the veranda on a wicker chair, waiting for him. He thought she was waiting to light into him a little further, and braced himself to take it politely. However, when she spoke her voice was gentle and intimate.

She said, "The little boy and his father came for the roan."

"The Tennessee Darnleys?" said Wheeler. "What did you think of them?"

"It's what I think of you," she said. "I think that was the finest thing any mortal ever did. The old man saddled up with Seth's saddle, put his boy in it, and couldn't thank me as he left. He was crying."

He suddenly had the feeling that she was crying, too. He said roughly, "That'll be enough of that. Can I ask you a question?"

"Yes," she said, now with herself under control.

He tried to think of something fast. He said, "What makes you act that way, like you did a minute ago, and like you did once before—so hot and angry with me?"

"I was scared for you," she said.

"Don't be," he said.

"I'm not," she said. "Not any more."

"That's better," he said.

"I've made my choice," she said. "Now I'm with you,

71

a hundred percent. I'm living it in my mind, now. Like you, I'm too busy in my mind to be scared."

He wasn't sure he liked this. He said, "I'll take care of all the thinking on the subject that is necessary. You leave it alone."

"I came out here and sat down," she said, not paying any attention to him. "I've been going over it mentally, every detail. There's something, maybe, that we've both missed."

"What?" said Wheeler.

"How the Simmons gang got out of the jail."

"Oakley Simmons managed it. He's a habitual jail-breaker."

"But how?"

"I've just told you."

"You've told me nothing. That window was deepset in a frame of stone. Does he carry a crowbar in his coat sleeve, everywhere he goes? Mr. Taliaferro, who was jailer at that time, has taken a nice expensive trip back to Chicago, to spend the remainder of his days, they say. But Mrs. Taliaferro, who likes Bearskin, couldn't bring herself to make the move, and not finding it too painful to separate herself from Mr. Taliaferro, in which opinion I would concur, has remained."

Wheeler thought this over.

Finally, he said, "These things happen."

"Before the jailbreak," said Tabby, "Mrs. Taliaferro owned nothing but an over-loused bantam rooster and a pair of sloppy mismatched shoes, they say. Now times have changed with her, I hear. Now the rooster is gone. She's opulent."

"Opulent?"

"I'd say so, from her viewpoint. She owns a nice new pair of shoes—and the Brazos Hotel."

"The Brazos Hotel?" said Wheeler. "I didn't know that."

"Well, she does. She just bought it."

"Well, think of that," said Wheeler. "Maybe I'd better take a look into this. Good night."

He walked rapidly across the dark lawn to the street.

When Wheeler came into Louey Hackett's *Shorthorn Social Club,* a little later, it certainly seemed different than it had that other morning when Hackett, alone at a lonely table, had offered his allegiance to him.

The place was packed, and hummed with business. Men of all sorts, farmers, third-rate rambling desperadoes, town drunks, most of them strangers to Wheeler, sat at crowded tables, intent on just about every card game from faro to poker. The cigar smoke was so thick he could just about snip a hole in it with a pair of scissors.

Hackett, walking here and there, keeping an eye on things, saw Wheeler the instant he appeared, and came forward to greet him warmly.

He shook Wheeler's hand, led him between the jammed tables through a door at the rear, into an office, closed the door carefully behind them, and they seated themselves. It wasn't much of an office, desk and two chairs, but somehow it really had the atmosphere of privacy.

Hackett said, "You're showing a little dust. I'd say you've been traveling, and traveling hard. Have you eaten? I've got a cot up in the loft. Could you use some sleep?"

"I'm all right," said Wheeler. "But thanks just the same."

He sat for an instant, just looking at Hackett. It was strange how he had come not only to like this man, whom he had once scorned, but how he had even come to trust him. He realized he had formed a lot of new opinions since this terrible thing had happened.

He told Hackett about the woman in the box canyon, and her conversation with him.

Hackett listened attentively, but amused. This was news to him, and his information in this category was astounding. Wheeler could almost feel him file it away in that complex brain of his.

"So she runs an outlaw stopover," Hackett said musingly. "And feeds them on the dodge. But whisks them off in a hurry."

"At least she wanted me away," said Wheeler.

"Her importance, I imagine," said Hackett, "is that she runs a word-of-mouth post office."

"That would fit in all right," said Wheeler, and told him about the gunfight at Alice in the Eagle Saloon and about the bartender there.

Hackett said nothing. He simply shook his head.

Then Wheeler told him about the tramp cowboy, and his visit at Halfway.

"Haggerty I know, and his place I know," said Hackett, his eyes twinkling. In admiration, he said, "You really don't care too much what might happen to you, do you?"

Wheeler said, "I don't know. I'm too busy to stop and worry."

"Maybe you need somebody to do your worrying for you," said Hackett.

"I got too many already," said Wheeler. "First Miss Tabby Venable, and now, it seems, you."

"And while we're on the subject," said Hackett lazily. "It looks to me as though somebody just to do your worrying for you isn't quite enough. And now, you say, you're riding south to Sandy Bend."

"Yes," said Wheeler.

"I'd like to go along with you," said Hackett.

"No," said Wheeler.

"A man can never tell when he might need a helping hand," said Hackett.

"Oh, I'll need a helping hand, all right," said Wheeler. "That's not the point. The point is I can tell you I'm not going to get you killed. Just when I'm beginning to like you."

Hackett pretended not to hear.

Finally, Hackett said, "Oakley is there, just like you think. But right now he's especially dangerous. He's broke. And when he's broke, he's poison."

"Broke?" said Wheeler, never doubting that Hackett knew exactly what he was talking about.

"Poker game down there," said Hackett.

"Poker game down there?" repeated Wheeler.

"Yes. Lost everything he had on him." Hackett nodded. "Everything."

Hackett just sat quiet, trying to make up his mind. Finally, he dug down deep into a pants pocket, came up with a gold coin, and laid it on the tabletop before Wheeler. "Sometime back, a stupid bigmouthed drifting no-good came into my place here. He lost that coin at one of my tables. He told me the story—after about nine whiskys—about Oakley Simmons going broke. He said that he personally had been in that game at Sandy Bend, and had won that coin from him. I saved it for you, Charley."

'Why me?" asked Wheeler, careful not to touch it.

"I thought it could be—of course, we'll never know

75

—I thought it could be part of the money they took the night they robbed your house."

"Part of Seth, you mean?" said Wheeler.

"Lord no," said Hackett, distressed. "I would never mean a horrible thing like that!"

Wheeler got up groggily, as though in an ugly dream. Hackett tight-lipped, watched him go.

The Brazos Hotel wasn't even on a street. It was in a sort of grassless eroded lot behind Main Street, hemmed in by a rectangle of trash piles and back doors of shops and offices. When Wheeler came up to it, the shops and offices were dark, closed for the night, but the Brazos, a tin two-story building in disrepair, showed pencil thin shafts of golden lamplight from the sides of drawn window blinds. Wheeler had always hated the sight of this place. Shaking his head to himself, he stepped inside.

The place had once been a poor man's parlor house, Wheeler had heard, but the girls, if he could call them that, unable to subsist, had moved on to more prosperous locales—Alice, and Austin. Part of the old trappings, however, were still in evidence. Wheeler found himself in a rather large room, sealed walls and ceiling with tongue and grove pine, yellow varnished, the varnish blistered and cloudy with neglect. There was a stairway, narrow and steep, ascending, and over it an arch of wooden curlicues. Between the front and the stairway, a fattish woman of indeterminate age sat spraddled on a milking stool before a small table, picking kernels out of a pile of cracked hickory nuts with a hair pin.

Her greasy gray hair was mist-thin over her pink scalp; her sallow face was puffy and piggish, and her tiny eyes were malicious and jet black. Wheeler knew her by sight. This was Mrs. Taliaferro. There was no one else in sight. The place seemed deserted.

Standing beside her, Wheeler said, "I'm Charley Wheeler."

"I know," she answered, not raising her eyes, continuing to stuff her mouth, chipmunk-like. "I've had you named to me."

Wheeler said, "It was my boy, Seth, that was killed in his home by the Simmons gang."

"I only know what I hear," she said, not raising her eyes. "What I hear and what I think. I think, when you come right down to it, you was the one that killed that boy. Leaving him alone like that. Off skylarking someplace, calling it business, leaving him alone and unprotected."

This was so vicious, so close to truth, it seemed to Wheeler, that he could hardly speak. Finally, he said, "I know it now."

"So now you admit, now you apologize," she said. "But that doesn't bring back your son, does it."

"No, it doesn't," said Wheeler.

"What did you want with me?" she asked.

"This," said Wheeler. "When the Simmons gang was in jail here, and your husband Tom was jailer, did they offer him a helping big bribe to get them a crowbar? And did he do it, and was that the way they got out? And did Tom take part of that money and go back to Chicago, and did you take part of the money and buy this place?"

"Right."

Startled, Wheeler said, "Is that all true?"

"Every word of it. This place was practically give to me, I might add. The previous owner was mighty tired of it."

"Then if Tom Taliaferro hadn't of taken a bribe, and the Simmons hadn't got loose, Seth would still be alive?"

"I'm not sure that I follow you," she said. "But if I do, that could all be right, too. But don't blame Tom for the boy's death. Blame yourself."

"You sit there and admit that Tom took this bribe, and got those prisoners that crowbar?"

"Sure."

"Aren't you afraid of consequences?"

"What consequences?" she said, raising her eyes and meeting his gaze evilly, fully. "This place is empty. They ain't nobody here but you and me. If you make anything out of it later, it can't be nothing but your word and mine. Deputy Tandy has already been here, I might add, and asked me all these very same questions. To you I say yes, to him I said no. No. And can't him nor anyone else *prove* different."

"But why?" said Wheeler. "Why admit it to me?"

"I wanted to see you squirm."

"Why?"

"Because up to now, I've always done all the squirming myself."

"I doubt it," said Wheeler. "I think you've been this way all your life. I know now why Tom Taliaferro grabbed that train away from here."

She raised her lips just a little, and showed the edges of rodent-like teeth.

As he left through the door, his back to her, she called, "You can't touch me!"

On Main Street, three doors down from the Magnolia House, was the *Owl Day & Night Cafe*. Over its doorway was a six foot pine two-by-four, with three lamps bolted to it, blazing with light, making a big blossom of yellow light in the surrounding night, bringing in butting and bumping night beetles, searing them with the searing heat, leaving them belly-up in the soft dust below. As Wheeler came up, he saw Tandy standing by the doorway in the lamplight, picking his teeth with a goosequill toothpick. He was spick-and-span in freshly laundered shirt and pants, laundered by himself, Wheeler knew, and the only thing wild and unkempt about him was that bushy, tangled frontier hair. He seemed in good spirits, even amiable, which was rare for him in Wheeler's experience.

Wheeler, coming to a stop beside him, said, "You look contented."

"I am," said Tandy affably. "I just had a steak about the size of a horse blanket. And when I eat a steak it seems to move in, and take over, and control me."

"I want to thank you again for what you did for me up at Alice, at the Eagle," said Wheeler.

"I couldn't do otherwise," said Tandy. "I'm a officer of the law."

He wiped the toothpick on the seat of his corduroy pants, and stowed it in a pocket of his unbuttoned canvas vest. "Run down your boys yet?" he asked. He spoke sarcastically, because that was his habit, but not really hatefully, Wheeler decided.

"That remains to be seen," said Wheeler.

"Be sure they don't run you down first," said Tandy.

"I've been told that before," said Wheeler. "And the truth is, I don't believe I'd much care."

"If you learn anything definite," said Tandy, "let me know."

"And we'll tackle it together?" asked Wheeler. "Is that it?"

"We'll see," said Tandy evasively.

"And if you learn anything definite, let me know," said Wheeler.

"That's different," said Tandy. "Be sensible about this."

Tandy dropped his eyes. He studied the dead beetles in the thick velvety dust around his boot-toes. Finally, he said, "I got something to tell you."

"Suit yourself," said Wheeler.

"It's this," said Tandy. "Cast your mind back to the Eagle Saloon, for instance. Remember the customers there? The drifters and the riffraff? What was the difference between you and them?"

Wheeler decided not to answer, to let Tandy do all the talking.

"The difference," said Tandy, "is that you won't lie or cheat or steal. That you got a code, and live by it. Now I want to ask you this. What's the difference between *me* and them?"

"You got a code, too," said Wheeler.

"No," said Tandy. "That's not it. And if I'd tell you my code, you couldn't stand there and listen to it. The difference between me and them, between me and the main body of the rest of the world, for that matter, is that I wear this badge."

"I call that a pretty thin difference," said Wheeler.

"Sure, I know you do," said Tandy. "But for one thing —just to show you a tiny part of what I mean—it's the difference between a gunfighter and a gunman."

"No badge is that," said Wheeler angrily.

"It's that, and more," said Tandy. "Folks that used to call me Blackie, and worse, now call me Deputy Tandy and Mr. Tandy and even Sheriff Tandy. Folks like you, I mean."

"Anything else?" said Wheeler shortly.

"Plenty else," said Tandy. "For one thing, now I ride with the posse instead of ahead of it. You eat better that way, and live longer."

When Wheeler looked at him in disgust, Tandy said, "I told you you wouldn't care much for my code. But now you get the idea. The idea is the badge. I got it, you ain't. And I ain't going to have you nor nobody else trying to freeze me out. Do you understand?"

"I understand your point, all right," said Wheeler. "But it was my son that was killed, not yours."

"I hate to say this," said Tandy, "But I've just give you a warning. And I don't warn twice."

Now Tandy had raised his eyes from the dust, not to Wheeler's face, not to meet him gaze to gaze, but to that attitude with which people were so familiar, that sinister, vague stare at the area in Wheeler's navel.

When he spoke, however, his voice was not sinister. It was highly amused at some selfish little joke. He said, "I hear you've gone out of the cattle business into the stole horses business."

For an instant, Wheeler didn't get it. Then he did. He remained silent.

"A man named Haggerty," said Tandy, "came riding into town a short time back at a full gallop from his place up at Halfway. He described you, in good detail, and warned me if you come to Bearskin you was a horse thief and had made him an offer."

"Is Haggerty a friend of yours?" asked Wheeler.

Coldly, Tandy said, "It's none of your hoity-toity damned business who my friends are. But I'll say this much for Haggerty, we sometimes trade favors and it works out satisfactory to the parties mutually concerned."

A man and a little boy came out of the syrupy blackness of the night, and joined them in the thick soft dust in the apron of lamplight. It was the male contingent of the Tennessee Darnleys, Mr. Darnley, sire, and son, Griffin. Mr. Darnley beamed at them. As usual, young Griffin looked as though he was just recovering from some sort of paternal reprimand.

"First," said Mr. Darnley, "say 'thank you, Mr. Wheeler, for that roan horse'."

Griffin said, "Thank you for that roan horse, Mr. Wheeler. I took all the burrs out of her tail and she's as good as new."

"You din't need to add that," said Mr. Darnley. "Mr. Wheeler didn't put them burrs in. That was when them horses was on their own."

Tandy said, "What is this? More horses, Mr. Wheeler?"

"We're talking about the saddle horses the Simmons gang stole from my stable on Elm," said Wheeler. "And turned loose, and wound up at the Darnley place." He didn't mention that he had given the boy the roan; when you made a gift, you didn't bring it up and keep talking about it.

"Oh," said Tandy and waited.

"The boy felt obligated to you, Mr. Wheeler," said Darnley. "He wanted to do something for you. Know what he done?"

"What?" said Tandy.

Darnley said, "He reads a little sign. It come into his head to backtrack them horses down the dry wash and see if after all this time they was still anything left that might tell him anything. They wasn't much chance what with Rawling's sheep and all, but he took a crack at it."

"What did he find?" asked Wheeler.

"Tell him, Griffin," said Darnley.

The boy seemed struck mute with so much adult male

attention focused on him. He tried to speak, went dumb, tried it again. "They ain't much to tell," he said weakly.

"Let's hear it anyway," said Wheeler encouragingly.

"Well," said the boy, "they wasn't too much to go on, but I jest kept right at it. I tracked them south off our place and into Rawling's dry wash. There, they wasn't hardly any sign at all, but I took my good old time. That's a long wash. After a while, at the south edge of Rawling's land, I come to where they was turned into it."

"And what sign was there?" asked Wheeler. "I mean there, where they were turned into the gully?"

"They wasn't any sign there, or anywheres around there." The boy looked unhappy. "That's plate rock and leaf rock, weathered since then and showing nothing whatsoever."

"Did you come to town to tell us this?" asked Wheeler.

"Yes, sir," said the boy. "I thought you'd like to know. Here's what happened to them horses. They was turned into the dry wash, went up the wash through Rawling's land, out into the mire, crossed the mire and come to us, where we put them up."

"We knew that already," said Tandy.

"But we thank you just the same," said Wheeler.

Darnley took the boy's small hand and said, "Let's go, son."

"Just a minute," said Tandy. "Boy, don't tell me you're a twelve-year-old law officer?"

Wheeler could hardly believe it. Tandy was jealous even of this youngster.

"No, sir," said the boy. "I'm an eleven-year-old rancher."

"And a good one," put in his father defensively.

Tandy walked away.

The boy said, "Papa, let's get the hell out of this place. I want to go home. I don't like this town."

"He likes you, Mr. Wheeler," said Darnley. "And I'm sure he likes Deputy Tandy, too. But it's jest that he was raised so close to his mama and me."

Now they, too, walked away.

Wheeler went to the Magnolia House stable, saddled his mare, packed her lightly with a few provisions from the hotel kitchen, and left town under a muggy black sky, heading south. Toward Two-Pines.

VIII

BY DAWN the country had become rough, and by the first sunset, as he camped in the dusk, he could see that to the south, which would be tomorrow's direction, it was a hell of a lot rougher. Beyond a belt of furrowed ravines, sudden unthrusting craggy mountains loomed, copper and vermilion in the setting sun, softening to slate-gray and lavender in the growing dusk. From where he sat, he realized, it looked not only rough, but impenetrable.

The next day, as he threaded his way into brushy hillsides rocketing sheer around him, riven and networked by a maze of midget lunatic abysses, he walked his mount often. A little after midday he veered West, starting the wide loop which Judge Venable had suggested, the loop which would take him from the main trail itself which would bypass the old settlement of Two-Pine itself and bring him eventually downstream from it. At dawn, he headed dead south again, and about noon, taking his bearings carefully, swung east.

He hit the creek, went upstream along its bank, and came to the pool in the last hot-oven interval of the afternoon.

It was exactly as Judge Venable had described it, except that the Judge had omitted the mention of the summer sun and the suffocating imprisoned heat. The pool itself, cold blue with depth, its surface glassy and unrippled in the breathless air, was an area perhaps the size of three big barn floors. Enclosing in on three sides were the rocks, a rock-wing left and right and a pocked and pitted limestone cliff at the rear. Down the face of this cliff came the trickle of water, scarcely larger than two of Wheeler's fingers—ending in a tiny mound of translucent bubbles and foam at the rock base, where it struck, and created the pool.

Wheeler stepped his mare into the water, and, hugging the west shore, walked her cautiously forward. He would be on a narrow shelf, the Judge had told him, and a misstep to the right could be the end.

Now, all at once, the rock mass at his left split, and he could see a path up the cleft, floored with ancient clay which bore a churned pattern of hoofprints.

Wheeler turned from the water, up the path. The walls were hardly a saddle-breadth wide; there was no sunlight here; it was cool and pleasant.

The path turned, and after a hundred feet of further ascent, a voice behind Wheeler said genially, "Do I know you?"

Wheeler stopped his mare. "No, you don't, I'd say," he answered. "Can I turn and have a look at you?"

"Good idee," said the voice. "Because when you gaze upon my countenance, I kin likewise and at the same time gaze upon your'n."

Slowly, Wheeler pivoted his head. There was a man leaning by the mouth of a cleft in the stone about a dozen feet behind him. He was a thin little fellow, steady-eyed, holding a rifle at his hip, a rifle aimed mighty accurately at Wheeler's upper left hand rib cage. Neither man nor rifle had been in sight when Wheeler had passed.

"Headed up to Two-Pine?" the man asked.

"Headed up to Sandy Bend, yes," said Wheeler.

The man came forward, relaxing only slightly, and said, "Kin I inquire yore business?"

Wheeler made a quick decision. He said, "I'm looking for a man named Oakley Simmons."

This was in every way better than a complicated lie —a lie in which the man might quickly expose him. If the man was a friend of Simmons, he would lead Wheeler to him, and likely immediately; if he was not a friend, and according to Haggerty of Halfway, many weren't, then he might indicate as much, and prove useful.

However, the man's face showed nothing. He said, "What do you want with Simmons?"

"Now that," said Wheeler, judging it best to put his foot down, "is none of your business."

"My!" said the man. "What have I got here? A bobcat?"

Wheeler simply waited.

"I got bad news for you," the man said at length. "Simmons and his friend was here for a while, but they left this morning. Could you name this friend, by the way?"

"Childress McGinn," said Wheeler.

"Good enough," said the man, now fully satisfied.

"Where did they go?" asked Wheeler.

"I don't know where they went," said the man. "They just left. Nobody ever tells me anything. But Slim will know."

"Then let's get to Slim," said Wheeler, showing his impatience.

Now the man appraised him, piece by piece, segment by segment. Wheeler, who never liked this kind of treatment from anyone, said, genuinely angry, "What are you looking at? What do you want from me? Trouble? Is that it, trouble?"

"No," said the man, suddenly trying to mollify him. "I just all at once got a real curiosity about you. They call me Teton, by the way. I was jest trying to figure you out, and I do believe I have done so."

"Tell me about it some other time," said Wheeler. "Right now I'm in a hurry."

"I know yore in a hurry," said the man called Teton. "And I've figured out why. Yore traveling around trying to catch up with Oakley Simmons. You want to be the new Snake Leffingwell."

"How's that again?" said Wheeler, blinking.

"Snake Leffingwell got hisself kilt. Now, at the moment, Oakley is shorthanded, and could use another man. Yore looking Oakley up, wanting to take Snake's place, wanting to join them boys."

"What I want," said Wheeler, "is to talk to Slim."

Together, they climbed the steep path.

They came out onto a grassy little shelf of tableland. On all sides, up to the edge of the cliff which they had just ascended, behind and around, rose a crescent of limestone knobs, part bare and chalky white, part covered with pine and seedling cedar. Through this little pocket of sward ran a ribbon of a creek, past the settlement to the rim of the bluff, and over, down into the pool through which Wheeler had just waded. Midway in this little pocket of flatland, the creek took a bend, and there was a shallow dune of white sand, snowy and corruscating and beautiful in the sunlight.

At the bend, a little back from the shore, was the settlement, the scattered assembly of old miners' huts. Wheeler had heard of them all his life, and now he took a good hard look. There were seven of them, some empty, some showing signs of being occupied. Built of cottonwood logs, shale-roofed, with eaves scarcely three feet from the ground, they must have been primitive hovels in the days of the miners; now they looked not only primitive, but sinister. At one side was a corral, with nine magnificent horses.

In front of the largest cabin, four men sat on their heels on the earth, in the shade—not talking, just sitting. Not enjoying each other's company, just sitting together because there was nothing else to do.

And a tough-looking crew they were, Wheeler realized. They weren't locals, he was sure. Locals would steer clear of the place likely; it was a little too close to home to be comfortable.

They were dressed in makeshift odds and ends. Three of them were run-of-the-mill hardcases, dissolute, stupid faced, and bestial, but the fourth, although of the same pattern, looked a little more intelligent. Not much, but a little. He was young, gaunt, blue chinned from fastidious shaving, and his eyes under their joined black eyebrows were blue and opaquely veiled. He was cutting a curl of worn leather from the edge of the sole of his boot with a jackknife, when Wheeler and Teton came up.

When Teton addressed him as Slim, Wheeler wasn't surprised. If this pack of curs could be said to have a head man, it had to be this one.

"He come up by the waterfall, Slim," said Teton. "He knowed the path. He also knowed Sandy Bend by name."

All of them, including Slim, got to their feet.

"Who is he?" Slim asked Teton.

"I don't know," said Teton. "He didn't tell me."

"He'll tell me," said Slim, for the first time meeting Wheeler's stare. "Who are you, friend?"

"I might be a man who has deed and title to one of

these cabins," said Wheeler. "Who inherited it from his kin and has come back to rebuild it and move in for the fishing. But I'm not."

One of the others, a carp-mouthed teen-ager with hand mended tin-rimmed spectacles, said, "I don't much care for the looks of this meat-head."

"You're a poor one to be speaking of looks," said Wheeler mildly.

"Leave it lay," said a new voice. "Simmer down, Johnnie." Wheeler glanced at the new speaker. He was an evil-looking middle-aged man with flakes of chewing tobacco caught between his foul teeth.

"They don't like you," said Slim, amused. "What are your plans, friend?"

After a moment, Wheeler said, "If worse comes to worst, I'll handle it the sensible way."

"If I was standing in your shoes, friend," said Slim, "I couldn't see no sensible way. Would you care to explain?"

"Johnnie here, and his older friend yonder, simply have to be a father-and-son team."

Wheeler had heard many times of these alliances. An older man and a young one, of no kinship whatever, teaming up to carry out their larceny and mayhem together, as a pair. They would travel together, become one in the eyes of the law, would be referred to as a father-and-son team. There would be no blood relationship between them, it was just the sort of life, the sort of existence they favored. The older man taught the younger one the seamy trade of petty crime, its ins and outs; the younger assisted and—when he was needed—protected the older.

"So what?" said Slim. He was no longer amused.

"So I'll get the old man, the 'papa,' first," said Wheeler.

The older man looked worried. The younger one looked even more worried.

"First the old man, then the boy, eh?" said Slim.

"No," said Wheeler. "First the old man, then you."

Slim flushed. "Do you think you can do it?"

"I can try," said Wheeler gently. "If I get the boy's 'papa,' the boy will go to pieces. As a matter of fact, it may put him completely out of the picture."

Teton said, "Hold it! Wait a minute, everybody. Whoa, there, Slim. You know why this man come here?"

The urgency in his tone turned their gaze toward him.

"He come here to find Oakley Simmons," Teton said. "He wants to join up with him. *He wants to take Snake Leffingwell's place!*"

"Well," said Slim. "Think of that! Some of us had had a kind of close call, could be. Snake Leffingwell's place. And Snake had a kind of special place with that outfit, I'd say. They say he was their heavy-duty gunman. And that I believe. He was not only topnotch in that department, but maybe he was a little better than topnotch."

"And Deputy Tandy of Bearskin," said Wheeler, "was a little better than Snake Leffingwell."

"So the story goes," said Slim. "But who will ever know? Even the best has his bad days."

"Well, that's over," said Teton, expelling his breath in relief. "Whew!"

"What I want," said Wheeler, "is to find Oakley Simmons, not to stop off on the way and quarrel. Teton, you can say that for me while you're at it."

"Whew!" repeated Tenton. "He wants one too."

"Thank you, Teton," said Wheeler politely.

In a further gesture of peacemaking, Johnnie said, "We're just fixin' to eat a little supper, corn dodgers and fried bear liver. Grab a plate and sit down with us."

"Thank you kindly, but no," said Wheeler. "Slim, where will I find him?"

"That's pretty hard to answer," said Slim agreeably. "I can tell you where him and McGinn have gone, and where they're going next, but I doubt if I can tell you how to find him. In fact, that's the way Oakley spends all day, every day, keeping people from finding him."

"That's understandable," said Wheeler. "But I have a feeling that this time he's going to be found."

"Then you better do it in a hurry. Say in the next few days or so. After that, I doubt if either you or me will ever see him again."

"How so?" asked Wheeler.

"He's hitting a place. For traveling money, you might say. He's headed for Canada after that."

"Canada?" said Wheeler. "You must mean Mexico."

"I mean Canada. Long-gone, never no more to come back. Since that boy was killed, things is red-hot for him. He's got no resting place."

"What job is he on?" asked Wheeler. "Or didn't he tell you?"

"Oh, he told me all right," said Slim in contempt. "He tells just about everything he knows. And a heap he doesn't know, for that matter. Him and McGinn are headed for Dwyersville, to take Kimble."

Wheeler knew the country about Dwyersville, but not the town too well. It was northeast of Two-Pine, up on the southern fringes of a wilderness country, a spanking new and prosperous little hamlet, separated from the rest of the state by a belt of hills and cedar brakes to its north.

"Who is this Kimble?" asked Wheeler.

Kimble, it was explained to him—just about all of them taking part in the conversation, interrupting each

other, overriding each other—was a comparative new-
comer, a private banker there in Dwyersville. He lived in
the biggest house in the village, a big, narrow, frame
house painted coffee brown. There were no banks nearer
to Dwyersville than Bearskin, so Kimble had set up a
thriving little banking business in his office.

They were using the word 'office,' Wheeler knew, old
style, to mean a little building in the yard near the
houe.

"The place seems like a natural target to me," said
Wheeler. "It's funny it hasn't been robbed before."

"It has," said Slim. "Too many times. Three times in
five months. I wouldn't touch it with a forty-foot pole."

"Anything they get there," said Teton unctuously,
"they're going to have to work for. Nothing in life is free."

All at once, thinking of something else, Slim began to
laugh.

"What?" asked Wheeler.

"I was thinking about the other fellow," said Slim.
"The one that hadn't scarcely left when you showed up.
Asking for Oakley, too."

Wheeler felt his body grown rigid. "Who was this
one?"

"He said he was Oakley's brother," said Slim. "And
that Oakley's mother had just died, and left a dying
message for Oakley, and that he was riding hard to ketch
up with Oakley and deliver it. He come up by the cliff
path, too."

"What did he look like?" asked Wheeler.

"A lean, medium-tall man, with a mop of gritty black
hair like a buffalo mane."

Deputy Tandy.

Wheeler moistened his lips. Always, Deputy Tandy
seemed to be a little ahead of him.

"What did you tell him?" asked Wheeler.

"We told him nothing. We told him that Simmons had been here and gone and we didn't know where. You see he had two little holes in the cloth above the breast pocket of his shirt that could mighty well have been pinholes from a badge. And the badge could have been in his pants pocket, there, but out of sight."

Despite himself, Wheeler smiled. He said, "He's lucky you didn't gun him down, like you started to do me."

"Gun down your friends and enemies and so on," said Slim smugly. "But never gun down a law officer if you kin he'p it. It just brings along more and more of 'em. They's no end to 'em. They go on forever."

"How do I leave this place?" asked Wheeler. "The way I came?"

"No," said Slim. "By the north. By the main trail, the Dwyersville trail. Teton will put you on it. He brought you in, he can put you out."

As Wheeler rode away, Teton walking by his saddlehorn, Slim raised his hand. "So long," he said.

"Come back agin, any time," called Johnnie.

IX

GRAY DAWN went into silver dawn, and the silver had burned off in the great dome of the sky to hot metallic blue fluffed with small motionless clouds, when Wheeler edged his mare down Dwyersville's broad single street. It wasn't a street, actually; it was a road, rutted and lumpy and grassy, and so wide that the fringe of newish-looking frame shacks and stores and saloons on either side of it seemed to be two little towns, facing each other.

The store fronts along either side of the road were ragged with buggies and hitched saddle horses and wagons. People stood in little knots, farmers and ranchers and townsmen, talking. It looked like market day but Wheeler knew better. Oakley Simmons had been here.

Been and gone, likely.

People looked shocked and angry. It was a new town, with new people, emigrants mainly, who hadn't yet learned the ways of their new countryside. New ones, without experience, were always the wild ones. Wheeler didn't like the temper that roiled about him in the dusty air. Nobody spoke to him; everybody stared at him as he passed.

He knew the Kimble house the instant he saw it. It sat back on the left side of the road, a two story frame residence, coffee brown, with curlicue cornices at its eaves, painted white, and white painted sills at its windows. In the back yard, not far from the kitchen door, at the end of a brick path, was the office: a squarish brown

95

building not much bigger than a chicken coop. Not much bigger than a chicken coop, but handling, Wheeler realized, probably at least a hundred square miles of banking business.

There was no one in sight, in the yard or on the porch. Everywhere else the town had been saturated with people. But there were none here. The blinds had been drawn at all the windows, bleaky dim in the smashing yellow sunlight. Wheeler tied his mare at a locust post with an iron ring in it, and mounted the new wooden steps to the porch. He had raised his hand to knock when the door opened.

Two women came out, a frail old woman with a walking stick and a younger woman holding her left arm in a bloody sling. The frail old one carried a hammer and a brassheaded carpet tack, the younger one a big wreath of freshcut garden flowers. They tried, falteringly and unsuccessfully, to tack the wreath to the door panel.

Gently, Wheeler took the things from their hands and did it for them.

They thanked him. The old one said, "Did you come here on business, or did you come to see him?"

"I came on business, of a sort," Wheeler said.

"It's too late for business with him," said the younger woman.

"I know," said Wheeler.

"We just got him back from the undertaker," said the old one. "He's in the parlor. You want to see him?"

How could you say "no" to a thing like that?

"Please," Wheeler said.

They entered the half light of the hall and turned into a darkened parlor, indistinct, murky from drawn curtains, still smelling of new wallpaper paste and varnish. A coffin was on two sawhorse trestles, open. The dead man in it was about thirty-five, the younger woman's husband, probably. He wore business clothes, a gate-ajar collar and good brown broadcloth, and had an intelligent looking long skull and a hawknose. Wheeler liked the looks of him; he wished he had known him before.

They stood for a moment in silence. When Wheeler turned to leave, the women went with him. Again on the porch, he said, "I hate to ask you, but I've got to know. When and how did it happen?"

The younger woman said, "This man, this man I know now was Oakley Simmons, came to the door here about four o'clock this morning, with this other man I know now was Childress McGinn. They said it was urgent, that they wanted to talk to my husband, Mr. Kimble. They said they were brothers and owned a ranch and had to have some money to build two barns. They hated to wake him up at that hour, but they had lost their father's money in a poker game. They wanted to borrow this money from Mr. Kimble. They seemed very worried."

"It was all a lie," said the old woman indignantly. "They were liars and robbers!"

"Yes," said Wheeler. "What did you do then, Mrs. Kimble?"

"Who was I to decide my husband's affairs? I went up to the bedroom and got him. But he had been through robbery before and came down the stairs with a pistol in his hand. They were standing just inside the door, in the hall there. When they saw his pistol, in the open like that, they shot and killed him."

"They're fugitives," said Wheeler. "Wanted for murder. Besides, they don't care too much about killing. How did you get yours?"

"She tried to push in between them," said the old one.

"I see," said Wheeler. "What's going to become of the business?"

Mrs. Kimble said, "I used to help him a heap with it. Now I'm going to try to run it alone."

Wheeler looked at her, at the fire in her eye, at the iron in her jaw. He had a feeling she could do just that.

"My name is Charles Wheeler," he said. "I'm a cattle dealer up at Bearskin. I'm known pretty well up there, on the other side of the cedars. If there ever is a way I can help you—anyway at all—just get in touch with me."

"I believe you mean that," said Mrs. Kimble quietly.

"Yes," said Wheeler. "I wouldn't say it if I didn't."

He walked to his mare, untied her, mounted, and rode away, back up the street.

He kept telling himself that he hadn't been responsible for Kimble's death just because he had been six hours late. He had to fight off the same mood that had come over him when he had found Seth; that it was his fault. When you were a running man, like Tabby said, it seemed no matter how fast you ran, it wasn't fast enough.

In the mercantile section of the town, on the left-hand side of the road, all wagons and buggies had been cleared and were now replaced with a mixed and variegated line of saddled horses, specimens up and down the scale, from shaggy, unkempt farm horses to sleek thoroughbreds. A posse was being assembled, Wheeler knew. He passed it by. He wondered idly who would lead it. Dwyersville was too small and too distant to have a resident deputy like Tandy. It would have a marshal, but, ten to one, the marshal would probably be a useless old man. It was Wheeler's guess that the leader of the posse would emerge from the citizenry.

He dismounted at the watering trough and watered his mare. Then he watered himself from an adjacent pump. He was mighty thirsty. He was just replacing the dipper on its baling wire hook on the pumphandle, eyes lowered from weariness, when he saw the boots. Three pairs of boot-toes in the dust, standing in a little circle about him. He looked up.

The three men were dressed differently, of different ages, different occupations. One, in rumpled brown wool, he judged to be a town merchant. Another, bleary-eyed and in patched khaki, with a pulled down mouth, as though he had just eaten a green persimmon, looked to be a small-time rancher or farmer. The third was another townsman, with glossy pop-eyes, pink-veined wattles to his pendulous cheeks, shoulders back, exploding with self-importance.

"My name is Ned Prynne," said this one, in a loud-mouthed offensive way. "I am said to be Dwyersville's, well, most favorite son. I didn't catch yours."

He extended a paw to shake hands, but Wheeler, disliking his looks, ignored it. "I didn't give it," he said. He had taken the bit from his mare's mouth to give her a rest; now he replaced it.

Prynne, steaming under Wheeler's rebuff, trying to hide it, said, "There was a heinous crime perpetrated in our community, this morning, suh. We are assembling a posse. You will take your mount down to Massey's General store and join the others. And I would advise alacrity. Time is of the essence."

So this was the 'leader,' the citizen who had pushed himself forward to take charge of the chaos. No power yesterday, maybe, and no power tomorrow, maybe, but now, in the fervor and stress, the leader, the man of power.

Wheeler said civilly, "I'm afraid that will be impossible. I'm in a hurry. I'm on my own personal business."

Prynne recoiled dramatically, as though he could hardly believe his ears. "And your business is more important than our business? Than the business of this entire community?"

"I haven't time to argue," said Wheeler.

As he put his hand on his saddlehorm to mount, Prynne said to him, "We were just studying the brand on your mare here, whilst you was taking your drink of water. I can't seem to place it." Turning to his companions, he asked. "Can either of you gentlemen place it?" They shook their heads.

"It's a Utah brand," said Wheeler.

"You from Utah?" asked Prynne.

"No," said Wheeler.

"Where might you be from?" asked Prynne. "If you don't object to answerin'."

"From Bearskin," said Wheeler, suddenly being cautious.

"And who can prove different?" said Prynne, with offensive jollity. "What brings you here, I wonder?"

"I'm just passing through," said Wheeler.

"Always they seem to be just passing through," said Prynne, into the air, to the rooftops. "I been to Bearskin. Twice. On very important business, I might add. I never forget a face. How come I ain't seen you there?"

"Get back," said Wheeler. "I'm mounting."

He felt a gun muzzle in the small of his back. From behind him, the bleary-eyed small-time farmer said, "Not until Mr. Prynne is through with you."

"And that might be some time," said Prynne pompously. "Thank you, Mr. Nicholson. Relieve this man of his weapon. That's right." Wheeler felt his gun slipped out of its holster.

"Now, Mr. Nicholson," said Prynne. "Escort him to that empty storeroom behind Massey's, and hold him. I'll want to question him later."

"You bet!" said Nicholson.

"I'll have your lunches and suppers sent over to you from the cafe," said Prynne. "Out of my own pocket, I might add."

"Lunches and supper?" said Wheeler. "Hold me how long?"

"Who can say?" said Prynne. "Until I get back with my posse, whenever that will be."

He walked away with his friend, the other townsman. Nicholson said harshly, "You heard him. Move!"

With Wheeler's gun in his belt, behind his belt buckle, he started Wheeler down the street. Every pair of eyes that they passed, taking in the two man procession, glared. Nobody was liking stranger, any stranger, today.

Behind a row of buildings, Nicholson tied Wheeler's mare to the spoke of a broken down wagon, and gestured Wheeler through a door. Wheeler found himself in a big empty room, windowless and dust-moted from a cracked glass skylight high overhead. It was hot, and from the smell of it, Wheeler decided it had once been used as a grain and feed storeroom.

"Set," said Nicholson, and pointed down.

Wheeler sat cross-legged on the bare floor. Nicholson pulled up an empty box and perched himself on the edge of it, about ten feet from his captive.

He inspected Wheeler morosely and belligerently. He saw a small weary man, with very pale, very steady eyes. He could well believe that he was looking at a desperate, dangerous man. He sucked in a rasping breath, and blinked.

Wheeler's fixed gray eyes returned his gaze. He saw watery red-rimmed dull eyes, a harsh self-pitying mouth, and enough encrusted grime on a crinkled neck to raise a crop of potatoes. There was a wicked vagueness about this man that Wheeler didn't much care for. Nevertheless, Wheeler sounded him out. He said, "I was riding for a doctor. I've got a sick baby. I've got to get out of here!"

Nicholson said, "Then go." He didn't exactly smile, but he looked faintly pleased.

"You mean it?" asked Wheeler.

"Sure. Jest git up and walk out."

If Nicholson had meant, or only half-meant, what he said, his trigger finger would have relaxed, if only slightly. To the contrary, it stiffened—stiffened like an expectant hunter waiting for a flush of game.

"You want to kill me, don't you?" said Wheeler sociably.

"No. I don't care one way or the other. If I wanted to kill you, I'd have did it before we come in."

"Are you a rancher or a farmer?" asked Wheeler conversationally.

"Neither, I guess. I had a ranch and it failed. I had a farm and it failed. The only thing that ever come into my life that didn't whipsaw me was that trolley I run back in Cincinnati."

"Then why don't you go back to Cincinnati?" said Wheeler.

"And leave all this golden opportunity out here? No, sir! For one thing it cost me too much to get here. It cost me a sixteen-year-old bride, six pigs, two cows, and a team of blue mules."

"So you're going to stick it out?"

"Of course. There's fortunes to be made here. If you know cows or cotton."

"Do you know cows?

"Not too well. They seem to know me better'n I know them. And don't bother to ask, do I know cotton. Cotton's done showed me it's too much for me. Did you know cotton gits diseases just like humans?"

"Do you mean goiter and backache and measles, and things like that?" said Wheeler, showing intense interest.

"Worse. Much worse. In fact, it has its own special ailments. Would you like to git up and walk around for a spell?"

"So you can take a potshot at me?" said Wheeler. "No thanks."

"The way I am now," said Nicholson, "the way I been the past few years, I never know one minute what I might do the next minute. If you should make some kind of move I took the wrong way, and I got excited and cut loose on you, it wouldn't be personal. You understand that?"

"I'm afraid I do," said Wheeler, and lapsed into silence.

About ten minutes went by, taut, almost unbearable.

Abruptly, there was a rapping on the door.

The activity that surged through Nicholson was a marvel to behold. He whipped from the box to his feet, looked around for shelter, found none in the bare room, and crouched, steadying his revolver barrel on the crooked elbow of his other arm, holding it rifle fashion aimed at the panels of the door.

"Some of them accomplices of yours, come to rescue you," whispered Nicholson. "Well, they're in for a surprise. I ain't a man to give up easy, as they will shortly learn."

"Better save a bullet for yourself," said Wheeler. "I've got some mighty bad accomplices."

He wondered who in the hell it was.

"Come in!" yelled Nicholson.

Sheriff Markham strolled in, chomping an apple.

"I heard they had you cached here," he said genially to Wheeler. "What you got yourself into, son?"

"That's hard to say," said Wheeler. "I'm not too sure myself."

"Well here I am, the long arm of the law, to git you out." To Nicholson, he said, "Give the gentleman back his pistol."

Nicholson, glowering, did so. "Mr. Prynne ain't going to like this," he said.

"Mr. Prynne kin suck a duck egg," said Sheriff Markham affably. "Shall we go, Mr. Wheeler?"

They went.

Outside, Wheeler untied his horse and mounted. The sheriff stood by. Wheeler said, "How did you happen to show up, like a gift from God?"

"I am a gift from God," said Sheriff Markham, hurt. "Why don't you git like my other constituents and admit it?"

"I mean where did you hear about me?"

"You're common talk uptown, up in front of Massey's Store."

"But what were you doing so far away from home? I thought you generally stayed pretty nearby to Alice."

"Oh, I wouldn't say that, wouldn't say that at all," said Sheriff Markham. "I hound law-breakers from corner to corner in this vast and glorious county. But in this particular instance, I was headed for my vacation when I happened to run into this mess. I'm taking over the posse, of course. Which brings me—"

"Vacation?" said Wheeler. "Where?"

"Fishing. They's a place some distance south of here called Two-Pines. And just south, downstream of Two-Pines they is a beautiful pool which old-timers say has the biggest and most fish in the state of Texas. I was jest going to bask in the sun, and while away the time, and relax and try to build up my overworked nerves."

"And then you ran into this?"

"And then I ran into this," said Sheriff Markham. "And a good sheriff is first and foremost a lawman. Blast it, I don't have no choice."

"That sounds like a reasonable point of view," said Wheeler. "Well, I won't keep you from it." He took up his reins.

"The posse is collecting in front of the general store," said the sheriff.

"I noticed," said Wheeler. "Well, good luck to you."

"Good luck to all of us," said the sheriff. "And that includes you."

"Why me?"

"Because you're going along."

"I can't make it," said Wheeler regretfully.

"That's too bad, because you're going to make it."

"What makes you say so?"

"Because I say so."

Suddenly it was a new sheriff to Wheeler, weak-mouthed but iron-eyed. A stubborn ineffectual man who didn't like to be contradicted.

Oakley Simmons and Childress McGinn would never be overtaken and caught by a posse, any posse. They were too posse-wise—they had to be—and certainly they must be expecting a posse. Besides, Wheeler had ideas on the subject, which he knew he would never be able to get across to a crazy, pigheaded, opinionated posse.

If Simmons was to be overtaken, Wheeler himself would have to do it, alone, and in his own manner.

Sheriff Markham was waiting, glaring.

Wheeler said, "I just can't do it."

"Don't you feel any responsibility as a decent respectable citizen?"

Wheeler made no answer.

"I'll remember this," said Sheriff Markham darkly.

"I know you will," said Wheeler. "And I'm sorry."

Suddenly Markham, hedging his bets, playing both sides, beamed. "What the heck," he said, "we're acting like children. Let's part friends."

"Friends it is," said Wheeler, dancing his mare a few steps, riding away.

X

THE CEDAR BRAKES started just out of town, in fact at the very northern edge of town. Wheeler had crossed them before and they were about as barren and desolate as any country he had ever encountered. The belt, miles deep, without order or pattern, was a crazy succession of wandering gulches, camelback humps of clay, flat pans of cracked dry silt, sometimes thick with cedars stinging his flesh as he pushed through them, blue-green and aromatic, in the sun's brutal hammering. Simmons and McGinn, he decided, if they knew this country, and they probably did—for it was by familiarity of such rough terrain that they managed to survive—would head for Spanish Wells. From Spanish Wells, likely they would start their night travel jump-off for Wyoming and Wind River. Nights they would travel, then, carefully and secretly. But now it would be night and day, fast, until Dwyersville was far behind them.

This was an area almost entirely of scattered and un-dependable waterholes, varying according to the season and the whims of the weather. The only dependable water was Spanish Wells, a wilderness engulfed group of three tepid mud holes. Simmons and McGinn would certainly head for Spanish Wells. They would try to pass them on the fly, but they would head for them.

Wheeler figured they would likely take the old Spanish burrow trail, long overgrown.

There was a shortcut though, a bowstring to the arc,

and Wheeler had to wrestle his way through the cedars and later trees and undergrowth.

He looked at the slanting shadows of the tree trunks, studying their angles of slant as accurately as possible, looked at the position of the sun, checked it all with his big silver watch, and swerved his mare directly into the flanking foliage.

He was satisfied that his calculations had given him his direction. A little later, he knew, he would have landmarks. He had been through this country several times, before there was a Dwyersville. But that had been years ago. He had always had a sense of terrain, though. And the rougher it was, the better he remembered it.

It was about four o'clock when he pushed aside the last branch and came out into the shallow bowl-like declivity which was Spanish Wells.

He was sure he must be ahead of his quarry, and was not concerned on this count. During his rugged ride, he made up his mind on his procedures, and now he began putting his decision into action.

The three basinlike holes were, at this time of year, small, each with only a little water in it, and a little brownish sediment. The two smaller holes were almost engulfed by hanging branches from the shore, and choked with grass. The larger hole, with four half submerged, beady-eyed turtles staring at him, was edged on two sides with an apron of boggy mud. He dismounted and watered his horse. Wheeler, himself, drank long and fully; for to him water was water, and he had seen worse.

He then started a careful and expert search, found plenty of animal tracks, but no recent horsemen tracks. His assumption had been correct. If they were heading here, he was ahead of them.

He had decided not to find them, but to let them find him.

It was dangerous, but not more dangerous than the other way.

He didn't know them by sight, except for Judge Venable's description; and he was pretty sure they didn't know him by sight either.

He then settled down for what might be a long wait.

Out of his pocket, he took a chunk of sandstone he had picked up earlier in the afternoon, and lifted his mare's right forefoot. Yes. He took off his hat, put about a cupful of muddy water in it, and placed it on the ground beside him.

Then he began. Once, long ago, at night, when a catamount had wailed from a bluff, his mare had taken sudden fright and shied. He had been riding on flint then, and the shying had left a scratch a fraction of an inch deep on the bottom of her shoe. Now, working systematically and conscientiously, dipping the stone in water from his hat, scrubbing the bottom of the shoe, dipping the stone once more, scrubbing again, he began the slow tedious job of burnishing out the scratch. It was going to take a long time, and that was the way he wanted it.

He knew he wouldn't hear them when they came. He didn't. All waterholes were approached with caution, even by innocent travelers. And these men had a price on their heads.

He happened to be looking at the waterhole, and the four turtles submerged completely, silently, leaving nothing but the surface of the water—and he knew he had company.

He looked up and around. They were sitting their

mounts, the two of them, watching him, grinning. Relaxed.

They weren't hostile, that was the important point: They were not hostile.

And they were exactly as the Huntsville records and Judge Venable had described them. One of them was tall, skinny, hunched and ugly, red-haired and sort of tubercular looking; that would be Simmons himself, Oakley Simmons. The other was big chested, with ringlets of jet hair growing down the back of his neck; this one looked more animal than man. He would be the bad one, the intelligent one, Childress McGinn.

"I don't like to be sneaked up on," said Wheeler. "How long have you been there?"

Neither of them answered this. Simmons said jocularly, "Now what on earth are you doing?"

"Nothing," said Wheeler. "Just resting a little, and passing the time."

They dismounted, both of them, and came lazily forward. McGinn picked up Cindy's off forefoot.

He said, "Whetting off a scratch on her shoe."

"I like my horse to have shiny shoes," said Wheeler.

"Even on the bottoms?" asked Simmons, chuckling.

"Even on the bottoms," said Wheeler. "What are you trying to do? Make trouble?"

"Even on the bottoms," said McGinn. "Maybe he means especially on the bottoms."

They watered their mounts; then they drank, and rejoined him.

Wheeler said, "What are you gentlemen talking about?"

"Will you do me a favor?" said Simmons. "Will you take your mare by the bridle and lead her around in a little circle?"

"Why should I?" asked Wheeler.

"Why shouldn't you?" answered McGinn.

Wheeler shrugged, and did as he had been asked.

McGinn studied her tracks, her new tracks. He then went to the edge of the waterhole and studied the tracks she had left on her arrival. "Hardly seems like the same horse," he said.

"Maybe it's not supposed to," said Simmons, with a smirk. "Somebody been chasing you, friend?"

Wheeler said nothing.

Simmons said, "Well, somebody's chasing us. So don't head south. Or you'll run into them, and be asked some questions of a mighty personal nature. I'm Oakley Simmons, and this-here is Childress McGinn."

"Is that supposed to mean something?" asked Wheeler.

"Leave it lay," rasped McGinn. "What you got in the line of food?"

"A few onions," said Wheeler, "a chunk of dried beef, and some crackers. Why?"

"Get it out," ordered Simmons. "All of it."

They ate, Wheeler joining them. They ate the onions, peel and all, swallowed the hard beef in great hunks, and softened the crackers, hardtack, in the muddy water. Afterwards, they all sat on the ground, with crossed ankles, and rolled and smoked cigarettes in contented silence. Finally, Simmons said, "That was good grub. Where did you buy it? At Bearskin, mebbe?"

They were trying to get him to back-trail himself, trying to learn a little about him.

"North of Bearskin," Wheeler said. "At a place called Halfway. I doubt if you've ever heard of it."

They said neither yes nor no.

After a moment, Simmons said, "Where are you bound for?"

111

"Nowhere," said Wheeler, smiling for the first time. "Just traveling, just seeing a little of this beautiful country."

"Listen," said Simmons, "if you're not afraid of gunpowder, why don't you ride along with us. Maybe we can use each other."

"It's worth a try," said Wheeler.

For sometime now, McGinn's evil little animal eyes had been burning into his. Were they trying to read him? Were they suspicious of him and trying to figure him out? Or had they identified him? It was not at all impossible that McGinn had seen him before, almost anywhere, maybe when Wheeler had been out on one of his buying trips. Or were they trying to convey some message, were they trying to talk to him, to say something?

Wheeler, who made it a habit never to allow himself to be stared out of countenance, who normally beat such a stare down, crumpled it, with his own fixed, responsive gaze, in this case averted his glance. If it was a duel, he wanted no part of it at this moment. If it was an attempt at communication, he wanted no part of this either.

After a bit, Simmons, in his arrogant manner, said, "It's time to move."

McGinn spat, then spoke. To Wheeler, he said, "Mount, ride a little piece up the trail, and wait." To Simmons, he said, "Oakley, I want to speak to you. Alone."

Wheeler, hesitated. After an instant, he decided that at this stage it might be better to play along. He mounted, and followed McGinn's directions.

He rode a little piece, a mighty little piece, and pulled up to a stop in a clump of undergrowth.

A pistol shot crashed out, a single blasting roar, and before he could turn his mare to return and investigate, McGinn, his teeth bared mirthlessly, was by his side. Wheeler asked, "What was that?"

"I couldn't say," said McGinn. He ejected an empty cartridge case from the cylinder of his pistol, and replaced it with a new one from his belt. "Forget it."

"I'm not built that way," said Wheeler. "Let's go back." They swerved their horses and returned to the waterhole.

Simmons lay spraddled at the edge of the largest hole, his legs and waist on the cracked dry mud, his chest and head and arms half floating in the brown water.

Wheeler said, "You shot him?"

"Right," said McGinn, watching Wheeler unblinkingly. "Why?"

"For one reason," said McGinn, "I jest couldn't take him no more. And this was as good a place and time as any."

"Time, maybe," said Wheeler coldly. "But not place. Let's get him out of there. By noon tomorrow that hole will be spoiled for a year."

"If you say so," agreed McGinn sardonically. Together, they dragged the body about a dozen yards back into the brush. This done, back at their mounts again, and in their saddles, Wheeler said, "Maybe I'd better know a little more about this, if you care to go into it."

"I was just fixin' to go into it," said McGinn, and paused.

Wheeler sat motionless.

McGinn said woodenly, "I was dissolving a partnership."

"Well, that's one way to do it," said Wheeler sourly.

"I've been studyin' you," said McGinn. "The new

partnership is you and me. Just you and me. We'll rip this country wide open. But first we had to get shet of Oakley. He was a bungler. Stupid. Trouble. Nothing but trouble."

"And if I don't turn out the way you want me, you'll dissolve me, too?"

"We'll cross that bridge when we come to it," said McGinn. "You got two hands jest like me, hain't you?"

"What kind of trouble did he get you into?" asked Wheeler.

"Well, for one thing, he talked me into trying to rob a banker named Kimble, down at Dwyersville. And killed Kimble, and got nothing whatever out of it. Nothing. Except a posse, of course."

Wheeler, remembering Mrs. Kimble, said nothing.

McGinn said, "Well, he won't bungle nothing more."

"If he is the man I heard about, the Oakley Simmons I heard about," said Wheeler quietly, "he lost four thousand dollars in gold in a poker game at a place called Sandy Bend."

Startled, McGinn said, "I thought you said you didn't know nothing about us."

"I didn't say anything, one way or the other. If he was such a bungler, where did he get four thousand dollars?"

Suddenly evasive, McGinn said, "I don't have no idee."

"You'd know if anyone would. You traveled with him."

"Saved it, I guess," said McGinn. "That's right. Saved it. He was a saver. I'm a spender myself. Easy come, easy go. But Oakley was a saver."

"A miser and a gambler," mused Wheeler. "I don't believe I ever ran into that combination in the same man.

I don't believe he saved up that money. You know how I think he got it?"

McGinn didn't like any of this, and his face showed it. "How?"

"I think the three of you—you, and Snake Leffingwell, and Simmons—killed a little boy in Bearskin, and took it."

Very softly, very softly indeed, McGinn said, "Now what makes you think that?"

Wheeler's gun was out, and resting, steady across his saddlehorn. "Because I'm the little boy's father," he said.

He took McGinn's weapon half drawn, from McGinn's limp hand.

"I should lay you beside Simmons," Wheeler said, "in the brush, and forget you. But that's not the way I do things."

Showing relief, McGinn said, "What, then?"

"Bearskin and Deputy Tandy," said Wheeler grimly.

McGinn jabbed his big dapple gray with his spurs, high in the tenderness of its underflanks, and the animal was off in a vault, in a spasm of bounding muscles, full into the cloud of shrubbery, and was gone. It was a thing only a frantic man, in panic, would do; Wheeler held his fire.

Wheeler, slipping his weapon back into its leather, was after him in a dead-run.

There was only one way to catch him, and that was to do it quickly, branches, foliage, obstacles or no, to overtake him immediately. He was out of sight now; if he got out of earshot, he was good-bye and gone forever.

Six minutes later, Wheeler had him, beside the vine-hung trunk of a rotting tree, arms over his head in surrender, fear and desperation in his eyes.

"You can't blame a man for trying," said McGinn.

"I don't," said Wheeler curtly. "Some would."

They sat quietly for a moment, their panting fading to heavy breathing, heavy breathing changing finally to normal inhalations and exhalations.

At last, Wheeler said, "Are you ready?"

McGinn nodded.

Wheeler said, "I suppose I should tell you this—at the start. You're not my prisoner."

"Then whose prisoner am I?"

"You're the prisoner of justice," said Wheeler. "And justice says you go back to the law, dead or alive. That's the situation. I think you'd better understand it. In a manner of speaking, it's out of my hands."

Mutely, McGinn touched his mare and started north. Wheeler rode a little behind him.

By mid-afternoon, the cedar brake—the great belt that isolated Dwyersville from the rest of Texas—was behind them, but the new country was scarcely any better. Now they ran into a shallow spur of the same knobby hills and cliffs which, much further south, had hidden Sandy Bend. And McGinn, as a captive, disturbed Wheeler. He simply couldn't be that tractable. He made little conversation, but his manner was agreeable. It was almost as though he and Wheeler were taking some sort of a little pleasure trip together.

Despite himself, as the hours passed by, Wheeler became tense.

When he had stood on the Kimble front porch at Dwyersville, and talked to Mrs. Kimble and her mother, Bearskin had seemed real and somehow not actually too far away. Now it seemed almost in another world, shadowy and vague. Judge Venable, Tabby, Hackett, even, at times, Deputy Tandy, seemed opaque memories.

The only thing that seemed real was the thing he so painstakingly concentrated upon: the animal that rode so self-assured and smugly in his saddle in front of him.

XI

THE FIRST NIGHT they camped by a seeping spring in a circle of low bluffs and split rocks. It was here that Wheeler got his first touch of real worry.

McGinn had been a good prisoner all day, riding quietly, a little ahead of Wheeler's stirrup, under Wheeler's directions, amiably, docilely.

Too amiable, too docile.

He's up to something, of course, he has to be, but what in the hell is it? Wheeler thought.

It was that night, when they had eaten and were in their blankets, McGinn with his hands lashed behind him, that Wheeler got his first glimmer of the trouble which faced him.

McGinn stayed awake all night. Talking a little at times, singing a little in a subdued hum. He couldn't sleep, he said. Maybe it was indigestion.

Wheeler, naturally, stayed awake all night, too.

In the morning, all things considered, he didn't feel too badly. McGinn was joyful, sparkling, full of life. All ready to go.

It was during the next day's ride that McGinn told Wheeler that it hadn't been indigestion that kept him awake at all. He had stayed awake simply because he had put his mind to it. Staying awake at night had never been difficult for him. It was a sort of gift he had ever since he had been a boy. He could doze in the saddle, it seemed, just short catnaps, and get up a backlog of sleep to hold him. Once he had done this, he said, for nine days. "Four days into Bearskin?" he asked.

"Four days," said Wheeler calmly.

Three sleepless nights, seventy-two hours or more, and Wheeler could be a dead man. And Childress McGinn into the brush and long-gone.

He didn't have to shoot the sleepy man to kill him. McGinn could beat him to death, for example, if he was dazed with weariness, and McGinn was okay but desperate.

That morning they passed through thicket after thicket of chaparral, which gave way to long-leafed pine and hickory. All afternoon, they transversed a network of furrowed valleys, bearing nearly as they could, south by southwest. The great forests seemed endless, dense, oppressive; they were mammoth cottonwoods, mainly, but where the ground was low, boggy, were ancient wind-twisted cypress.

The ground got damper, with spots of marsh, and hummocks of swamp grass, and then drier. When they camped that night, in a dry stretch of wilderness countryside, there was only bluestem sage and wild rye, with no sign of water whatever, and they camped by utilizing their canteens.

Wheeler, a day and a night without sleep, with tense steady alertness for his prisoner, dreaded the soporific coolness of night, and darkness.

That night he tied McGinn as securely as he was able, with his picket rope this time, not only hands, but feet and ankles, too.

And this night troubled Wheeler even more than the previous one. For this night, in his blanket, McGinn neither hummed nor chatted.

Periodically, as Wheeler bent over to check on him, he

could see McGinn's eyes glinting at him by the firelight
—evil, malignant, threatening.

Savage and bloodthirsty, the report at Huntsville had
said about him.

He was waiting.

Next morning, it was the captor who was haggard
and stiff as they mounted, not the prisoner. The prisoner
was catlike and supple.

Though McGinn had spoken not at all during the
night, now, during the day's ride, he asked Wheeler
questions, intermittently, as though he were testing
Wheeler's mental acuteness. As he might stick a pole into
a muddy pool to test its depth.

It was in the middle of the third day, with Wheeler's
brain taut and seeming to sear the inside of his skull as
he fought himself now, not only to hold his prisoner but
to protect his own life—when they came out of a stand
of timber suddenly into a clearing.

At the far edge of the clearing was a truck path, dry,
but recently fenced and well-tended. In the center of the
clearing was a small cabin, of elm logs, peeled, apparently long abandoned, with a corner of its roof and
part of one end, caved-in. Two men were trying to re-
pair it, trying to make it livable; though, to Wheeler's
eye, it had been lived in anyhow, with steel traps
hanging on its lintel.

And hardcase looking characters they were, decided
Wheeler. One had cruel lidless eyes and a little puckered
mouth; the other was big and mean and stupid-looking.
They were dressed in a hodgepodge of pelts mixed with
ragged denim. They looked like any other lowdown
scummy forest-rats, except for one thing. Their gunbelts,
holsters, and weapons were mighty well cared for; and,
for that matter, no ordinary man wore his sixgun while

he was engaged on a simple little bit of carpenter work on his home.

Instantly, Wheeler decided to get out of here, that this was no place for him. He was about to retrace, about to call to McGinn—but he was too late.

McGinn had touched his mount on the flank, urged it forward, and joined the working men. "Could I have a drink of water?" he asked. And dismounted, deftly and innocently, on the far side of his horse from Wheeler.

The man with the lidless eyes produced a red cedar bucket and a dipper, and McGinn drank noisily. When he had finished, he returned the dipper, and whispering, started toward them.

Wheeler called, "McGinn! Come!" When he got no response, he dismounted and walked forward and joined their group.

When trouble loomed, a mounted man was at a disadvantage to men on foot—unless the mounted man intended to get away quick. Which was far from Wheeler's mind. He said, "Time's up, McGinn. Let's move."

"Who is this feller?" asked the big brawny man, looking annoyed.

"Name's Childress McGinn," said McGinn. "The last of the Simmons gang."

"My," said the man with the lidless eyes. "Is that so? I've always heered that the Simmons gang was an abomination unto the earth. He's shore ugly, hain't he?"

"But he jest called you McGinn," said the brawny man.

"He calls everybody McGinn," said McGinn. "Jest to mix 'em up."

Their faces were stiff, but they were having the time of their lives, laughing at him, Wheeler realized. Harshly, he said, "Who are you two?"

"Don't put on a tough voice like that when you speak to me," said the big man threateningly.

The other one, pretending to peacemake, said, "Let's be decent about this. So if anything should happen, which o' course it won't, we can always say afterwards we was decent about the whole thing. Stranger, I'm DeWitt, and my partner here is Caddo Johnson." Amusing himself immensely, he added, "Would somebody keer to explain this peculiar situation?"

McGinn said, "To start with, I'm Sheriff Markham of this county."

"Well, pleased to meet you, sir!" said Dewitt, putting on a big show of cordiality. "Welcome to our humble home."

Caddo Johnson, the brawny man, simply glowered.

McGinn, his eyes glinting maliciously, said, "I been looking for him for days. I finally came up to him back yonder in the swamp. I tried to be easy on him, but it was my downfall. He overpowered me."

"And managed to git yore gun from you, I observe," said DeWitt.

"But what's one gun agin two?" asked the brawny man.

"Where is he takin you?" asked DeWitt.

"That's the thing I cain't understand," said McGinn, grinning. "Here he's a outlaw, and a notorious one, like I said, and I'm a respectable law officer, like I said. Whoever heard of that situation? Whoever heard of a outlaw taking a law officer prisoner? What is he up to? It's unnatural. I'm scared."

"All right, McGinn," said Wheeler. "This has gone on long enough. Mount up!"

"He's not going anywhere," growled the brawny man.

DeWitt, enjoying it too much to let it end, said drolly, looking Wheeler in the eye, "Me and Caddo always tries to be fair about everything. Would you like to make a little speech and give yore side o' this? It ain't likely we'll believe it, but go right ahead."

Wheeler reached for his gun and the brawny man, surprisingly swift, drew also, and Wheeler nailed him. He went back against the door lintel, as though he had been rammed by an invisible bull, bringing down with him the cluster of steel traps, jingling and jangling, and was dead from Wheeler's slug before he hit the ground.

Several things happened, following instantly, with speed.

Moving his gun in a short arc toward DeWitt, Wheeler held his fire. The man had already drawn, but, under Wheeler's gunsight, froze. One moment he had been bullying, viciously aggressive. Now, covered, actually facing gunfire, his backbone seemed to melt.

He yelled, "Don't shoot," dropped his weapon, and took off at a lope for the hedge of brush which enclosed the clearing.

Wheeler's eye flicked after him as he disappeared among the tangled branches.

In that split second, McGinn threw himself down at the dead Caddo who lay almost at his bootside. He wrested out the dead man's sixgun, protruding from under his chest, and in the same fluid motion rolling the dead body half over him, as part protection, took a crazy, wild snapshot at Wheeler.

Wheeler killed him carefully, deliberately.

He had no choice. In his suicide gamble, nothing else cold have stopped him.

Wheeler took the two picket ropes, his and McGinn's, and tied McGinn's limp body over his saddle.

A voice called, "Kin I help?" and DeWitt walked

forward out of the bush into the clearing, his hands over his head.

Wheeler made no answer.

Tremulously, DeWitt said, "No hard feelings, Sheriff?"

"So now I'm a sheriff?" said Wheeler.

"Man," said DeWitt affably. "We was shore mixed up there a minute ago, wasn't we? But now we're straightened out, ain't we?"

DeWitt's gun lay there, some distance away, in the moss and leaves. Oily black, with a gleam of copper cartridges and lead bullet noses peeping out of the front and back of its cylinder, it seemed as big as an anvil. Both Wheeler and DeWitt ignored it.

Fawning, DeWitt said, "I imagine you got some hard traveling ahead of you. How about a nice cup of coffee before you start?"

"No," said Wheeler. "Better get a shovel and bury your partner."

"Why, naturally," said DeWitt. "Why, naturally."

Wheeler, once more in his saddle, led McGinn and McGinn's mount out of the clearing. He expected no shot from behind him, and no shot came. There was no sound, no birdsong even. He was glad to get away.

It was a little past suppertime when Wheeler, leading McGinn across his mount, came into Bearskin and turned down Main Street. His muscles were stiff, his knuckles and knee-joints burned with weariness, and he could hardly keep his eyes open, could hardly make this last short stretch.

This was the hour when townsmen, just up from their tables with full stomachs, visited with each other along the boardwalk. Everyone turned and gawked at Wheeler as he passed. Some waved at him. He kept his gaze straight ahead, and returned no salutations.

As Wheeler approached the busiest section, a man disengaged himself from the crowd, came forward around the corner of the watering trough, and stood in the center of the rutted road, blocking Wheeler's advance. The man was Deputy Tandy, his face feathery, expressionless in the glow from the lighted shop fronts. Wheeler came to a halt. "I was headed for you," he said.

"Why, that's McGinn," said Tandy. "What happened?"

"I ran him down," said Wheeler. "And had to kill him."

"*Had* to?" said Tandy. "It should have been a pleasure. What are the details?"

"Later," said Wheeler. "Tomorrow. I have to get to the Magnolia House and hit the hay. Three nights and four days without sleep."

"Make out your report first," said Tandy, showing a little ugly iron in his voice.

"Tomorrow," said Wheeler.

He opened his aching hand, releasing the bridle reins to the ground.

"What's that supposed to mean?" asked Tandy.

"It means he's all yours."

"This is no way to bring in a man," said Tandy.

"It's the way you brought in Leffingwell," said Wheeler. He rode around the standing deputy, and continued toward the Magnolia House.

XII

WHEELER AWOKE in the morning physically rested, but possessed by an empty dissatisfied mood. The scales had been balanced, three vicious renegades had been removed from the world's face, and would cause no more sorrow; but Simmons had had no chance to talk, and McGinn, doubtless looking forward to escape and the future, had amused himself by also remaining silent on the subject. This left many details unclear, and Wheeler was a man with an orderly mind. He would always wonder, always worry. Just what had happened that night? Just how had Seth acted? Like a man, for certain, but what had he said when he faced them before his death? What was his manner?

As Wheeler passed through the hotel lobby on the way to the cafe and breakfast, the clerk said, "People have been asking for you, sir. A rather seedy-looking rancher with rundows bootheels, dragging a little boy by the wrist."

"The Darnleys?" said Wheeler. "Did they give their name as Darnley?"

"I believe they did," said the clerk. "To tell the truth, I was otherwise occupied at the moment."

What had the boy been up to now, Wheeler wondered. He grinned. He was beginning to really like these people.

After breakfast, Wheeler located Deputy Tandy in the backroom of a saloon, with a glass of cherry phosphate, nonalcoholic, before him, just sitting, staring at the woodgrain in the tabletop. Wheeler seated himself across from Tandy—without any invitation, or greeting —and made his report, in great detail.

Without moving a muscle, without altering his gaze to Wheeler, or showing any expression, Tandy listened through it, writing down nothing, making no comment, asking no questions. When Wheeler had finished, Tandy said, "Though I hate to admit it, for a amateur you done a reasonable-good job. Now will you get out of my hair?"

"I won't even speak to you on the street, if you don't want me to," said Wheeler.

"Suit yourself on that point," said Tandy. As Wheeler got to his feet to leave, Tandy said, "Tell me something. What has this whole thing taught you?"

"A lot," said Wheeler.

"I doubt it," said Tandy. "You'd do it again tomorrow, if you had to, wouldn't you?"

"I wouldn't want to, but I would if I had to."

"I thought so," said Tandy. "Just get out and leave me alone."

Wheeler left.

As Wheeler walked down Main Street, toward the Venables, he pretty quick got the idea of why Tandy was in a black jealous mood.

Everywhere people congratulated him on his venture and its success. Shoppers came to their doors, people tried to stop him and question him, or walked a few steps with him, expressing congratulations and approval and satisfaction. He was courteous to them, but untalkative. He wanted no praise, and showed it in his manner. To him it had been a hard, unpleasant job. He was glad it was over. He hoped he would soon forget it.

But there were no congratulations waiting for him at the Venables.

Neither Tabby nor her father received him with acclaim. They received him warmly, studying him carefully, as though he were a friend returned from an arduous journey—and that only. They were seated on chairs on the veranda, enjoying the early morning sun—the Judge with an after-breakfast cup of coffee on his knee, Tabby with an embroidery hoop in her lap—when he pulled up a chair and sat beside them.

The Judge said quietly, "I hear it's all over."

"Yes," said Wheeler.

They asked him no questions about his experience, and he volunteered no comment.

Tabby said, "What now?"

"Back to business, I guess," Wheeler said.

They both nodded in agreement.

"But not here in Bearskin," said Wheeler. "That part of me has withered."

"Sometimes I don't understand humanity, not at all," said the old judge pensively. "A man can do a courageous thing, such as you have just done, and then deliberately injure himself with a cowardly decision, such as you have just expressed."

Wheeler flushed a fiery red, but remained silent. These people had a sincere, deep, unselfish interest in him.

He tried to change the subject. He said, "When you've been through what I've just been through, a funny thing happens to you. You've been living a quiet life, but all at once people look different to you. Some look better, some look worse."

"So you're going to move to another Bearskin, called perhaps Waco or Austin, or something," said Tabby, "and change all that. It couldn't be you, of course."

"I've just said it was me," said Wheeler. "I know it."

After a long pause, Judge Venable said, "You know what's going to happen to you, of course. No matter where you go, no matter how often you shift your base, the wormwood is going to spread through your system and the good people are going to seem fewer and the bad people worse and more multiple. I'm really worried, but you're a grown man and I don't know what to do about it."

"I do," said Tabby. She got to her feet, left them, and went into the house.

When she returned, she carried the bailingwire key ring, with Wheeler's keys.

She dropped them with a jingle in his lap, and said, "You're not leaving us. You're going back to Elm Street, and reopen that house. That house is your home. It's the only home you have. You're going to do exactly what I say."

After an interval of sultry, heavy thought, Wheeler slipped his wrist into the wire ring, accepting it, and nodded. "I don't know what got into me."

She touched him gently on the shoulder. He looked up, smiling, to thank her, when they heard Judge Venable's voice boom out, "Well, good morning, folks. Good morning. Have you eaten?"

Mr. Darnley's voice said, "Yessir, thank you kindly."

Wheeler turned. Mr. Darnley and the boy, Griffin, walked up the path, toward the porch, to join them. There were wisps of sage on both father and son, as though they had slept on the open ground, which, Wheeler was sure, they had.

Darnley said, "Mr. Wheeler, we been wantin' to see you mighty bad."

"Well, here I am," said Wheeler good-humoredly.

"What can I do for you?"

"First, the roan is doin' well, is eatin' well, and seems satisfied," said Darnley.

"Glad to hear it," said Wheeler, waiting politely.

"The boy has did it because he likes you," said Darnley. "It's not payment for the roan, the Darnley's don't spoil gifts by paying for them. He done it because he likes you, simply as a favor."

"Favor?" said Wheeler patiently. "Well, that's nice of him. What is this favor?"

"As you'll agree," said Darnley, suddenly nervous. "It ain't no boy-size favor neither. He's a boy, but it's a man-size favor."

Wheeler, the Judge, Tabby, waited. These things, they knew, took time.

Finally, with the greatest possible courtesy, Wheeler said, "And what is this favor?"

Darnley said, "He has found out who has killed your boy, Seth."

"Who?" asked Wheeler, all at once rigid. "Simmons or Leffingwell or McGinn?"

With his eyes as big as saucers, he said, "It was none of them fellers, Mr. Wheeler. It was Deputy Tandy."

Even before the child explained, Wheeler knew that this must be the truth. He could feel it in a great coldness through his flesh and bones. Tabby looked confused, but the old Judge believed it, too, and his face became weary and set.

When the boy had backtracked Wheeler's horses down the dry wash, he had found bootprints at the point where they had been turned into it. He and his father had come to town to inform Wheeler of this. They had found Wheeler under the lights with Tandy before the

Owl Cafe. He had started to say so when Tandy had moved, and left duplicates of those very same boots in the dust.

"A panic come over him then," said Mr. Darnley. "And I don't blame him."

"Neither do I," said Wheeler softly.

"Of course I cain't swear, when you come right down to it," said the boy, "that Deputy Tandy was the one that fired the shot that killed your son. I wasn't there when it happened. But I kin sure as hell swear, and will be glad to, in any court in the land, that he was the one that turned yore stole horses into that dry wash."

"That's good enough for me," said Wheeler, dry-voiced.

"And for me, too," said the old Judge calmly. "Tabby, get my gun."

XIII

TANDY WAS STILL at his little table in the back room of the saloon when they walked in on him—Wheeler, the old Judge, and Mr. Darnley. Young Griffin had been wild to come, but they had left him with Tabby and a plate of cookies. The deputy sat darkly, brooding, one arm out, fingers splayed and glued palm down to the tabletop. Frozen, he seemed hardly to have moved a muscle since Wheeler had left him. Judge Venable said, "Mr. Tandy, I arrest you for the murder of Seth Wheeler, and the robbery of his father."

Tandy got to his feet. He wore around his waist three broad belts—gunbelt with gun and pistol cartridges, cartridge belt below it with pistol cartridges, and cartridge belt below that with rifle cartridges. There was a lot of weight there, Wheeler knew, brass and lead and thick greasy leather. Tandy unbuckled the gunbelt, swung it out, and laid it with a rattle and thump on the table before him. "What next?" he asked dully.

Judge Venable gathered in the weapon. "Alice is next," he said.

"He didn't even fight," said Mr. Darnley.

"Once," said Tandy, "when I was on the outside, I would have tried it. But since then I've been on the inside, I want no more of the other thing. You live too hard, and can't win in the end."

"That's right," said Judge Venable. "Very sensible."

"You know something?" said Mr. Darnley in an audible, conspiratorial whisper to Wheeler. "I never knowed a justice of peace could arrest a deputy sheriff. I knowed a deputy could arrest a justice of peace, in fact, I seen it happen back in Tennessee one time. But I never knowed till now, it could work both ways."

"Anyone can arrest anyone, with cause," said Wheeler. "You could arrest me, for instance."

"Oh, I'd never do that," said Mr. Darnley. "Never!"

"I suppose you searched my house and found your money up my chimney?" said Tandy. "And your wife's locket."

No one answered him. Wheeler hadn't even missed the locket.

"What put you on to me?" Tandy asked.

"I'll tell you how you did it," said Wheeler. "In the first place, you probably had it figured out for a long time, sometime when the boy was alone, when I was away somewhere on a long trip. Any way you looked at it, from your point of view, it seemed perfectly safe."

"It was perfectly safe," said Tandy. "I cain't for the life of me see what in the hell went wrong."

"Here's the way I reason it out," said Wheeler. "I may be wrong in some of the little details, but I'm right in the general picture. Stop me if you don't like what I'm saying."

"Just tell me where I made my mistake," said Tandy.

"Like I said," declared Wheeler. "You had been thinking it over for a long time, probably. You, like a lot of people, knew a lot of times I did a cash-on-the-barrelhead business. And knew it wasn't reasonable I went around all the time with this load of money on me. I must cache it somewhere in my house until it was needed, you decided."

The room was tomb-silent.

Wheeler's voice was steady, impersonal. He said, "You

knew Seth wouldn't be any problem to you. A man like you who could handle such mad dogs as Snake Leffingwell, and probably others even worse before him, wouldn't be too worried about a little boy."

Mr. Darnley said, "The plan was to hit the house sometime when you were far away, like back on the Staked Plains. But you been away on many a business trip before. Why did he put it off?"

"Because the boy had to die," explained Judge Venable. "That was part of the plan. The boy had to die."

"I'm not a child-killer," said Tandy.

"You'll kill anything," said Wheeler. "Anything, any time it stands in your way, or if you just happen to feel like it. And you know it."

"Why was it part of the plan?" asked Mr. Darnley.

"For four reasons," said Wheeler. "The money, certainly, would be hidden in the house. The boy would be in the house. The money would have to be searched for and the boy would hear the ransacking."

"Which brings us to reason number four," said Judge Venable. "The important reason. The reason the boy was slated for slaughter. He knew Deputy Tandy very well by sight."

"You kin be mighty sure o' that," said Mr. Darnley. "All boys knows all law officers. It's in a boy's elements."

"And then the Simmons gang came to town," said Wheeler.

"And here was his perfect alibi," said Judge Venable. "So he arrested them and put them in jail and made a spectacle of them. Arrested them as undesirable, of all things, undesirables."

"And they broke out," said Mr. Darnley.

"That actually made no difference one way or the other," said Wheeler. "They would have been blamed for it even if they hadn't broken out. And he didn't break them out, by the way. They bribed Taliaferro, the jailer, for a crowbar. As I say, the thing was to put them in jail and to call attention to them. Seth's body, probably, wouldn't be discovered until I returned. After so long a time, who could say definitely just when it had really happened?"

Tandy listened, ashen. He said hoarsely, "I ain't a child-killer. I'm a top-notch gunfighter. And that's the way I'll always be remembered."

"You'll always be remembered," said Mr. Darnley severely, "as the wrong man wearing a badge."

"The way he saw it, the tidy way to do it," said Wheeler, "was to clean up the boy first, so he would have plenty time to do his ransacking, uninterrupted. He worked this out like you would work out a move in checkers. He went to the stable first and made a commotion, I'd say. That brought the boy out in his night-gown, with his squirrel rifle."

Here Wheeler's voice was so placid, that to Judge Venable and Darnley, it seemed as though he spoke of a boy he scarcely knew, in another place, long ago.

"He had the hammer at full cock," said Tandy. "And any rifle is just a hammer, a trigger, and a finger." So great was their contempt that they didn't even deign to glance at him.

Wheeler said, "So then he did his ransacking, found the money, and returned to the stable. And led out the horses and turned them into Rawlings' dry wash. The missing horses were the thing that fooled everybody. Everyone knew the Simmons gang had to have horses."

"That's one point that might be hard to prove," said Tandy.

"He went crazy when I tried to chase the Simmons

gang down," said Wheeler. "As long as they were free, they were suspect. In his first spurt of panic, he even tried to kill me at Cherry Point Ford. If they were captured, they might talk. And who knew for sure, they might have something up their sleeve that could prove their innocence."

"And it became a race between the two of you," said Judge Venable. "Who would get to them first."

"He got to Leffingwell first," said Wheeler. "I got to the other two first, but they didn't talk."

"I saved your life at the Eagle Saloon," said Tandy.

"What else, as you yourself have said to me, what else could you do?" said Wheeler.

"And why was he there in the first place?" asked Judge Venable.

"Tailing me, I'd guess," said Wheeler.

Tandy said, "I killed that boy in self-defense."

"And maybe you used good judgment there," said Wheeler bleakly.

One night, a few months later, Wheeler sat at the Venable table, with Tabby and the Judge, for the old man's birthday supper. There were things on the white tablecloth he hadn't seen for so long that he had almost forgotten they existed. Chicken stew in a brown crockery bowl, floating with dumplings, corn lightbread, made of part wheat flour, part cornmeal; mashed sweet potatoes laced with wild honey, Spanish onions boiled in cream and glazed with butter. Since Tandy's arrest, Wheeler had been living in a dark unhappy mood which he found impossible to shake; now, somehow, he felt relaxed.

Before supper, they had been sitting on the porch, in the tangy October dusk. Now, through the open windows in the dining room, came autumn air with a downright chill to it. Shivering a little, the old Judge said, "Charlie, I must have left my shawl on the veranda. Would you do an old man a favor and fetch it?"

Wheeler smiled, and left the room.

Turning to Tabby when Wheeler had gone, the Judge said, "Get ready, get set, go!"

"Father!" she said angrily. Nevertheless, she too left the room for the porch.

The Judge arose, went to the sideboard, and took his heavy woolen shawl from the sideboard, reseated himself, and put the shawl across his shoulders. Five minutes went by, and then five more.

He went to the kitchen and came back with the big two gallon coffeepot, which he placed by his elbow.

He settled down, enjoying himself.

He was sure they were, too. He had seen that blurry doe-like look in their eyes every time they happened to get together.

The doctor had said no cigars, but he lighted a cigar.

When they came in a little later, flushed and happy, the old man said contentedly, "Where were you?"

"On the porch," said Wheeler.

"Well, I sure didn't hear you," said the old man. "I thought the Comanches had carried you off."

"Father!" said Tabby.

Two Action-Packed Western Novels
Back to Back in One Book—at 75¢

27276 Gallow's Gulch West
Man at Rope's End West

30701 Gun Feud at Tiedown Nye
Rogue's Rendezvous Nye

41910 Justice at Spanish Flat Garfield
Gun from Nowhere West

48755 Lobo of Lynx Valley West
Ragbag Army Trimble

49301 Lost Loot of Kittycat Ranch West
Saddle in the Wind Searles

72260 Rio Desperado Shireffs
Quick Trigger Shireffs

72525 Rincon Trap Owen
Call Me Hazard Wynne

77910 Stage Line to Rincon Hardin
Man Called Ryker Hogan

81861 Toughest Town in the Territory West
Guns at Q Cross Constiner

82435 Trouble on Diamond Seven Jenison
Coffin Fillers Cord

The No. 1 Experience

The Sensuous Mouth

by Paul Ableman

Spine-Tingling Mysteries

06610 Black Man, White Man, Dead Man Kingsley   75c

10435 Chinese Agent Moorcock   75c

11550 Coming Out Party Frede   75c

13570 The Damned Innocents Neely   75c

14155 The Old English Peep Show Dickinson   75c

14283 Devilday Hall   75c

36300 If Dying Was All Goulart   75c

37375 Isle of the Snakes Fish   75c

40589 Too Sweet to Die Goulart   75c

51800 Man in a Bird Cage MacLean   75c

54710 Murder League Fish   75c

57570 Night's Evil McShane   75c

76721 The Sinful Stones Dickinson   75c

Ace Westsellers

01985 **Ambush at Coffin Canyon**
Lomax   60c

08360 **Bucking for Boot Hill** West   60c

08380 **The Buffalo Runners** Grove   60c

14271 **Desperate Deputy of Cougar Hill**
Trimble   60c

30800 **Guns Along the Jicarilla** Hogan   60c

31620 **The Hands of Geronimo** Patten   60c

52234 **Mavericks of the Plains** Lomax   60c

60941 **Odds Against Circle L** Patten   60c

62730 **Once an Outlaw** Kincaid   60c

71076 **Reckless Men** Adams   60c

73890 **Rustler's Moon** Holmes   60c

76175 **Showdown at Texas Flat** Hogan   60c

76840 **Six Ways of Dying** Patten   60c

76851 **Sixgun Duo** Haycox   60c

85901 **Valdez Horses** Hoffman   60c

88560 **The White Man's Road** Capps   95c

88800 **Wild Bill Hickok** O'Connor   75c

95000 **The Youngerman Guns** Patten   60c

Available wherever paperbacks are sold or use this coupon.

- - - - - - - - - - - - - - - -

ace books, (Dept. MM) Box 576, Times Square Station
New York, N.Y. 10036

Please send me titles checked above.

I enclose $...................Add 15¢ handling fee per copy.

Name ....

Address ....

City.................... State.............. Zip........
Please allow 4 weeks for delivery.   9B 5/72

FALSE TRAIL ON THE HIGH PLAINS

Watts Denning had hung up his sixes years ago and had settled for the easy rolling life of a roving bartender. When a worried father offered to pay him to go up to Folsbee, Montana, and watch over his teenage son from behind the bar counter, Watts had accepted. Easy job, easy money—only there wasn't any teenage son in Folsbee. . . .

There was only a hired killer, a dead hotel owner, and someone who was trying to pin a murder on Watts Denning.

Watts had a choice. He could leave Folsbee far behind, or he could take out his short-trigger gun. He chose the latter.

MERLE CONSTINER has been a full-time professional writer since 1939. A frequent contributor to the action magazines of the forties, he became notable for the authenticity of his backgrounds and the ease of his narration. Not limited to one type of market, his material has ranged through all varieties of writing and he has appeared in *The Saturday Evening Post, Argosy* and many more. A native of Monroe, Ohio, he holds a Master's degree from Vanderbilt.

Short-Trigger Man

by Merle Constiner

ACE BOOKS

A Division of Charter Communications Inc.
1120 Avenue of the Americas
New York, N.Y. 10036

CHAPTER I

IT WAS A small desolate settlement named Knuckle Springs, up in the northwest corner of Montana, perhaps thirty miles south of the Canadian border. This was the High Plain country, semi-arid, a rolling plateau of juniper and sage, with scattered, isolated hills crowned with dusty stands of timber. It was lonesome country, but Watts Denning liked it. The handful of buildings—a few homes, a store, a blacksmith shop, a saloon—had weathered completely into the drab landscape. For the moment, Watts was working at the saloon. He wasn't really needed but he wanted a little rest, and the pleasure of some elk hunting. Old Man Gresham, its owner, liked his company. That was Watts Denning's trade, roving barman.

It had not always been his trade, for he was a man of varied background. In his youth, he had been a short-trigger man, a mercenary in the Arizona and New Mexico cattle wars, and one of the best. Later, battle weary, he had moved to Idaho and established his own small spread. His ranch prospered. Then came the terrible blizzards of '87, which wiped him out.

The ice of that winter had scarred four states. No one could estimate the number of cows that had perished. In the distress of the tight-money period that followed, he had become a drifting bartender. As such there was always a livelihood and, subtly, he learned to enjoy new places, new faces. Almost immediately, to his surprise, he learned that he had joined a brotherhood, that there was a network of roving barmen. He would move a little, work a little, work once more, always as free as the air. His wandering had taken him from border to border, up and down the country, through towns, wilderness, and settlements.

He had just come up, taking it easy, following his nose, from the deep South. This place, Knuckle Springs, he had decided, would be his northernmost point. He had stayed because the last stretch had been rough terrain, and because Old Man Gresham was earthy and hospitable. His next town would be Folsbee, a thriving cattle and railroad center, two days directly east, on the Milk River. At Folsbee, he would work a little, and swing south again.

But he was in no hurry.

He was a medium sized man, slim, slightly stoop shouldered, dark of hair and skin. He was grave, soft voiced, and had a tense hawklike frown which led strangers to believe he was perpetually brooding. Some even made the error of thinking he was myopic. On the trail or in the backcountry, as now, he wore range clothes, frugal and faded. On the job in town, he dressed otherwise, but quietly. He only wore his six-pistol when conditions required it.

He was a man of great patience, but had lived through too much danger to be a fatalist. He believed strange appearances could hide strange dangers.

Therefore, on his tenth day at Knuckle Springs, when Old Man Gresham began to change, suddenly acting jumpy over nothing, Watts began to wonder.

The saloon, known within a radius of a hundred miles of hinterland simply as Gresham's, was at the edge of the settlement. It was made of cedar logs, sun beaten, frozen, polished to silver gray, and dirt roofed. It had two rooms, the front room, the saloon, and the back kitchen and personal living quarters, and each was earth floored. Though desolate and lonesome, it was the final outpost to the Rockies, and had many more customers, drifters, travelers, and emigrants, than Watts would have expected. It was sort of a club for hunters, too. While Watts was never truly busy, he was never idle, either. He had a comfortable cot in the kitchen, the food was good, and the first ten days went peacefully, almost dreamily.

Gresham was an old-timer, one of the early buckskin boys. He was about sixty-eight, greasy, and long haired. His teeth were bad from too much pemmican in the past, his eyes were swollen from too much sun and snow, and easy living had turned him squaw-fat. He walked slew-footed, and made his own moccasins. Watts wasn't exactly friendly with him—long ago the old man's past had molded him into a lone wolf—but he liked him.

One thing Watts liked about him was his serenity. He seemed completely nerveless. You could relax around him and really rest.

Then, after ten days of this, came the change. For no reason at all, out of a clear sky, the old man became nervous, jumpy, quarrelsome. These were traits Watts couldn't and wouldn't abide.

A man didn't change that way over nothing. What was happening? What was going on?

That night about eleven, when they had locked up and retired to the kitchen to go to bed, Watts decided to bring it out into the open.

The small kitchen was Gresham's pride and joy; as far from a teepee as he could make it. Its log walls were whitewashed. It had two patent cots given to him by wealthy hunters, and a cast iron range, broken, wired, broken again and wired once more, which had somehow found its way to this nowhere from Philadelphia. Gresham's cot was in a corner diagonally across the room from Watts, and while he always used it, he slept in his greasy buckskins, in case there was a fire, or a mythical Indian raid, or a midnight settler woman should knock on his door for a bottle of whiskey, which so far had never happened.

After they had put out the kerosene lamp, and had lain on their cots in the dark perhaps five minutes, Watts said, "It's hard against my usual policy, Mr. Gresham, but I'd like to talk to you about something personal."

Gresham's heavy baritone came cordially to him across the room. "Why, yes. Yes, indeed. I'm always glad to lissen to a feller's trials and tribulations."

"Not mine," said Watts. "Yours."

There was a moment of silence.

"You been taking my head off the last day or so," said Watts. "What's got into you?"

After a pause, Gresham said, "Does it show? I had a little talk with a rancher passing through from Folsbee—and it upset me."

"I just wanted to be sure it wasn't me," said Watts. "That's all I wanted to know."

Watts heard him take a deep tremulous breath. "But that ain't all I'm going to tell you. I'm half crazy, worrying about Fleetwood."

"Fleetwood?" said Watts. It sounded like a racing horse.

"That's my baby," said Gresham.

Baby, thought Watts. Well, there's a surprise for you. The old codger has a baby.

"What's wrong with Fleetwood?" Watts asked, in spite of himself.

"Nothing yet. But they tell me he's just about all set to go on the gun."

Watts put the image of an infant badman from his mind. "How old is this baby?"

"Sixteen," said Gresham. "His mother died when he was borned. I brought him up the best I could but he was always a little gingery. Not bad, just high strung. About a month ago he run away to Folsbee. What I was afraid would happen, has happened. This rancher said he seen him there and he's fell into the wrong kind of company."

"Sorry to hear it," said Watts sympathetically. He, as well as anyone, knew just what this could mean.

"Well, I won't keep you awake no more," said Gresham. "Thanks for lissenin'. Goodnight."

It was Old Gresham's woodsman's habit to beat the sun up by a good half hour, and Watts, who had no objection, followed his custom. Watts had just fixed breakfast, rabbit stew left over from supper, mush and molasses, and coffee, and put it on the table, when Gresham came in from the saloon and sat down. He had a tin cup of whisky in his hand, and drank deeply. This was something new for him, such a big drink, so early.

"Watts," said the old man. "I don't know just how to say this."

"Say what?"

"You're fired."

Watts put down his knife and fork.

"I guess that's clear enough," he said.

"What you goin' to do now?"

"I'll have to study it over."

"You was saying a while back when you left here you'd head for Folsbee?"

"Probably."

The old man threw four gold coins on the table, two double eagles, a single, and a five dollar goldpiece.

"That's fifty-five dollars," he said. "The five is for the work you done. The fifty is for something else. I'm hiring you for a new job."

Watts waited. This was like old times. "I'm not a fighting man anymore," he said.

"This isn't fighting," said Gresham. "In Folsbee there's a big hotel called the Regina House."

"I've heard of it," said Watts.

"It's owned by a gentleman named Underhill. Me and Mr. Underhill is good friends. I'm his favorite guide when he comes out here elk hunting. And once I saved his life from a wounded bear, but I don't see no need to mention that."

He took a sheet of paper from his pocket. "This here is a letter I've wrote to Mr. Underhill, asking him as a personal favor to give you a job behind his bar at the hotel. He's an old-timer like me, and if I know him at all, he'll do it. Will you take it?"

"I'd jump at it," said Watts. "If it's as harmless as it sounds. What do I have to do for that fifty dollars?"

"Just stand behind that bar at the Regina House and keep an eye out for Fleetwood. And listen for what you can hear about him. A bartender, even more than a barber, knows ever' thing that happens in a town. When you see him, or hear about him, send me word so I can come in and talk to him. Is that too much to ask?"

"No," said Watts. "It's not too much. I'll take the five dollars, but I won't touch the fifty. It's you that's doing me the favor."

He stowed the letter away, and said, "When do you want me to start?"

"Not before you finish your mush," said Old Man Gresham, grinning.

The black sky was still crusted with glassy stars, and the settlement was dark and sleeping, when Watts led his saddled mare to the yellow panel of lamplight which was the kitchen door. The old sorrel was lumpy and misshapen and big footed, but she had the speed of a Hopi, the strength of a grizzly, and the stamina of an Apache. Her name was Poison Ivy, though he always referred to her in public simply as Ivy. The predawn air was in her nostrils, and she was excited, ready to go.

Gresham came out of the kitchen door with a bundle.

Embarrassed, he said, "He's likely seen bad times. He'll be wanting a clean shirt. Give it to him. There's a little cash money wrapped up in it until I can get to him. Give him that, too. Watts, I'll never forget this."

Watts put the bundle in his saddlebag.

He said. "He isn't home yet. But I'll do my best."

As Watts rode away, the old man called earnestly, "And don't let on to anyone. Especially Mr. Underhill."

II

WATTS REACHED Folsbee in the early evening of the second day.

He walked his mare down Main Street. To his left was a shored-up boardwalk, a good four feet above the rutted roadbed, and to his right were weedy lots and hideyards and livery barns. The soft glow of lanterns above the doorways made a vapor of light, half smothered by the night dust, and soft shadows blocked out the entranceways to shops and offices. It seemed a nice

11

little cowtown, peaceful, respectable, sleepy, but Watts knew differently. He had been here four years ago. Beneath all this lazy exterior, it was mighty hard-case. It had about doubled its size since he had been here. New buildings had gone up, old buildings had been enlarged.

He stabled his mare at a livery barn, asked directions, and, with his saddlebags over his shoulder, headed for the Regina House.

The Regina House was across the street from the courthouse, facing it, and had gone up since his last visit. As he approached it, he appraised it with interest and mild surprise. It was not the makeshift scrap lumber and cracked-pane cowtown structure he was so familiar with, but handsome and large, shiny in good brown paint, and trim in its new tin spouting and impressive limestone carriage block. Unless there was something wrong, something that didn't meet the eye, he was going to like working here. *If* he got the job.

He wiped two days' dust from his jaw and eye sockets with his neckerchief, and stepped inside.

The lobby was airy and pleasant. It seemed decent and clean, and this, Watts well knew, showed a clean and decent owner. In the center of the rear wall was the stairway. On one side of it was an open arch to the bar, which seemed all right, as much as Watts could see. On its other side was a brown varnished door marked in goldleaf, *Keep Out*. This, Watts knew, would lead to the hotel's interior, the back corridors, the office, the kitchen and storage rooms.

The desk was against a wall just inside the front door. At its far end, in a sort of a cage, behind a wicket of fancy brass rods, a man sat poring over a ledger. He got up as Watts approached, and came to meet him across the counter. He was a small man, expensively dressed, with sulky mouth and unpleasant little squirrel teeth. His unfriendly eyes, behind his tin-rimmed spectacles, were like boiled duck eggs. He brought with him the suffocating odor of a fashionable barbershop perfume, Balm of a Thousand Flowers, which, Watts knew, had a base of citronella and rosemary, and was about as revolting a smell as a man could imagine.

Watts gazed at him in cold alarm. If this was Mr. Underhill, it was all over. In the first place, he wouldn't hire Watts, and in the second, Watts wouldn't work for him.

Watts took Old Man Gresham's letter from his saddle-bag, and said, "Are you Mr. Underhill? I have a letter for Mr. Underhill."

"I'm Mr. Selden, the manager," the man said. He held out his hand. "But I'll take it."

"It's for Mr. Underhill, not Mr. Selden," said Watts, dryly.

All at once, Watts realized that Mr. Selden was drunk. Not paralyzed drunk, but firmly and solidly drunk, and that he was probably that way twenty-four hours a day, seven days a week. That would explain the Balm of a Thousand Flowers, to cover his breath.

Shelden looked at him in distaste.

He pointed. "Go through that door. You'll be in a hall. You'll find a door marked, *Office.*"

"Thank you," said Watts, and walked away.

He passed through the door marked, *Keep Out,* and found himself in a bare narrow corridor leading to the rear. To his left, as he advanced, was the business door, the back door to the bar, half open; through it, things already sounded lively. Down the hall, at the very end, was a door which led either to the kitchen or to the alley. When he came to the door on his right, marked,

13

Office, he knocked. A courteous voice called out for him to enter.

The room was small and crowded with furniture. On the pine walls, golden in the lamplight, hung Navaho rugs, Yavapai shields, Zuni lances. In one corner was a big black safe, its face painted with a landscape of an elk drinking at a brook; in another was a big rolltop desk, its pigeonholes crammed with a confusion of papers and letters. On five chairs were three battered Texas saddles, a burlap sack of black-eye peas, and a bushel basket full of gunbelts. Each item had a little paper pinned to it, bearing a name. Watts knew they were being held in pawn, and were certainly acts of kindness on the part of the man who had done it. And this, Watts was sure, was the man who sat before the desk.

He was elderly, wiry, leathery, and already Watts knew a lot about him. The Indian weapons and rugs were from the South, so he was probably somewhere from the South. He didn't get that leathery skin behind a hotel desk; he got it in a saddle. And he was a man of compassion and understanding. When a man hard-up came to him for money, he wouldn't insult him with charity, but would take a token in pawn.

"What can I do for you, son?" he said.

Watts handed him Gresham's letter. "I'm kind of looking for a job as bartender."

Mr. Underhill read the letter, laid it aside, and forgot it.

"I've worked in the big ones," said Watts quietly. "And in the little ones. If I don't give you good honest service, you can either shoot me or fire me."

The old man studied him with pleasure. "It's a joy to

look at you, son, just to look at you. I haven't really seen that mold since me and Ursula left home."

"And I bet home is Utah," said Watts.

"No, sir, but you're close. It's Colorado. I had a little ranch there, and finally got tired of all them cow eyeballs drinking you in, and sold out, retired and come up North here. You're no more a bartender than I am. How did you get into such a siwash life?"

"Blizzard of '87. Wiped me out in Idaho. And bartending isn't siwash. It's never the job that's siwash, it's the man that does it."

"Before you had that spread you lost, what did you do?"

"Now you know better than ask a question like that," said Watts, suddenly stony.

Underhill's face crinkled happily. "'Scuse me." Turning businesslike, he said, "You're hired. For the first couple of months your pay will be fifteen dollars a week and found. After that, maybe, we'll see about a little raise. You want to hear my rules?"

"I sure do."

"The first is keep clean, yourself, your bar and glasses, and your language."

"I think I can handle that."

"And the second is Mr. Tom Selden, my manager. He's got his peculiarities, but he's a wizard. The simple fact is, the Regina couldn't get along without him. Most important he's my friend, and your boss. I don't want no serious squabble between the two of you."

"If I squabble with anybody, it will be on my own time."

"That's not good enough," said Mr. Underhill gently. "He can be mighty aggravating. I want your promise."

"Sure, why not?" said Watts steadily. "I can always quit."

He was given a room at the top of the backstairs on the second floor, a cubbyhole, but he had occupied a heap worse.

It turned out he was working with, and under, a head barman named Rouse, a man whom Watts had met and liked, who had once been a rover like himself, who was now satisfied and settled down. In every way it was an honest, clean run bar. Most big bars, and the Regina was a medium-big bar, had a hundred little sharpshooting practices, and here at the Regina these were reduced to the functional minimum. Big bars frequently had a little side room, called the wineroom, for ladies and their high spending escorts, and here the worst of the barefaced piracy took place. The prices were not only high, but many of the drinks were completely counterfeit, made down in the cellar: artificial cider, made with brown sugar and tartaric acid and yeast; strawberry syrup, sugar and water, colored red by cochineal cooked in copper, and flavored with tincture of orris and acetic-ether; pineapple syrup, colored with tumeric, and flavored with butyric-ether, blended with alcohol, and served as expensive cordials; bitters and schnapps, alcohol loaded with gentian root and cinnamon and anise seed and goodness knows what else, at fifty cents a glass.

There was nothing like this, Watts was glad to learn, going on at the Regina.

Time passed uneventfully. A month went by, and Watts came to understand the pattern here. Underhill had sold out down South for a very sizable amount, and was a wealthy man. He had moved then to Folsbee, built the Regina, and a luxurious ranch house on a small place about thirty miles north of town. These were his two hobbies, and he divided his time between them, living sometimes at his ranch, sometimes at his hotel. He was a widower and his daughter Ursula spent all her time at the ranch. The Regina House never knew when it would see him and when it wouldn't.

The manager, Mr. Selden, was in constant residence. Because Watts didn't like him, he tried to steer clear of him, but it was impossible, of course, to avoid him completely. Watts found him mighty hard to get along with, but remembered Underhill's admonition.

When Watts had been in Folsbee four years past, he had worked for a short time at a little backstreet saloon named the Fort Kearny. He and its owner, Hal Irwin, had become close friends. One of the first things he had done this time, was to look Hal up at the Fort Kearny. Hal had welcomed him heartily.

He has asked Hal about Fleetwood Gresham, and Hal, not knowing the man or name himself, had said he would put out an under-cover inquiry.

In the days that had ensued, Watts had asked other people, too, always carefully selecting his person, time, and place. No one was able to tell him anything.

The month had hardly passed when Hal said flatly that he believed this Fleetwood Gresham had never come to Folsbee. He had a mighty big grapevine and no one—no one at all—had ever heard of him.

Watts, puzzled, decided to search a little longer.

Late one Thursday night, Watts, finishing his day's work, left the bar to go to his room. That week he was on the nine to eleven shift, Rouse would close officially at one. To get to his room, Watts went through a door behind the bar, down the hidden back passage, to the back stairs. He had opened this door, closed it behind him, and was standing for a moment in the hall, when he saw the man.

The man was walking down the passage, away from him, in the general direction of the kitchen—and Watts knew him instantly.

He knew him from the slouching swing of his shoulders as he walked, and from the Green River fighting knife in its sheath at the small of his back.

The man was a famous hired killer named Cranfield. Watts had known him, had served him often, across the bar at Paris, Texas. He was considerably north of his customary territory and a man like Cranfield never travelled for pleasure.

From the front, Watts knew, he would show no arms, but carried a heavy gun in a shoulder holster. The knife at his back was simply a decoy. He was savage and efficient. He was tight-mouthed, too; no one knew the count of his victims.

When he came to the door marked, *Office*, he stopped and entered.

Watts broke into a wild run, following him, and threw himself into the office.

Cranfield, his back to the door, was standing in the center of the room, with a bone-handled .45 in his hand. His knees were slightly bent and spread, and his left arm was outstretched like a wing. Mr. Underhill was half out of his chair by his desk, frozen. There was bewilderment in his eyes, but no fear.

Cranfield said, "I'm getting two hundred for this. I can't for the life of me see why."

He thumbed his hammer to full cock and Watts smashed him with a bone crushing blow behind the ear. He swayed, partially turned, and Watts hit him a second time, in the soft hollow of his throat, in the V under his chin. He went to the floor, to his hands and knees, dazed, hurt, barely conscious, with the .45 still in his hand, as steady as though it were held in a vise.

This was a terrible moment.

When he shook his head, and closed his slack mouth, Watts was on him like a wildcat, threshing him half erect, shooting him with his own gun.

There was a long moment of silence.

Mr. Underhill finally said, "That was a close one."

"Yes," said Watts, breathing deeply.

"What kind of a man are you, anyway?"

"Ever see him before?" said Watts, ignoring the comment.

"Never."

"Well, he was hired to kill you. You understood that, didn't you?"

"Yes."

"Who would do a thing like that?"

"I can't even begin to guess," said Mr. Underhill. He was utterly, genuinely, baffled.

"I'd try to guess, if I was you," said Watts gently.

He went out of the office, up the backstairs to his bedroom.

He wanted to get away from people. He was trembling, unhappy. It was as though the old life had come back to him, and he was through with the old life.

III

In his room he lit the lamp on the washstand, took off his shoes, and lay on his bed. Things were happening around him fast and illogically. While in his past experience he had known things to happen quick, and some-

19

times plenty quick at that, things rarely happened illogically. When something happened illogically, it was almost always because he hadn't had sufficient information to understand it. The more he thought about it, the more it worried him.

The thing that had bothered him most the past few weeks was this Fleetwood. He had finally come to the conclusion—in spite of what Old Man Gresham had said—that the boy hadn't come to Folsbee at all but had gone elsewhere. If he was flesh and blood, he certainly would have left some trace.

And now a strange and disturbing idea came to Watts. What if the boy wasn't flesh and blood, but just a lie of Gresham's? What if he didn't exist, and had never existed?

But why would Gresham go to so much trouble, writing that letter to Underhill and everything, over a lie?

Watts arose from his bed, opened the bottom of the washstand, and took out the bundle which he was supposed to deliver to the boy. The bundle was supposed to contain a clean shirt and money.

It was wrapped in brown paper and tied with a dirty, knotted string. He put it on the bed and unwrapped it.

It contained a hickory shirt, dirty, not clean, patched and worn—a rag. He unfolded it. It contained something else, all right, he could feel it. There was no money in the shirt, but there were two brass keys, about two inches long, one a little larger than the other. He knew them instantly for what they were, safe keys.

A chilling hunch told him they were duplicate keys to Mr. Underhill's office safe.

Everything fell into place. There was a plan to kill Mr. Underhill. He, Watts, had been sent here with suspicious evidence in his possession to take the blame.

This was to be a murder thoroughly concealed, with no loose ends. Cranfield was to do it, Watts was to be the scapegoat.

Moving swiftly, he put two silver dollars in the shirt, rewrapped it, and replaced it in the washstand. Then, still in his stockingfeet, taking the keys with him, he went out into the hall.

Across from his room was a mop and broom closet. He opened the closet door, placed the keys inside the door, up on the ledge of the door frame, and reclosed the door.

Back in his room, again on his bed, he rolled a brown paper cigarette. He had smoked about half when the pounding on his door started.

Three men pushed roughly into the room. The first was Sheriff Finch, a squarely built man, red-haired, with a red square face; Watts had seen him about the town, considered him honest, and liked him. Close behind the sheriff's shoulder came Mr. Selden, the manager. Mr. Selden was really loaded tonight, both with Old Crow and Balm of a Thousand Flowers, and had the manner of an executioner. Bringing up the rear was a frog-faced man in black broadcloth, hunched, mucus lipped, who Watts had been told was one of the town's most powerful citizens, a Mr. R. R. Alford.

"What do you want here?" said Watts coldly.

"Just stand there quiet," said Sheriff Finch. "We'll get to you in a minute."

Wordlessly, they searched the room. It was Alford who found the bundle in the washstand. He pounced on it. "What is this, and where did you get it?" he asked grimly.

"It was given to me by an old man at Knuckle Springs

named Gresham," said Watts. "He said it was a shirt and some money."

"Really?" said Alford woodenly. "And what were you supposed to do with it?"

"I was to hold it until called for," said Watts. "I guess it's being called for now."

Sheriff Finch unwrapped it.

"Shirt and money like he says," said the sheriff. "No keys."

A quick, almost imperceptible convulsion of anger puckered Alford's mouth. "He's outwitting you."

"Let's go, gentlemen," said the sheriff. To Watts, he said, "Sorry we bothered you."

Watts nodded. "Forget it."

They left the room.

As he crossed the threshold, Mr. Selden paused and turned. "I suppose you could hear the shot up here?"

"What shot?" said Watts.

"Mr. Underhill was killed about five minutes ago. He was standing in the alley, by the kitchen door, and someone came up in the dark and shot him six times."

Mr. Selden closed the door. Watts heard their steps fade away down the hall.

His face was bleak.

He undressed to his drawers, and stood in the center of the room, in moody thought.

Cranfield had failed, their careful plans had miscarried, so they had been forced to try it again, even at a risk. For some reason, they, whoever they were, were desperate. They wanted no delay. They wanted Underhill to die, and now. It seemed very probable that they were working on a time schedule of some kind.

And when you came right down to it, he himself was in grave danger.

He had guilty knowledge. He knew that something was afoot. He knew—if nobody else did—how he had been manipulated by Old Man Gresham.

Somehow he couldn't get Mr. R. R. Alford out of his mind. He went to bed, thinking about him, came up with nothing, and fell asleep.

Early next morning, he visited Hal Irwin.

The Fort Kearny Saloon, where Hal Irwin was proprietor, was behind the courthouse, one block south, across the railroad tracks, in a hell for leather neighborhood of corrals, rickety parlor houses, and fenced in lumber yards. The building, put up by Hal himself, was whitewashed and had a dirt roof of red scoria. Irwin was an old ex-cavalry corporal. He catered to rough trade, and that was what he got, the roughest. He was a laconic man, withdrawn before strangers, and about the closest friend that Watts had ever had.

During this present stay of Watts in Folsbee, Irwin had never been to the Regina House to visit him. He didn't like to cross those railroad tracks into that other world.

He knew more about the town than the mayor, but he didn't like to leave his neighborhood.

When Watts entered, the saloon was empty except for Irwin, who was setting rat traps scarcely smaller than beaver traps here and there in the corners of the room. He straightened, smiled, drew two mugs of beer, poured two glasses of whiskey, and they seated themselves at a wire-legged table.

"I see you've gone into the rat business these days," said Watts, drinking. "Well, it's always good for a man to have a side-line."

"How they hear about me, I don't know," said Irwin.

"I think they come in on the train just to get here. I caught one last week that was wearing a little derby and spoke with a New York City accent."

"You shouldn't have caught him," said Watts reprovingly. "He was probably just passing through on his way to San Francisco."

"He was on his way right here," said Irwin. "The word has got out about my luscious free lunch counter. For that matter, I catch San Francisco rats, too. Plenty of 'em."

"I was going to ask you how you can tell," said Watts. "But I've changed my mind."

"I can tell a San Francisco rat because they smell like the Balm of a Thousand Flowers. They're deluxe, they live at the Regina. But they eat and drink here. Just like you."

"Hal," said Watts. "Did you hear about the trouble we had up there last night?"

"I did."

"What did you think of it?"

"Not much one way or the other. I've been hearing about trouble all my life."

"Hal," said Watts. "I was the one that killed Cranfield."

"I hadn't heard that," said Irwin lazily.

"It's not known up to now," said Watts. "His body wasn't found for a while and they think Mr. Underhill did it in self defense, just before he went out in the alley and got killed himself. I'm going to the sheriff when I leave here and tell him. I had a chance to tell him last night, but it didn't seem quite the right time."

While Irwin sipped his beer, Watts told him the story of the fight in the office. Then he went back to the beginning and told him about Old Man Gresham and the keys. He told him about the visit to his room, and the search.

"I don't know what it's all about," he said slowly. "But I can tell you one thing. I'm sure Mr. Alford tipped the sheriff off about that bundle, and the keys that were supposed to be there."

After a pause, Irwin said, "It could very well be."

"Why?"

"I don't know why. But this Cranfield, with his Green River knife, has spent many a night here—loud mouthed, drinking my liquor, and arguing over paying for it."

Watts waited.

"A couple of times when he was really drunk he spoke Alford's name and called him boss. And once he told me to collect his night's tally from Alford. I didn't. He paid next night, I'm glad to say."

"Thanks," said Watts. He got to his feet and headed for the door.

"Do you want to borrow my gun?" asked Irwin.

"I've got one of my own, somewhere. If I should happen to need it."

"Why, yes, of course," said Irwin. "I hadn't thought of that. If you should happen to need it."

Watts found Sheriff Finch in the lot behind the courthouse, currying his big gray gelding, preparing to ride out to the east end of the county and deliver a writ. A half dozen shopkeepers and loafers were standing around him, asking questions about last night's excitement at the Regina. Busy with his currycomb, red-faced, he was answering in grunts. When he saw Watts, he said, "Howdy," and Watts said, "I'd like to talk to you a minute in private."

He laid the currycomb on a window ledge behind

him, mounted, and said, "I don't have no time for private right now. I got a long ways to go. I better get started."

If he wanted it this way, Watts decided, why not give it to him? He said, "It was me that killed Cranfield last night, not Mr. Underhill."

"Is that so?" said Sheriff Finch, mildly interested. He picked up his reins. "That's what my wife figured."

"Your wife?"

"Cranfield was shot with his own gun. One cartridge fired, no bullet nowheres but in him, and powder burns on his shirtfront. And the bullet in at a funny angle. Someone twisted his own gun back on him and let him have it. My wife said maybe you—Mr. Underhill likely wouldn't be strong enough. What was he up to?"

"He didn't tell me. I came in behind him, saw he had his gun out and leveled, and rushed him from about a yard away."

"Maybe he was just wanting to pawn it," said a bystander, belligerently. "Mr. Underhill sometimes loaned money on .45's and such."

"Oh, I don't think so," said Watts pleasantly. "I didn't get that idea at all."

"We call it attempted robbery and misadventure," said the sheriff. "Well, you gentlemen have yourselves a nice little debate."

He waved as he moved off. "See you later."

When the sheriff had gone, Watts returned to Main Street and walked west. It was about nine-thirty, and Mr. R. R. Alford should have arrived at his office.

The Folsbee Feedingyards, owned by R. R. Alford, straddled the railroad at the edge of town. It was a typical feedingyard, and a big one. There were literally acres of pens, big and little, square, hexagonal, oblong. The sun was already glaring from a cloudless sky and the air was opaque with dust and gnats, and musky with the odor of animal urine. The chutes were on the north side of the track; on the south side were a few buildings of warped, unpainted lumber. Like all feedingyards, it seemed shabby and makeshift, but Watts knew it for what it was, the county's greatest financial and market center. Its financial complexities, buying and selling, the mortgage of futures, both of cattle and crops, shipping, storage, investment and speculation, formed an intricate design almost unintelligible to the average rancher. A big feedingyard, homespun and friendly to the public eye, could hold a hidden kingship in the county.

A building of raw, unseasoned lumber stood back from a rough clay path. A sign over its door said, *Office*. Watts entered.

He found himself in a small anteroom. Behind a waist-high railing of unplaned two-by-fours, two clerks sat at desks, pens in their hands, open account books before them. Watts said, "Mr. Alford. Important." One of the clerks gestured. He passed through a gate in the railing, opened a second door.

Alford, with his prematurely wrinkled frog face and black broadcloth bridegroom suit, stood by a long table, sorting and annotating business letters. The room was bare and frugal looking. The crude wall cabinets were like kitchen cupboards, and the few primitive chairs had shuck-bottom seats. What could anyone say but that the place was hard working and honest, and maybe even on the point of bankruptcy?

As Watts came into the room, Alford gave him a hungry, wet-lipped smile, and said, "So it wasn't Mr. Underhill who killed Cranfield after all, but you. And you've admitted it to the sheriff."

He had already heard it. The news must have come to him on the run.

"That's right," said Watts. "In a misadventure, and just in time."

"What brings you here, may I ask?"

"I guess I just wanted a good look at you when I wasn't flustered. Last night when you came in with the sheriff and Mr. Selden, I was flustered."

"And now you've had your look?"

"Right."

"So there's nothing to delay your leaving."

Watts frowned. "I wonder what the sheriff was looking for? Did he say?"

"Yes. I believe someone left an anonymous note on his desk saying that you had come to town to loot Mr. Underhill's safe. And had duplicate keys in your room, wrapped in an old shirt."

"You know something?" said Watts sociably. "The man that wrote that anonymous note is something to think about. He sits wherever he is and imagines I got a bundle with a shirt in it, up in my room at the Regina, *and, by golly, he's right*. It's there, just like he imagined. Pretty scary, I'd say. Of course, he missed on the keys, but all told he made a mighty good score."

"I'm a busy man," said Alford shortly. "I have no time to chat."

"Of course," said Watts levelly, but not moving. "Would you like to hear my personal opinion on this Cranfield?"

"Not particularly."

"It's this. Maybe he wasn't set on robbery at all. Maybe he was brought here to kill Mr. Underhill. Maybe you and me and Sheriff Finch should get our heads together and figure out, if he was a hired killer, who it was that hired him?"

When Alford failed to answer, Watts said, "Well, I'll be getting along. Like you say, you're a busy man."

He walked toward the door.

Alford remained silent.

He doesn't have anything to say, thought Watts, because he's already decided to have me killed. He decided that last night.

Back at the Regina House, Watts had a few minutes talk with Mr. Selden. Something had come up, he declared, and he might be away for a while; would that be all right? "Of course," said Mr. Selden. "Take your time. Your job will be waiting for you." It was a different Mr. Selden, friendly, comparatively sober, eager to please. He was almost too new to be true.

Up in his room, Watts put on his traveling clothes, boots, faded Levis, faded shirt and neckerchief, and his gunbelt. He got his old range war pistol out of his saddlebag and examined it.

Ordinarily, he didn't like to wear it because anyone with half an eye could pretty well see what it was. It was a gunman's gun, and nothing else. Like his father had taught him, he had just about remade it. Trigger and trigger guard had been taken off, and the hammer-dog had been patiently filed for swift liquid action. It was in no sense a trick gun, just speeded up. Nor was it a fanner's gun—he had only contempt for fanners. He fired it like most other professionals, by thumbing the hammer.

Next, he went to the broom closet across the hall, got the keys from their ledge over the inside of the door, and went down the backstairs.

As he passed through the kitchen to the alley, he got

an empty flour sack. He put into it coffee and sugar, in little packets of newspaper, and cornmeal, bacon and a handful of onions. He went to the livery barn and saddled up. He filled his canteens, tied the sack of provisions to his cantle, and left town.

He expected a rifle bullet as he rode down Main Street, but none came.

When the town was behind him, he rode due north, for the Lazy U, and Miss Ursula Underhill, whom he had never seen.

The remainder of the day, he rode through rich grassy swales speckled with fat comfortable looking cattle. That night, he camped in a thin clump of alders beside a stream.

By midmorning, next day, the land had become poor and patchy, and the cattle had become noticeably fewer. About eleven, he topped a low hill. Below him, to his left, were two small log buildings, a cabin and a shed, joined together by a pole corral.

This, though he had never seen it before, he knew to be the D-Bar-D ranch house. He knew its owner to be a man named Slatterly. He had never seen Slatterly, either; apparently he rarely came to town. Now there was no one in sight. It was a tiny spread, he'd heard, with only a handful of miserable cows.

Already the country was becoming desolate, with broad barren valleys and distant, prominent scarps.

North of the D-Bar-D lay Underhill's Lazy U, tucked up against the Canadian border. Rouse, the head barman at the hotel had told him all about the Lazy U. The land was poor, but Underhill didn't care. He had bought it because it was scenic and, to him, pleasant. He had built a big showy house there. He had been raised in wild country, and liked it. Actually, the place was hardly a ranch at all; there was only a token herd of cows, kept because Underhill had ranching in his blood, and because his neighbors would think him queer if he had no cattle at all.

Watts reached the Lazy U ranch house about noon. The house, in a grove of trees, seemed to sit in more of a little park than in a ranch yard. It was big and white, with several roof levels, bay windows, and a broad veranda with a railing and pillars. Some distance away were a barn, the corral and stackyard, a small bunkhouse, and sheds. Behind the house, north towards the border, stood the badlands on the horizon, great cubes and loaves of purple and red and old gold, the hazy notches between them shimmering with sun and dust.

Watts dismounted at the front steps, hitched Ivy, strode across the porch, and knocked at the front door. Everything, house, yard, outbuildings, was silent in Underhill's death.

He had raised his hand to knock again, when a girl opened the door. She was in her middle twenties, straight-backed, black-haired. Her lavender eyes had been blurred by recent weeping. She was about the loveliest thing he had ever seen. He said, "I'm Watts Denning, a barman at the Regina. Could I talk to you?"

"Of course," she said. "Did Mr. Selden send you? Won't you come in?"

"Mr. Selden didn't send me," Watts said. "I'm here on my own. And I won't come in right now, with your grief and all."

"That's very considerate of you," she said, her face showing sudden friendship. "How can I help you?"

He told her how he had killed Cranfield, and her face became immobile.

"Oh, why weren't you with him a few minutes later, in the alley," she said. "When he was killed!"

Now he went back to the beginning. Very carefully, he told her the whole thing, who he was, about old Man Gresham and Knuckle Springs, about the shirt and the keys, and how the sheriff and Alford and Selden had searched his room for them, unfruitfully.

"I knew Cranfield in Texas," he said. "He was a hired killer. That and nothing else. Someone brought him here to kill your father. When he failed, someone else, maybe the employer himself, took over and did the job himself. I was supposed to take the blame."

He handed her the keys.

A great change had come over her. Now she was listening to him in scorn.

She said, "And who would this supposed employer be?"

He hesitated a moment, and said, "I don't know."

"But you've got a suspicion?"

"You could say that."

"Do you know something, Mr. Denning?" she said. "The more you talk, the less I like you."

Stunned, Watts said, "Don't like me? Why?"

"I find your story hard to believe. For one thing, no one would have wanted to kill my father."

"Yet someone did."

"And the more I think about it, the more I find your victory over this Cranfield hard to swallow. He, according to you, was an expert assassin. You were unarmed."

Watts remained silent.

After a long pause, he said, "You think I killed Cranfield *and* your father, don't you?"

"No I don't, exactly. But it's not impossible, is it? You could have run out here and bewildered me with this story because you're scared."

"No," said Watts quietly. "Whatever I am, I'm not scared."

"You want to know something, Mr. Denning?" she said. "I was born in Colorado, born and raised among badmen."

"Is that so?" he said politely.

"And you fit the bill," she said.

"Not me," he said through his teeth, icily. "I'm not a badman, and never was. Like I told you, I'm a bartender."

"I was noticing your gun," she said. "Are barmen wearing them like that these days? I've seen guns like that before, fighters' guns. Trimmed down to about nothing but barrel, butt, and bullets."

She raised her voice. "Bradley!" she called. "Bradley!"

A man, middle-aged, came out of the barn and walked toward them across the ranch yard. He limped a little as he walked, crippled maybe from an arrowhead, or a mean horse, or an old gunshot. He reminded Watts a lot of his father. His smile was compassionate and sad. He had been feeling the tragedy, too.

Ursula said, "Mr. Denning, this is Mr. Bradley Ives, our foreman. He was my father's best friend."

Watts and the veteran shook hands.

"Brad," she said, "Take a good look at Mr. Denning."

Painstakingly, the foreman studied him, every inch of him. It was like having your picture taken by a camera.

"I never want to see this man on our land again," she said. "Do you understand?"

The foreman nodded.

"Can I ask a question before I go?" said Watts. His voice was soft, deadly, expressionless. "How do I get to Knuckle Springs from here?"

The foreman answered courteously, pointing, gesturing, explaining. Knuckle Springs was southwest by west, an arduous two day trip.

No one said good-by as he left.

IV

THE LANDSCAPE, as he moved southwest from Lazy U, started bleak and grew bleaker. It wasn't rocky country, it was just dry and flat and thin. The grass swells were lower, the sage bowls shallower, and the arid earth beneath his mare's hooves was like one gigantic drumhead. This High Plain's heat had a quality of its own, drying his skin, searing it, flaking and cracking his lips. Even old Ivy showed distress. Overhead, the sun hung like a blinding gaseous ball, and all afternoon he headed almost directly into it.

He spent the night on a low solitary hill, whose crown was a nest of dwarfed, wind-twisted cedars, and was off again well before daybreak.

He came into Knuckle Springs just before sunset, when the shadows were the longest, and the accumulated heat the greatest.

It was, of course, the same mangy desicated settlement that it had been before, but now that he knew it as the place where all his trouble had started it sure as hell didn't look the same. Before it had looked simply shabby and desolate; now it looked sinister. Before it had looked like a good place to take a little rest; now it looked like a good place to stay away from. Actually, and he knew it all the time, it was no different from hundreds of other lonesome flea-bitten hamlets.

The first building in the line was a tumbledown blacksmith shop, and here Watts halted his jughead. A few feet away, through the open doorway, a husky smith was tempering the spring of a steeltrap, plunging it into a vat of water. Watts said, "Howdy," and the smith nodded.

"I see you're tempering a steeltrap," said Watts good humoredly. "I bet I can tell you something. I bet it's for a customer, not for yourself."

The smith turned and faced him. "Why?"

"My uncle down in Texas was a smith. Smiths, like doctors, have their secrets. To get a perfect temper in a steeltrap you got to do it a special way. You got to heat your metal at night, in the dark, so you can get it just the second it *begins* to turn red."

The smith laughed. "That's right. But it's the hardest way, so it's the most expensive. This is the easiest, so it's the cheapest. And folks hereabouts, anyway you look at it, is mighty cheap folks. Didn't I see you sometime back, working for a spell at Old Man Gresham's?"

"You might catch me working anyplace," said Watts. "Where there's a free blanket and a pan of cornbread."

They gazed at each other in mutual respect.

"How long you lived here?" asked Watts.

"Maybe six years."

"Ever hear of a sixteen year old named Fleetwood Gresham?"

"Can't say I have. Is he kin to the Old Man?"

"It's his son, the Old Man says."

"Then he told you a bare-faced lie. He don't have no son. At least he ain't in the six years I've known him."

"Thank you kindly," said Watts.

35

"Why would a nice old man say a foolish thing like that?"

"To get me in bad trouble."

"Did it work?"

"It sure as hell did."

"Let's go talk to him about it," said the smith, picking up a short handled sledge.

"I'd best go alone," said Watts. "But I appreciate it."

The sun, at its moment of setting, was like crimson glass as he dismounted before Gresham's saloon and the building's wind scoured logs were red-tinged in its glow. The door, as usual, was wide open to the dust and heat and flies. Watts entered.

Gresham, alone in the room, sat slumped at a table, staring at his fat hands, listless on the tabletop before him. With his matted hair, greasy buckskins, bulbous, veined jowls, he had never been exactly a pretty picture, but now, it seemed to Watts, a change had come over him. It was as though he were sitting there decaying.

Coming to a swinging stop in front of him, Watts said, "As no doubt you've already heard, things went wrong. They managed to get Underhill killed all right, but they didn't lay it on me."

Gresham made no answer.

"The way I am right this minute," said Watts quietly. "I don't much care what I do. Do you believe me when I say this?"

Gresham spoke, sepulchrally. "I believe you."

"Then you better tell me who!"

Gresham raised his glance. There was hatred in it, not hatred of Watts especially but hatred of the situation in which he found himself. But for that matter there was no love for Watts either; Watts was nothing to him, nothing. Watts had seen men with that look before, men who were only accidentally involved with, maybe, but had guilty knowledge of someone else's serious crime—rustling, say, or barn-burning—or murder. In these troubled days it was not a rare look. The fear of death was in him, and nothing would make him speak.

However, Watts took a final try.

He said, "Who is the sheriff of this county, and where is he located? Maybe he would be interested."

"If I was you, I'd stay away from our sheriff," said Gresham venomously. "You'd have a pretty foolish story to tell and it would be your word agin mine. My story would be a heap more sensible."

"Your story?"

"Yes. I'd deny it completely, say I had to fire you because you was such a funny kind of liar, and that when you left you stole a hundred dollars from my strongbox underneath my kitchen floor."

"A hundred dollars!"

"Let's make it five hundred."

"He wouldn't believe you."

"Why shouldn't he? We're good friends. I'm his old elk hunting guide."

"Did a Mr. Alford pay you to do it?"

"I don't know any Mr. Alford."

"Or did a gunman named Cranfield scare you into it?"

"You'd better go now," said Gresham harshly.

It was like a dream, making this trip from Knuckle Springs back to Folsbee all over again, such a load of peril and worry coming from such a harmless and innocent seeming start. This time he took the journey slowly, to do a little thinking. What would his situation be when he got back to town? Would he still have his job, with Underhill gone? Did he still want it, for that matter? What should his next move be? Should he travel straight on, leave Folsbee behind him, and call himself lucky? Or should he hang around, and work on it a little, and give them a hard time?

Automatically, he decided to give them a hard time. Fighting had once been his trade; running had never been.

The decision brought him immediate contentment. It wasn't that he enjoyed trouble, God forbid, it was just that somehow he always felt peaceful when he was really swamped in it.

He got into Folsbee a little after lamplighting on the third day, left his mare at the livery stable, and made his way to the lobby of the Regina House. Just within the front door, Mr. Selden was chatting with a rancher and his wife. He greeted Watts almost pleasantly as he passed them, and told him to report to him for work in half an hour. It was as though Mr. Selden himself owned the hotel, and nothing had happened here.

Watts found his room exactly as he had left it. He bathed, shaved, put on clean clothes, town clothes, and smoked a cigarette. When his big silver watch told him his half hour was up, he went down to the lobby.

Mr. Selden was behind the desk. As Watts approached, he lifted a flap in the counter by the wicket cage, and motioned him through. Watts followed him across a narrow strip of floor and through a door, into his private living quarters. He had never been here before.

It was a large room, and, for the habitat of a perpetual drunk, surprisingly neat and tidy. Its walls and ceiling had been painted green with wagon paint and its floor was bare. There was a large oak wardrobe carved with a trim of fruit leaves, an oval table, marbletopped, a bed with a head eight feet high, and a miscellany of chairs and ottomans. At Mr. Selden's gesture, they seated themselves.

Watts sat a long moment in silence as Mr. Selden inspected him fixedly, his sulky little eyes intent, his tiny squirrel teeth partly visible behind his loose lips.

Finally, he said, "There was a sizable crowd at Mr. Underhill's funeral."

"Sorry I couldn't make it," said Watts noncommittally.

Then, smoothly, glibly, Mr. Selden began to talk. He had talked with the new owner, Miss Ursula, and she had indicated that the situation at the hotel was to remain the same. That meant by inference—though he hadn't been mentioned by name, no one had been mentioned by name—that his job was of course still open to him, if he wanted it.

"I want it," said Watts.

"There has been one slight change which perhaps I should mention," murmured Mr. Selden. "I'm the new manager."

Watts looked at him. He thought the man was confused with alcohol.

But Mr. Selden was far from being confused. "To Miss Underhill and the world at large, I'm still the old manager. But to you, and the rest of the staff, I'm a completely new manager. From now on, my slightest order, regulation, or instruction must be carried out promptly and without question. I'm going to make this place mechanically perfect. Mr. Underhill's sad demise has offered me this position of power and I humbly accept it. When I snap my fingers you and the others jump. If I say black is white, that's the way it stands. You understand?"

"Absolutely."

Mr. Selden raised his hand and held up three fingers. "How many fingers am I holding up?"

"Maybe you better tell me," said Watts cautiously.

"Six."

"Six it is," said Watts cheerfully.

"You'll do," said Mr. Selden. "Go in and get to work."

V

WHEN WATTS came into the backbar through the passage door, he saw that the room was, as he had expected, almost empty. It was the after supper hour, and few people, townsmen or travelers, cared to follow their greasy fried potatoes and thin hard country style steak so soon with hundred proof bourbon. Rouse, his elbows on the bar, his buttocks almost filling the aisle, his big bull-nose shoes planted on the slatted floor, was whiling away the time talking to a hardware drummer. He looked exactly what he was, a top-notch head barman. Watts walked to the far end of the backbar and immediately Rouse joined him.

"Well," Rouse said, beaming. "Welcome back. I thought maybe you was in Mexico or somewheres by now, long gone with itchy feet. I had 'em myself, you know, until I hit this place. Where you been?"

"For one thing," said Watts, "I been to Mr. Selden's room, learning how to say black was white, and counting fingers."

"We all been there the last couple of days," said Rouse, laughing.

"I'm not sure it's anything to laugh about. That man's turned power crazy, and I mean crazy. Could be from now on we're living in hell."

Rouse chuckled. "Oh, I don't think so. I've out talked

40

worse crackbrained drunks than him, many a time. And so have you, for that matter."

A man came in from the street door, wove his way between the tables, and faced them across the bar.

He said, "You must be Watts Denning. They just told me at the livery barn you was back in town." He said it with a sneer.

Watts looked at him. He was a medium sized man, bareheaded, with his cowhand's Stetson hanging across the back of his shoulders by its leather chinstrap. He wore expensive black leather batwing chaps, black gun-belt, and high on his upper arm, not his gun-arm, was a black leather armband. Hanging from this armband was a rattlesnake's rattle. You could call it an ornament, or you could call it a perpetual challenge to anyone looking for any kind of action. His head was large but his face was tiny, as though his eyes, nose, and mouth had been sucked together in its middle. It was a hateful, hostile, cruel face. Watts had never seen him before.

Rouse said soothingly, "Howdy, Mr. McCracken. Nice to see you in town. How about a little drink on the house to start the evening?"

"No thanks," said McCracken, scarcely moving his lips. "I'm going to start my evening by hiding me a bartender."

"I don't fight," said Rouse, and looked scared.

Watts watched him in amusement. He'd seen him in more fights than he could count.

"I'm not talking about you, I'm talking about him," said McCracken, pointing to Watts.

"I don't fight either," said Watts. "Leastways not much. And hardly ever when I'm on the job. It's bad for business. Generally speaking, while customers are fighting they're not buying drinks. What you got against me?"

"That's my affair. You coming out, or am I going to have to climb this bar?"

"If you want to go out and accommodate him," said Rouse politely. "I'd be glad to relieve you of duty for about five minutes."

McCracken had been glaring at Watts. When Rouse spoke, McCracken looked at him. Now, when Watts answered, he swung his gaze back to Watts. He had no suspicion that he was being whipsawed.

"That wouldn't be fair to you, or to Mr. Selden," said Watts. "I'm afraid I'll have to reject your kind offer, Mr. Rouse."

McCracken said angrily, "He hasn't got anything to do with it. It's me that's making the offer, not him. So you're yellow?"

"I didn't say so," said Watts. "I said I'm busy."

"Then maybe you'd like to set a date for the future?"

"How can I? Those things are in the hands of fate."

Frowning, Rouse got into the conversation again. "What do you mean, fate?"

"Well," said Watts. "Say he'd chase me down an alley and catch me. I'd have to fight then, wouldn't I?"

"If it was a blind alley, yes," said Rouse. "I see what you mean."

McCracken turned on his heel and walked away. When he had left the barroom, Watts said, "Who in the hell is that?"

"His name is Joey McCracken," said Rouse. "He's new around here. He came while you were away. He's Miss Ursula's new foreman."

"New one? You mean she fired old Brad Ives?"

"He got killed."

"Killed? Who did it?"

"His horse did it. He was out alone and got throwed.

They found him in the sage with his skull busted like an eggshell."

"And his horse came in riderless."

"Right."

"There's an oldtime English saying that I heard from a rancher in Wyoming: There's nothing as sad to look at as the return of a riderless horse."

"Right."

"And you know why? Because a horse can't talk."

When Rouse said nothing, Watts changed the subject. "This McCracken. What will he do now? Will he go back to the Lazy U tonight?"

"I doubt it. He usually throws his weight around up and down Main Street, until Main Street closes up for the night, then plays cards until dawn."

"Cards? Where?"

"He likes the riffraff that gathers in the backroom of the Bon Ton Barbershop."

"I think I'll pay it a visit after I finish my shift."

"You stay away from there."

Watts said kindly, "You know better than that. When you get crowded, you crowd back. Or you won't last long."

Business that night was slow, which was all right by Watts, because he was tired, and had a lot to think about. The bar closed at eleven. About ten minutes before closing, Mr. Selden came in, the new Mr. Selden, sort of marching, with chin up and shoulders back. He gave Watts a puzzled, appraising look and said briskly, "Take off your apron and follow me."

Watts untied his apron, hung it up, went around the end of the bar, and followed Mr. Selden out of the room.

They cut across the rear of the lobby and stopped

before a door. This, Watts knew, was the ladies' waiting-room where unescorted females could sit in respectable isolation if they felt the main lobby was too masculine and public.

Mr. Selden knocked on the door, and called, "Here he is," making it sound more like, "here it is." He said curtly to Watts. "You're wanted inside," and left.

Watts twisted the doorknob and stepped inside.

Around the four walls, the wallpaper was patterned with brown trellises and pinkish, liver-colored sweet peas. There was a lamp with a stained-glass shade on a small table, two chairs and a ramshorn horsehair couch. A man sat on a chair in a corner, at the edge of the shadows. Miss Ursula Underhill, in black dress and veil, sat on the couch. Watts ignored the man and stood before the girl.

He waited.

Impersonally, she said, "As you know, I'm the owner now. I just wanted to tell you there will be no changes in the staff."

"Which means no one is going to fire me," said Watts. "I've already been told."

"That's all," she said. "You may go now."

"You called me in here just to tell me this?"

"I wanted to make your position clear. You must have been wondering."

"I sure was," said Watts. "And still am. You hire me in your hotel, but you order me off your ranch."

"I was dazed with grief," she said. "I realize now that when you came to me with that foolish story, you thought you were being helpful."

"What foolish story?" said Watts. "I don't remember any foolish story."

"You know very well what I mean," she said.

He looked away. She wouldn't put it again into words. Apparently, she was keeping it to herself.

"Don't get into any trouble," she said. "I'm going back to the Lazy U in the morning, with Mr. McCracken and Mr. Slatterly."

"Slatterly?" said Watts. "That's the owner of the D-Bar-D, up next to your place, isn't it? I hear he doesn't get to town much. I don't believe I've ever seen him."

"You're looking at him now," said the man in the corner. He seemed to be a man of about forty, prematurely gray, meaty faced, in wrinkled stockman's serge. His voice was thickly genial, but he didn't offer to shake hands. "I come in for the funeral."

"Mr. Underhill's?"

"No. Brad's. I didn't hear about Mr. Underhill until too late. I was out riding line, and didn't make it." He paused. "They was wonderful neighbors, Mr. Underhill and Brad. For that matter, so is Miss Ursula."

"For that matter," said Ursula, "so are you, Mr. Slatterly."

"And now," said Watts gravely. "If you'll pardon me. I've got a little work to do before I go to bed." He left the room.

In the bar, Rouse had ejected the loafers and a few late buyers, and was downing a thimble sized drink of the best stock, a nightcap, the only drink he allowed himself all day. Watts passed behind him, opened the cash drawer, and took out one of the two pistols there. He thrust it into his waistband.

Holding his drink to the lamp, studying its color, Rouse said, "Who should I notify as next of kin?"

"See you in the morning," said Watts.

"That weapon still has its factory action," said Rouse. "I doubt if it's been fired."

"I imagine it's good enough. We never know, do we?"

VI

THE TOWN OF Folsbee had a front side and a back side, a new side and an old side. The first clump of business buildings had been built along the river, because it seemed right for men to face running water. Then the railroad had come, some distance back from the river, and the new buildings turned about and faced the railroad, which was the town's lifeblood. The Bon Ton Barbershop was in the old section of town, facing the river.

It was a small building with an eleven foot front, attached to a larger, empty building which had once been a slaughterhouse. It had originally been the butcher shop of the slaughterhouse. Watts pressed the brass thumblatch of its door gently, found it locked, peered through the dark window, and saw only blackness.

He went down a stinking, littered alley, turned left, and came to the backdoor. This door was unlocked.

He stepped from the river mists and the black night into a small brightly lit room. It was like a hobo version of a gentlemen's clubroom. On the walls were lithos of girls in tights, race horses, and prizefighters. A piece of old tarred canvas had been tacked over the only window. Along one wall was a once elegant red plush sofa, broken-down, its legs charred, a castoff survival from some fire. A man lay on it, drunk, his chin in his own vomit. In the center of the room was a round library table with pieces of veneer stripped from its face. Around it, on battered chairs, sat five men playing poker. One was McCracken. Another, a weasel-faced man in a frayed alpaca coat, was obviously the barber. All others, with the exception of these two, looked like the lowest dregs of humanity. The stakes on the table were very low. Instantly, Watts knew why McCracken favored this place. Here he would be a man of tremendous importance. Here he would be treated with fawning deference.

He stood for an instant a few feet from the table, appraising the Lazy U foreman. There was an old rule in his short-trigger days. When you're crowded, crowd back, or you wouldn't last long.

Now they were all looking at him, all except the drunk on the sofa.

He said gently, "Mr. McCracken, I'm off duty now."

McCracken arranged his face into a horrible glare, and waited.

"You got the toothache?" asked Watts solicitously.

McCracken made a new face. This time it was one of fury and blood curdling malevolence. He said, "What brings you here?"

"I thought that was what you had in mind. For us to kill each other."

There was a moment of pulsating silence.

"I didn't say that," said McCracken. "I said I had a mind to give you a good hiding."

"But hidings are just for little boys," said Watts reasonably. "To the best of my belief, we're not little boys."

The barber said, "This is private property. You ain't wanted here."

Watts said, "You in on this?"

"Maybe," said the barber. "Why?"

"I just wondered."

"And maybe I ain't," said the barber.

McCracken said, "I don't see no gun. You carrying one?"

"I hope so."

"Where?"

"There's a way for you to find out."

McCracken pretended not to hear.

Watts said, "I just remarked there was a way for you to find out."

"You listen to me," said McCracken, blustering, sounding tough but not too tough. "You pick up a little argument we had at the Regina and come here and try to build it up into serious trouble. I've heard about you. You're a killer. Look how you jumped that man Cranfield. I'm foreman at the Lazy U, I'm not a gun thrower." Here Watts smiled. If McCracken wasn't a gun thrower, he'd never seen a gun thrower. "But I'm a decent respectable citizen," said McCracken, covering his retreat. "And I'll lay down my life for my honor, so don't push me too far."

"You came into the Regina bar, where you thought you had the edge," said Watts. "It was public, you thought you had me handicapped, and you thought you could get away with anything. I think I had a mighty close call back there."

McCracken remained silent.

"You never saw me before," said Watts. "What do you have against me?"

"I don't have nothing against you," said McCracken. "I was just feeling my oats. We all cut up that way one time or another."

"Not me," said Watts. "Never." Now his voice became hard.

Now he began to crowd back. He said, "I'm leaving this place, here and now, but before I go I want you to do me a favor. I want you to say, 'Mr. Denning, it was a pleasure to make your acquaintance.'"

McCracken said, "Mr. Denning it was a pleasure to make your acquaintance."

He said it mockingly, derisively, but he said it mighty quick.

Back in his cubbyhole bedroom, on the second floor of the Regina House, he gave McCracken a little thought. A little thought, but no real worry. It was his guess, just as he had said, that McCracken had come into the Regina bar, trying to catch Watts at a disadvantage, intending to work a fight into a one-sided gunning. McCracken looked to Watts a mighty lot like another Cranfield. Maybe not so good, maybe a hell of a lot better. The fact that he wanted an advantage, that he wouldn't fight in the barbershop, didn't mean anything one way or the other. Contrary to general opinion, few of that brotherhood were stand-up, face-to-face killers. What they wanted was you dead, and no trouble for themselves. A doorway and a shot in the back was fine, a dark street was better, and if you were asleep in bed, say, that was best of all. They preferred it all their own way, if they could get it. But that didn't mean they couldn't deliver face-to-face, if they had to. In fact, that was the way most of them got started, in purely amateur quarrels.

Weary, Watts stripped to his waist and sat on the edge of his bed. His watch said ten minutes after twelve. The hotel would be sleeping now, he knew, with a nightlight down in the lobby. He was about to get to his feet and blow out his lamp when his door opened and Selden came in.

He was wearing a green quilted smoking jacket, brown lounging trousers, and red carpet slippers, embroidered with purple asters. Under his arm he carried a small wicker hamper. He quirked his mouth into a cordial conspiratorial smile, winked, and put the hamper on the bed. Before Watts could speak, he began unpacking it.

He took out a box of deluxe sea biscuits, a jar of marmalade, and a brown glazed crock, sealed at its lid with red sealing wax.

Busily, he scraped off the sealing wax with a penknife and opened the crock. "Smoked oysters," he said, as though they had been in the middle of a pleasant conversation. "From Boston. Everything here is from Boston. The best food comes from Boston."

"Is that so?" said Watts mildly. "I didn't know that. I always thought the best food came from a cow. It was nice of you to come all the way upstairs to show it to me."

"We're going to eat it," said Selden. He covered a cracker with oysters, handed it to him, fixed another for himself, and sat down.

Watts took a bite. It was pretty good.

"You better not let Mr. Selden know you're here," he said. "I don't think he'd approve of us fraternizing this way."

Selden chuckled. "We all have our moments of humanity."

"What I'm wondering is," said Watts, "are you going to be human again tomorrow?"

"I doubt it," said Selden, munching.

Watts tried some of the marmalade.

"Trouble with me," said Selden, his voice heavy with self pity, "is the lonely life I lead. Sometimes there comes over me a terrible craving for companionship. I'm not intruding?"

"Help yourself," said Watts graciously.

For about twenty minutes, they talked casually, Watts talking mainly about cattle and, Mr. Selden talking about dances and whist, and social high life back East.

Finally, Selden arose and repacked the depleted hamper. "I didn't know you knew Miss Ursula," he said.

So this was it, Watts decided. This explained the free crackers and oysters and the moment of humanity.

The manager was burning with curiosity as to why Ursula Underhill had summoned Watts Denning to the ladies' parlor that night, and what they had talked about.

"Ah, yes," said Watts, pretending great wariness. "I know Miss Ursula."

"I hope she didn't call you in because she was dissatisfied with your employment here?" This remark, Watts knew, was simply made to provoke him.

"No," he said. "It was another matter."

"Another matter?" said Selden, making a great show of friendly bewilderment.

"That's right," said Watts seriously. "And I can tell you something else. My father always said it was indecent for two men to get off together someplace like we are now and discuss a girl this way."

"Indecent?" said Selden, startled. "Nobody has said anything indecent."

"Well, I haven't anyway."

"Neither have I," said Selden, disturbed. "What's got into you?"

"I'll tell you what's got into me," said Watts. "I'm trying right now to make up my mind whether I should go to her and apologize or not."

"Listen," said Selden. "I'll drop it if you will."

Watts showed him formally to the door. "Thank you for the oysters," he said stiffly.

Alone, he had a good laugh.

VII

NEXT MORNING, Watts saw them leave, all three of them together, Ursula, McCracken, her foreman, and Slatterly, the D-Bar-D man. About nine o'clock, Watts, headed for the Fort Kearny Saloon and a short visit with Irwin, came out the front door of the Regina House, and there, on the boardwalk, were Ursula and Slatterly. They were waiting, it turned out, for McCracken, who had gone to the stable for the horses.

They happened to be standing in such a way that they blocked his path, so he took a half step and slowed down to circle them. Ursula, with whom he almost collided, said, "Good morning." Slatterly said nothing.

On an impulse, Watts came to a stop.

For one thing, he wanted a good daylight look at Slatterly.

Outwardly, he seemed about the same as he had last night in the shadows, meaty tanned face, prematurely gray hair, musty blue serge. Except that last night he had seemed a respectable stockman; now, in the sunlight, he seemed an imitation. Maybe it was the stockman part that didn't quite come off, maybe it was the respectable part. Anyhow, instantly, Watts put him down as a fake. He remembered how he had flattered the Underhill name the night before, and added, slippery.

Now Slatterly spoke. He said, "I'm powerful sorry, Mr. Denning, but we don't have no time to chat. We got a long trip to make."

You could take it as an insult, but he said it amiably enough and made it sound almost friendly. Almost, but not quite.

"Well, it's going to be a nice day for travelling," said Watts, putting his body into a position of complete relaxation, looking as though he might spend the day on this very spot. Conversationally, he said, "Do you enjoy riding, Miss Underhill?"

"Yes," said the girl.

"She said yes," said Slatterly.

"I heard her," said Watts.

"I believe it's going to be a nice day for travelling," said Watts.

"Shall we step back into the lobby, ma'am?" said Slatterly. "Would you like to wait inside?"

"Whatever you say," said the girl.

McCracken came up the street, riding a mare and leading two others, and joined them. There were no pack horses so Watts knew they meant to spend the night at some ranch house along the way.

He said cheerfully, "Good morning, Mr. McCracken."

McCracken seemed deaf and blind to his presence. Slatterly helped Ursula into her saddle, and mounted.

The whole picture disturbed Watts. It was as though the girl were wearing invisible handcuffs, as though she were somehow their prisoner.

He said casually, "Everything okay?"

She shot him a disdainful glance.

It told him she was a prisoner, all right, but a prisoner of her own stubbornness.

He watched them ride off, turned, and saw Alford diagonally behind him across the street, sitting in a buggy before a hardware store. Through chance or design, the little scene had been carefully observed.

Watts descended the wooden steps from the board-walk to the rutted street, crossed the street, and confronted him, standing abreast the end of the buggyseat.

The feedingyard man was drably dressed as usual, but his buggy, with its bright yellow spokes and the glossy bay between the shafts, was a vision of glamor. Mr. Alford had his personal vanity, like anyone else.

Watts said, "Were you waiting to speak to me?"

"Does that sound likely?" said Alford.

He untied the reins from the whipsocket, flipped them, and rolled away. There was a crack in the tire of his left rear wheel which left little spaced bars on the deep dust with rhythmic regularity. Overhead a hawk circled, looking for someone's backyard chickens.

There had been two interesting things about Alford. First, he didn't use his buggy in Folsbee; which possibly meant, just possibly, that he was taking a little trip. And second, that there had been a light blanket across his knees as a lap robe, and it was too hot for a lap robe.

Watts squinted his eyes down Main Street. When the buggy reached Union Street, it turned south.

Hal Irwin was sitting in the shade on a long bench at the side of the Fort Kearny Saloon, when Watts came up. A spindly-legged, saucer-eyed little girl about five years old was standing in front of him. He was making her a corn shuck doll. Watts seated himself beside his friend and watched the dexterous, scarred fingers, as a human figure materialized from the husks —head, waist, arms, skirt. None of them, Irwin, the child, Watts, said anything as the magic went on. When it was finished, the child took it and scampered off.

"I've seen that done before," said Watts. "But never so nice."

"That was the way my mother's father used to make them for my little sisters back in Indiana," said Irwin. "It's grandpa-work. I must be getting old."

"I've been noticing that," said Watts sympathetically. "For one thing, you're getting meaner."

"Talking about mean," said Irwin. "What would you think of a top class gunfighter that would go down an alley, into the backroom of a riffraff barbershop, and try to pick a fight with a bunch of lowgrade nobodies?"

"He doesn't sound like much to me," said Watts.

"That's my opinion, perfectly."

They sat there on the bench in the shade, each of them staring into space, each of them poker-faced and solemn.

Finally, Irwin said, "Things have been very peaceful around here for the last week or so. It was almost like you were out of town."

"I was," said Watts, and told him about the trip to Knuckle Springs, about McCracken, about the girl and McCracken and Slatterly.

After a moment of heavy thought, Irwin said, "I consider you a perilous man, Mr. Denning, and when you come right down to it, I ain't sure it does me any good to associate with you. If I was a sensible man, I'd forbid you my premises, in spite of the tremendous amount of money you always spend here."

"You can't do that," said Watts triumphantly. "We're friends."

"That's right," said Irwin gloomily. "It slipped my mind."

Watts returned to the Regina House. This was his swing-shift day. He worked until one.

Over and over, his mind came back to Alford and his buggy.

That afternoon Watts was off until seven. About four o'clock, more in a mood of mild curiosity than anything else, he went to the barn, saddled Ivy, and rode south out of town, down Union Street. Union Street led to the main pike going south.

He didn't bother to look for the buggy tracks in town, but the last house was scarcely behind him when he picked them up, tapelike imprints in the dust, one of them marked by the small lateral bar of the cracked tire. They were simple to follow. Sometimes he saw double sets, and knew this meant that Alford had come and returned along this road.

About four miles out of town, a small side road, barely discernible, scarcely more than a trail, forked to the left, and here the buggy had left the highway. Watts also left the highway.

Before long he came to a dense grove of cottonwoods. This indicated a creek nearby, and he knew instantly where he must be, near a small stream he had heard of, Sterrett's Branch. Rouse had told him about Sterrett's Branch, and about the mill. A few years back a man from Ohio had built a mill on the stream, not understanding the eccentricities of certain small creeks in this country. Two dry years had ruined him, and he had moved away.

Watts entered the cottonwoods, and soon came out into a small clearing. Flowing into it from the east, and leaving it on the west, was the Branch. In the center of the clearing was the abandoned mill with its rickety wheel, already lonely and delapidated. It was a mill of the overshot style; the wheel was powered from the top by a sluice and a dammed pond behind it. The wheel no longer turned, and the pond was coated with scum. Sickly sunlight filtered through the motionless cottonwoods.

Here, not far from the mill's door, Alford's buggy tracks came to an end.

Watts hitched Ivy and stepped into the mill.

He found himself in an empty room which the miller had stripped of all cartable machinery—the cooler, conveyor, and the spur-wheel driven shaft which had extended to the grinding room upstairs.

There was nothing here of the slightest interest. Watts climbed the crude stairs to the second floor.

This room, too, had been stripped, except for the circular grinding stones, which had been too heavy and expensive to move for future use, and too easy to acquire elsewhere. Now, removed from their hopper, they stood at an angle, leaning against the wall.

There was nothing in this room either.

Except a cigar band. Lying new and crisp in the center of the dusty floor. Alford had been here. It had to be Alford.

But why?

Watts walked to the millstones and rolled them to one side.

There, on the floor, in a tidy little pile against the wall, were two smoked hams, sweet potatoes for baking, a canister of uncooked noodles, a dozen plugs of chewing tobacco, and two quarts of whiskey.

Watts replaced the stones as he had found them.

It looked as though someone of limited taste, fresh out of the wilderness, say, or a group of someones, was all set to have a quiet little banquet.

He went down the stairs, left the building, and returned to Folsbee.

When he came into the lobby of the Regina, Mr. Selden's attitude toward him was one of uncertainty. This was the first time Watts had seen the manager uncertain about anything, and it was a pleasure to behold. If their conversation on the night before hadn't really frightened him, it had certainly made him nervous, and his manner toward Watts was now one of caution. Gone, in respect to Watts, at least, was his emperor pose. If he wasn't exactly friendly, he wasn't domineering either, and that was something.

Hesitantly, he said, "Denning, I've been thinking and thinking. About our visit last night. I respect, almost worship, Miss Ursula. What did I say that gave you the opposite idea?"

"Words like those are best forgotten," said Watts, making his eyes flinty.

"I wasn't myself," said Selden. "I've been working too hard. I take my job too seriously. That's my curse, hard work. Sometimes when I'm fatigued I speak a little irresponsibly."

"Oh, then, that explains it," said Watts kindly.

"But what did I say? What were the very words?"

"They're not the kind of words I like to repeat."

Changing the subject with effort, Selden said, "I'm supposed to give you a message from Sheriff Finch. He wants you to drop in."

Stunned, Watts said, "Did he say why?"

"Yes, this is a supper invitation."

"Oh," Watts said, still bothered. It didn't make sense.

"One more thing," said Selden, beaming, trying to be casual. "I believe I noted you and Miss Ursula on the walk in front of the hotel this morning, chatting. I was wondering—"

"Now you're at it again," said Watts reproachfully.

"What did I say wrong?"

"It wasn't what you said, it was what you were getting ready to say. That's the way you started last night."

Mr. Selden looked blank and flinched.

Watts went to his room, washed, rubbed up his boots, and put on a clean shirt. He'd done a lot of strange things in his life, but he had never eaten supper with a sheriff. The truth was, he could hardly believe it. He wondered if Mr. Selden could have got it mixed up someway.

As he passed through the lobby on his way out, Selden again got him into conversation.

"In regard to Miss Ursula," said Selden. "You've got the wrong idea entirely—"

Watts paused a moment, and faced him. "I hate to say this," he said patiently. "But you're twice her age. You're worldly, and maybe a little lewd, and she's young and innocent. You've got her a heap too much on your mind." He walked toward the street door.

Selden called after him desperately. "Of course I've got her on my mind! Don't you understand? She's my boss!"

Watts passed on.

Around the west side of the courthouse, by the back corner, was a door; just inside the door was a staircase to the sheriff's domestic quarters on the second floor.

The front part of this story was the jail, the back part, the Finches' living section. Like other sheriffs Watts had known, the underpaid sheriff augmented his meager income by feeding the prisoners, and his wife fulfilled this contract.

Watts climbed the stairs. Through an open door, he saw Sheriff Finch in his parlor, reading a paper.

"Come in!" he called, putting down his paper.

The room brought back Watts' boyhood to him. It reminded him of his aunt's parlor long ago down in Texas, except for the addition of an oval dining room table with a white cloth, set with bone-handled knives and forks, and a big bowl of flowers. On one wall was a crayon drawing of young Mr. and Mrs. Finch, bride and groom, under belled glass, on another, a framed montage of sea shells pasted to cardboard, and, in a corner, a three foot urn of gilded bullrushes. There were only two places set at the table. Mrs. Finch, apparently, would eat in the kitchen. So there was an element of official business in the invitation, after all.

"I'm hungry, and I hope you are, too," said the sheriff. "So let's get to it." He seated himself and pointed Watts into his chair. "Sophronsia!"

A motherly little woman with sparkling eyes bustled in with platters of food. They ate in silence, as was proper.

It was a meal Watts never forgot.

When the last crumb of the lemon meringue pie was gone, Sheriff Finch got out his pipe, and loaded it moodily.

"You know why I asked you here?" he said.

"No," said Watts, a little tensely, despite himself. "Why?"

"To get some of Sophronsia's company pie. She misers

her lemon extract like it was her life's blood."

Watts smiled, and before he could answer, the sheriff said, "You're looking at a pitiful man. When you come right down to it, I don't have any friends. I had one, a mighty close one, but he's dead."

"I'm sorry to hear it," said Watts. "What happened to him?"

"He was murdered. We don't know who did it. His name was Underhill."

"Oh," said Watts.

"It gnaws at me more than people know," said Finch. "My dearest friend gets shot down, and I'm the sheriff, and I don't do anything about it."

"I liked him, too," said Watts quietly.

"This is a silly question," said the sheriff drowsily. "And you got to 'scuse me for it, but I don't suppose you have any idea who could have done it?"

"I wish I did," said Watts bleakly.

"Or why?"

"Or why."

"But you're working on it, hey?" said the sheriff, encouragingly.

Watts tightened. Sheriff Finch was proving to be quite a man.

"I'm a bartender," said Watts. "I'm working on serving whiskey."

"You just took a four or five day trip. I wish I could have been along. I love trips."

"I went to Knuckle Springs."

"You got kinfolk there?"

"No, thank goodness."

"And you ain't going to tell me why you went, I see. That note left on my desk, that brought me to the Regina when you and me first met. It was about a man

61

at Knuckle Springs named Gresham. I bet you seen him."

"You bet I did," said Watts.

"I wonder why they left that note for me."

"Cranfield was supposed to shoot Mr. Underhill, and I was supposed to take the blame."

"Why, do you know, that's what Sophronsia said."

"I can't prove it," said Watts. "But I'm sure of it."

"And you don't have nothing else to tell me? Nothing at all?"

Watts considered. This was the moment. If he was going to talk, he should do it now. And tell everything. But it just wasn't in him to voice suspicions as facts.

"I'm afraid not," he said.

"When I was a sheriff across the mountains," said Finch conversationally, "there was a fellow had a gun like that 'un of yours I seen in your room the other night, all honed up and hammer spur lowered and all. He could make that gun do everything but think. But guns don't take care of men, men take care of guns. He got himself a little tangled, and I asked him could I help him, and he said no thanks. He was shot in a blizzard with a shotgun. I never did know why."

"I can take care of myself."

"Glad to hear it. Because I seem to like you."

Watts got to his feet. "I've got to get back to the Regina. I go on at seven. That was a real meal. Tell Mrs. Finch I thank her kindly."

"Down in my office," said Finch, "I got an old desk, and I keep it in a mess. The other day I was going through a drawer. Mixed up with some old string and penpoints and pencil stubs and such, I found a rusty old deputy badge. You could take a piece of bacon rind and polish off the rust and I could swear you in as special deputy. You could just carry it around in your pocket, as sort of a charm, so it would be there should we need it. How about it?"

"No," said Watts, startled. He couldn't afford to have his hands tied. "Why me?"

"I got to do something with it. Nobody's using it." Watts grinned, shook his head, and left.

He was walking down Main Street toward the Regina, and had just passed the Cloverleaf Livery Barn, when he sensed someone walking behind him and come up beside him. He turned his head. It was Miss Ursula Underhill.

He gave her a quick, puzzled look. She was a little rumpled from travel, but was in good spirits.

She said, "We're both headed for the hotel, I imagine. Can I accompany you?"

"What happened?" he asked. "About now you should be twelve miles north. Laughing and singing and cracking jokes with Mr. Slatterly and fancy-dressed Mr. McCracken.

"I got to thinking. I decided I ought to be back here. For a while at least. And learn how to run a hotel. I've got to knuckle down to work, and I'd better start right now."

"So you just turned around and came back to Folsbee."

"Yes."

"Alone?"

"Yes."

"And they let you do it, McCracken and Slatterly? Unprotected."

"Well, they argued a little."

"But you argued them out of it."

"That's right."

"Well, there's two real gentlemen," said Watts. "First,

they let the lady win the argument and have her way, and second, they save themselves a useless, time-wasting ride."

When she spoke, her voice was icy. "What would you have done?"

"I'd have let you go, of course," said Watts dryly. "But I'd have dogged you back at a distance, and kept an eye on you, and seen that no harm came to you."

This struck her silent.

After a moment, he said, "Here we are."

They turned from the sidewalk through the front door of the Regina. The lobby was empty except for Mr. Selden. He was fussing over a four foot rubber plant, watering it, examining its thick leaves, being sure it was doing its best to put out its best performance. He gaped in surprise as he saw Miss Underhill and took a little lurching step in their direction.

"Welcome back," he said, trying to put enthusiasm into his words.

"She's coming back to stay," said Watts woodenly. "She's moving in forever. She's going to take over your job. She's going to be the new manager."

"He's joking," said Ursula.

Watts parted from them and went upstairs. It was a quarter of seven.

That night, business at the bar was slack. The wind started about seven-thirty, first coming in little gusts down Main Street and striking through the open door in hard, hot puffs. In the West, the sky turned to crimson mist, then burned to bronze, and finally became sluggish in slatey gray. A storm, and a vicious one, was on its way. The very quality of the air bred fear. People stayed indoors. Those few outside, when they met, spoke in hushed tones, and passed on hurriedly. The first rain came a little after eight—came and passed, like a tinkling handful of carpet tacks against the windows, and then there was nothing again but a feeling of emptiness. Silently Rouse shut the street doors.

Back behind the bar, he said, "I wish I was somewheres else."

"How about a game of cribbage?" said Watts.

"My heart wouldn't be in it."

For the next hour they were in the storeroom, checking the stock, simply trying to pass the time. They were here, among the cases and barrels, working by the light of two barn lanterns, when the thing cut loose outside. It was a world of silence, then, suddenly, a world of deafening sound. An awful screaming was unleashed, and that, they knew, was the cloud burst; through it, pulsing like a snare drum, was the maniacal rhythm of the wind. Even the storeroom floor seemed to shake.

Within five minutes it was over. The rain seemed sucked away by a giant inhalation. The rain reduced itself to a dribble, and dwindled to nothing.

"Well," said Rouse grimly. "I do believe it missed us."

Watts, also thinking of cyclones, said, "Yes."

"Let's take a look," said Rouse.

Carrying his lantern, he left the storeroom; Watts followed him. They went down the passage, to the back door, and opened it to the alley behind the hotel.

The clouds were thinning, becoming patchy, and stars were already showing. Great puddles blackened the alley, reflecting Rouse's lantern. Across the alley, the buildings were intact. "Everything looks okay," said Rouse.

A man and a horse came down the alley, the horse

at a walk, the man, in a glistening india rubber poncho, bent exhausted over his saddlehorn. He dismounted, tied his horse to an iron hitching ring by the door and brushed past them, into the hotel. From the little blur of face between black poncho and dripping hat brim, Watts recognized Slatterly of D-Bar-D.

"You been out in all that?" said Rouse, concerned.

"In all of what?" said Slatterly with a short unfriendly laugh, moving away from them down the passage. "I didn't notice anything."

So Slatterly was back, too, thought Watts. First Miss Ursula, and now Slatterly.

Could it be that she was under some sort of strict surveillance?

And if so, why, he thought a little later as he lay on his bed. And what was it all about? There was money involved, he was certain, big money. Men like Cranfield and McCracken didn't work for chicken feed.

And there was something else. The man who had hired them had known where and how to hire them; and that wasn't as easy as the average decent citizen might think.

That man, Watts was sure, was Alford. It had to be. He felt it in his bones. And that meant there was a side to Alford the people of Folsbee weren't aware of. It followed logically. This, too, had to be.

But anyway you twisted it, it came right down to one question. Why was Underhill killed, and apparently on a time schedule?

Or look at it this way. They wanted him dead, right then, and killed him. What had happened since? Nothing.

Or had it happened, in secret?

Or was it going to happen, and soon?

It was going to happen, and soon, Watts decided. McCracken and Slatterly, and Alford, for that matter, had all the appearances of men completely undisturbed, going about a job in an orderly fashion. What job?

He was almost asleep when he was summoned to the door, and opened it to find himself confronted by no one other than Slatterly himself.

The D-Bar-D man was in pants and collarless shirt. His eyes were red-rimmed and unhappy, and he held the side of his jaw.

He said in surprise, "Why, it's Mr. Denning."

"Sure," said Watts. "I live here. Who did you expect?"

"I didn't expect anyone in particular. I was just going down the hall, knocking on doors."

Watts waited.

"I'm in hell," said Slatterly, grinning in misery. "I've had a bad tooth for six years and now and then it gets its elements up. It's got them up now."

"Might have been that ride in the rain," said Watts.

"Must have been. I don't see how I can stand it until I get to a dentist in the morning. So I'm knocking on doors. You got any opium powder?"

"No."

"Any oil of cloves?"

"Sorry, no."

For an instant, Slatterly almost seemed likeable.

"If we can get a pair of pliers, I'll try to pull it for you," said Watts. "I've pulled them before."

"Thank you, no," said Slatterly. "No tooth ever comes out of my mouth until it drops out. God put 'em there, and there they stay."

He wandered away down the hall.

Watts thought of his childhood, and toothaches. There was nothing worse than a hell-busting toothache, unless it was an earache.

VIII

ONE OF THE bar's first customers next morning was Mr. Alford. Watts, who was busy at the backbar, getting things in order, seeing him in the backbar mirror, didn't bother to speak to him. Alford ordered a cherry-bounce, a woman's drink with scarcely more alcohol than a glass of rain water, and Rouse poured it for him. He paid for it from a clippurse, a nickel and five pennies, and took it down the full length of the room to an isolated table in a corner. When he had seated himself, he called, "Mr. Denning. I'd like to see you a moment."

Watts called back. "I'm busy."

"Go ahead," said Rouse. "I can handle it."

When Watts arrived at the table, Alford said, "Take a chair," and Watts said, "I won't be here that long."

Fiddling with his cherry bounce glass on the table, untouched, Alford said, "You don't like me, do you?"

"No," said Watts blandly. "Not a bit."

Alford's expression became grieved, but the vein in his neck stood out like a rope. He was enjoying himself immensely.

Watts said, "You called me over. What do you want?"

"Stories come to my ears. I hear little things about you. They say you're mighty touchy these days, that your nerves are hair trigger. What are you scared of?"

"Among other things, you," said Watts.

"Me?"

"Not you personally, God knows. You're nothing." The remark left Alford completely undisturbed.

Seeming not to hear it, he said, "I don't know how to put it. Let's say it this way. Everyone has his own sphere of life. You have yours, I have mine. I'm not stating it as a fact, I'm only saying it's possible that our spheres momentarily touched. And that, through no fault of either of us, we became at odds with each other."

"Momentarily?"

"What was true two days ago, is no longer true." Watts cocked an eyebrow, and listened.

Alford said, "Certain events have changed my attitude toward you. You are no longer either a friend or an enemy. As far as I'm concerned, you are non-existent."

"What events?"

"Events which are my business only," said Alford. "You need no longer fear me. And, I might add, I need no longer to worry about you. And you did worry me. You were carrying a little to much pressure for my comfort."

"I still am."

"You won't be, when you get it through your head what I'm saying. Have a good time. Enjoy yourself. Our ways have become divided. Nothing is going to happen."

Alford arose leisurely, and went out onto the street.

Back at the bar, Rouse asked, "What did he say?"

"I'm not sure," said Watts. "Maybe I've got this whole thing figured wrong."

The morning rush started. Today he would be off at noon.

There was a little restaurant not far from the railroad

station, run by a German, and sometimes Watts had noonday dinner or supper there. He got his meals free at the Regina, of course. It was part of his employment with them, but sometimes something came over him and he wanted to get away. He had dinner there today. The place served a lot of things that it turned your stomach to think about, offal and viscera, brains and sweetbreads and liver and lights, but it served the best pork chops this side of heaven. He ordered pork chops and coffee and chocolate cake as he passed the desk, and seated himself at a table by the window.

He was halfway through his meal when Slatterly came in and seated himself across from him. The D-Bar-D man looked battered but affable. He said, "I think it's going away."

"You mean the toothache?" said Watts.

The waitress came by. Watts asked for another cup of coffee. "Make it two," said Slatterly.

When she had gone, he said, "I've been to the dentist. Like you, he said it ought to come out. I've had other fellers with pliars and other dentists say the same. But I've got a wonderful set of choppers, and I don't want them meddled with. No offense. Look."

He lifted his lips and squared them back, like a dog. From across the table, Watts studied them. They didn't seem especially wonderful; they seemed ordinary, a little less than ordinary.

The waitress put down their cups of coffee. Watts took a sip.

"She still hurts a little though," said Slatterly. "But the dentist gave me something to fix that. Opium powder." He took a folded paper from his pocket, opened it, and poured white crystals into his coffee cup.

"You know, I'm getting to like you. You aren't the kind of fellow I thought you were at all."

A feminine voice behind Watts said, "Mr. Slatterly?"

Watts turned. Miss Ursula had come in and was standing behind him. He arose and faced her.

She spoke past him to Slatterly. "They told me at the hotel that you wanted to speak to me, and that I could find you here."

Slatterly, too, arose. He said, "I've been trying to get you all morning at the Regina."

"I was tired. I was asleep."

"I guess it wasn't as important as they made out at the hotel," said Slatterly.

She said, "I thought you would be home by now. Is it what brought you back to town?"

"No. I come back on another matter," said Slatterly. "It's this. It was a little business matter I had with your father before he died, and his death drove it clean out of my mind until this morning. A few cows of mine got on your place some time back and ruint some winter feed he'd put out near your south line. I want to pay the damages."

"Oh, for goodness sakes," she said. "He told me about it when it happened. You tried to pay him and he wouldn't take it. What are neighbors for?"

Slatterly laid a nickel on the table to pay for his coffee. "Well, I can tell you one thing. Neighbors shouldn't hurt each other. I'd be happier if you'd leave me settle."

They left the restaurant, walking side by side, and talking earnestly. Watts watched them leave, watched them as they passed the window.

He sat down, finished his cake, and reached for his coffee.

Suddenly he realized he was groping, that the cup's

handle was not where it should be. It was not at the right side, but at the rear.

The cup had been moved, and he himself hadn't moved it. He looked across the table at Slatterly's cup. It, too, had been moved, for its handle was at the left.

He sat for a minute thinking, and a chill went up his spine.

He was pretty sure now he'd seen crystals like Slatterly's toothache powders and they were strychnine crystals.

He got up and went to the desk, taking the cup with him. On the floor by the desk was a big brass cuspidor. He poured the coffee into it, washed the cup out with a carafe of water from the desk, and poured that in also. The proprietor stared at him. "Coffee bad?" he asked solicitously.

"I'm trying to break the habit."

"Break the habit?" said the proprietor, shocked. "Why, coffee's a good habit. Coffee's medicine."

As Watts paid his bill, the proprietor said, "You mean it keeps you awake?"

"I mean it puts me to sleep," said Watts.

This was his afternoon off, but he returned to the hotel bar.

He drew Rouse to the far end, the empty end of the mahogany and said softly, "Billy, if I wanted to buy some strychnine, where should I go?"

"To the drugstore," said Rouse. "Or even a good general store."

"But say I wanted to murder someone. You, for instance."

"Am I a friend of yours, Watts?"

"Up to now. But you never know."

"Don't use strychnine. Did you ever see an animal

die of strychnine? Hold me under gunpoint and feed me to death on T-bone steaks."

When Watts simply waited, Rouse said, "My God. They tried to do that to you. Was it McCracken?"

"No."

Rouse said, "You know the answer to your own question."

"I'd go to see a wolfer," said Watts. "Is there one in town?"

There sure was. His name was Pennyman and he lived as a squatter out on Cherry Street, in what was an old freighting office before it had burned.

Cherry Street footed on the river, two blocks west of the Bon Ton Barbershop, and Watts spotted the old burnt out freight office as soon as he came up to it. You couldn't miss it. Along the sidewalk front were two great rectangles of charred frames which had once been windows, and beyond them, inside, was a chaos of blackened wreckage. At the far rear was a smoke stained plaster wall with a scarred door. Watts stepped inside, made his way through the wreckage, and swung open the door.

He found himself in a medium large room, which had once been the shipping room. The damage effected by the fire here was mainly overhead, on the ceiling and part of the roof. The broad-planked floor was warped, but still sound. In the center of the room was a two wheeled cart, covered with a tarpaulin and hung with wolfer's equipment. In a far corner was a makeshift stall and a shaggy, ill groomed horse. On a buffalo robe by the cart, on his back, lay the wolfer, gazing tranquilly through the hole in the roof.

This, Watts thought, was a perfect picture of one of

his trade off duty. They were a mighty independent breed. They lived by making contracts with ranchers to exterminate their wolves, and exterminated them by the skillful placing of "buttons," tallow balls containing poison. They lived solitary lives, associating with no one, rarely even with other wolfers, and were considered highly eccentric. The truth was, Watts had long ago decided, that they live in warfare with such wily creatures that they were just about half wolf-brained themselves. For some reason, Watts always got along with them medium good. Or thought he did. How could anyone tell?

"Mr. Pennyman?" he said, and the man sat up.

His cheeks were withered, the hair at the back of his neck looked as though it had been hacked off with a skinning knife, which it had, and his eyes were little flakes of jet.

"You come to buy some wolf hides, Son?"

"No," said Watts. Mr. Pennyman was having a little fun with him. It wasn't even the season for wolf hides.

"Then what you want with me, Son?"

"They're saying around here you're a wolfer."

"Been for twelve years."

"Then you're a new kind to me," said Watts scornfully. "And I've known quite a few in my day."

Pennyman's face grew hard and hostile.

"The wolfers I've known," said Watts. "Are like good blasting-men at a mine. A good blasting-man knows the power of his rock powder, and knows he's the only one that does, and knows he would be going against his trade if he passes it out with both hands to ordinary citizens. Wolfers, good wolfers, are like that with their strychnine. Go to a drugstore. Don't expect a wolfer to sell it to you."

74

"Why, naturally. Strychnine ain't for everyone."

"A little while ago," said Watts. "I was offered some of your strychnine in a drink of coffee."

Pennyman looked flustered. "I don't believe it. Sure I sold some. But the party that bought it wouldn't do a thing like that. She bought it in mercy, to kill weasels in her henhouse."

"Would you mind giving me this merciful party's name?" said Watts.

"Of course not. It was Miss Ursula Underhill."

Watts was out of the building, and on the sidewalk, and as far down the street as the Bon Ton, before the numbness went out of his mind.

He wheeled, retraced his steps, and entered the shipping office.

Pennyman nodded aimably, uninterested, unsurprised at his return.

Watts said, "Do you know Miss Underhill? I mean by sight?"

"I've known her a heap longer than I've knowed you. And like her a heap better, when you come right down to it."

"What was she wearing—how was she dressed, for instance?"

"Don't get smart with me. I didn't say I seen her. I said she bought it. It was Mr. Alford, her friend, who come and done the actual buying."

As he returned to the hotel, the whole incident arranged itself for him and was explained. He understood the entire picture. How Slatterly prepared him for it with his toothache story, how he had brought Ursula into the restaurant to divert him while he made the switch of cups. And how Ursula, innocent of the whole thing, had unconsciously been an accomplice.

Alford had bought the poison, but Alford could easily cover himself here. He could cover himself by simply buying more strychnine, say at a drugstore, and delivering it to the Lazy U, and making a show of it.

Now, too, Alford's visit with him at the Regina that morning became clear. All his vague conversation meant nothing at all.

He had come to gloat.

In front of the court house, between the big double doors and the rutted road which was Main Street, there was a patch of hot, grassless earth which constituted a sorry sort of court square. Two years ago Mrs. Sheriff Finch had prevailed upon her husband to set out a shade tree here, a maple about eight feet tall with a trunk about the size of a broomstick. You couldn't truly say it had died, but you couldn't really say it was alive, either. You could stand on the sidewalk across the street, in front of the Regina, and easily count its leaves, which always looked to Watts like secondhand rejects from other, more bountiful trees. Shadows from this sparse foliage lay on the baked ground beneath it like dead gray butterflies, and here someone had placed a church pew for the weary passerby. As Watts approached it down Main Street, he saw there was a man sitting there, legs outstretched, ankles crossed, hat brim over his eyes, and the man was McCracken.

First Slatterly back in town, and now McCracken. The girl was a belle ewe, sure enough, Watts decided. Wherever the girl was, they went.

McCracken straightened up and adjusted his hat. He called, "Mr. Denning!" His voice was neutral, non-hostile. Watts swerved and joined him.

"I don't much care for a man that calls me to him,"

said Watts affably. "But this time I'll overlook it. What's on your mind?"

"You and me got off on a bad start together," said McCracken, crinkling the corners of his eyes, trying to look attractive and candid. "How about it? Let's say bygones are bygones and shake hands."

"About bygones being bygones," said Watts. "A man who ever agrees to that, the way I look at it, is a man who can't learn by experience. And about shaking your hand, no thanks."

McCracken seemed undisturbed.

"Well, then, how about this?" he said stolidly. Watts appraised him. Now it was coming, the real reason for the conversation.

"I was talking to a man a few minutes ago," said McCracken. "A rich man. He wants you out of town, as I get it."

"If you mean Alford," said Watts. "He wants me dead."

"I didn't say Alford, I didn't mention any name. He'll go so far as to buy you a little business of your own, if you'll take it."

Sheriff Finch came up the walk from Main Street, on his way to the front door of the courthouse.

As he passed them, he said, "Afternoon, Mr. McCracken, Mr. Denning. Hot, ain't it?"

They nodded to him, McCracken sullenly.

"I didn't know you two was acquainted," said the sheriff, his eyes twinkling. "I'd like to join you, but I got paperwork to do."

When he was out of earshot, Watts said, "Let's hear about it."

"It's a small place out at a settlement known as Knuckle Springs," said McCracken. "I understand you've been there. Run by a man named Gresham."

"Gresham wants to sell?"

"Who can tell, if the money's enough, and showed to him in the right way?"

"On the point of a scalping knife?" said Watts.

McCracken made his terrible blood-curdling face. Apparently, he made this face strictly in the line of business.

Watts laughed, and left him.

Mr. Alford was just within the front door of the Regina as Watts came in, obviously waiting for him. From where he had stationed himself, he could see across the street, and clearly observe Watts' conversation with McCracken. Watts had a feeling that after he had left McCracken, McCracken had passed a signal to Alford behind his back, and that the signal had said, "He wouldn't take it." Alford, therefore, was in the alternative position of following up McCracken's groundwork if the results were favorable, or, if unfavorable, of dealing a new hand.

He called Watts by name, and when Watts stopped, came up to him, smiling.

Watts said, "I've just talked to Pennyman, the wolfer. He says you're the one that bought the strychnine."

"I bought some, yes. But what about it?"

Watts didn't bother to argue. He said, "And I've just turned down McCracken's bribe."

"All this puzzles me greatly," said Alford, looking baffled.

Suddenly, Watts realized that they were growing afraid of him. And along with this, they were losing their deftness, their certainty, and beginning to blunder. They were reluctant to shoot him down publicly, as they had shot down Mr. Underhill, afraid their situation couldn't stand it. But frantic men do crazy things. If their position had somehow worsened, so had his.

"Denning," said Mr. Alford. "You wouldn't work for me under any circumstances?"

"That sums it up."

"Under any at all?"

"You're wasting my time."

Mr. Alford half dropped the upper lids to his eyes. "Mr. Selden, I believe it was Mr. Selden, anyway, someone remarked to me that you and Miss Underhill were, how shall I say it, becoming rather friendly."

"That's news to me, and it would be news to her. She loathes me."

"I want to hire you to protect her," said Alford.

When he could speak, Watts said quietly, "Who from?"

"From herself, and from her horse. Remember what happened to old Brad Ives, her family friend and foreman. He was out alone on the plain and his mare threw him and killed him. It could happen to anyone."

"Does she ride the same horse?"

"Any horse is dangerous."

After a long pause, Watts said, "And how am I supposed to keep it from happening? Move out to Lazy U? What do you want me to do?"

"Nothing. That's the easy part of it. You just stay here, and go about your daily routine."

"How will that protect her?"

"For one thing, you'll be minding your own business." Back through the open door, they were spreading cloths and placing tableware in the dining room for supper. "It's a little early, but I think I'll have a bite to eat." He moved away.

Watts said amiably, "What does it pay?"

"In money, nothing. In peace of mind, a great deal."

That night, the bar was busy. At eleven-thirty, Watts

left the hotel and crossed the street. There was a light in the sheriff's office at the courthouse.

The sheriff was in his office, at his desk, when Watts came in. Before him, on the desktop, were two big kerosene lamps, and between them was a heap of small papers, grocers' bills. He was casting up the annual food bill for the jail, to present to the county commissioners, and his face registered pain, as though someone were beating him over the head. When he saw Watts, he said, "How much is three hundred and sixty-five servings of mashed potatoes at thirty-three cents a bushel, with side meat and gravy?"

"That's a hard one," said Watts, seating himself. He grinned. "I'd like to study it over."

"And how did you spend this lovely, burnin' hot day?" asked Sheriff Finch.

Watts told him. About Slatterly and the strychnine, about Pennyman the wolfer, about McCracken and his proposition. Finally, he told him about Alford and the threat to the girl.

When he had finished, the sheriff said sympathetically, "You're letting this thing upset your judgment. That's the way I was when I was a whippersnapper. I can't believe Mr. Alford's in this at all."

"He isn't *in* it. He *is it*."

"He wouldn't threaten Miss Ursula. What did he say, exactly?"

"He didn't say anything exactly. That's the way he talks."

"Let's be reasonable about this," said the sheriff. "Why? What could he gain?"

"I'm willing to be reasonable," said Watts. "You're the sheriff. So let's start at the beginning. Why was Mr. Underhill killed?"

"That ain't fair. You know I don't know."

"But that's important. That's what this is all about."

The sheriff was scarcely listening. "Doggone it," he said moodily. "If you had just drunk a little of that coffee, we'd have something to go on. Not enough to kill you, o'course."

"Just enough to give me a few harmless convulsions."

"You're hard to talk to. You take everything I say wrong."

Watts got to his feet. "I came to make a report. And I made it."

Sheriff Finch strode to him, put his arm around his shoulder, and walked with him to the door.

In a new voice, a different voice, quiet, and firm as rock, he said, "And I heard you, son."

Watts went down the backstairs, out the backdoor, and sat on the back step. Indianlike, he waited in repose for a safe amount of time, say two hours, to go by. The hitching lot was dark, and without life, and the backs of the shops on its far side were closed for the night.

He worked for a while on the question he had twice posed to the sheriff, *Why was Underhill killed?* The answer to this, of course, was the answer to the whole mess. It wasn't something out of Underhill's past—revenge, say—he was pretty sure of that. Revenge was a thing of passion, and rarely expressed itself with such scheming and cunning.

The idea suddenly grew on him that even Underhill himself couldn't have answered the question.

He wasn't killed for revenge, or in anger, he was killed for gain. He was an innocent obstacle, and stood unknowingly in somebody's, Alford's, way. Obstacle to what?

A little after two o'clock, when the time seemed about

right, Watts got to his feet.

He headed for the Folsbee Feedingyards.

At the edge of town in a patch of dead pipestem weeds was the water tank for the locomotive boilers; down the tracks, fifty feet further, was a culvert over a wet weather stream bed, now dry. Beyond the culvert began the warren of pens which was the Folsbee Feedingyards. When Watts came to the culvert, he descended to the stream bed, made a quarter circle, and entered the feedingyards from the rear.

Clouds hung low and humid, and the night lay heavy and almost impenetrable over the pens. He made his way zigzag between them, toward a small shack a short distance behind the office which he had seen on his previous visit, and which he was certain must be the watchman's hut. Cattle, some humped shapelessly on the ground, some standing, eyed him lethargically as he passed.

There was a light in the shack window. Pausing well back in the lip of darkness, Watts took a quick look. A spidery old man in overalls sat by a lamp, on the edge of a lodgepole bunk. His pursed mouth held glinting little nails. There was a hammer in his hand and an upturned, broken down boot between his knees. He was half soling it, and from the feeble way he was operating, would be at it for a good half hour.

Watts left the watchman's shack and walked to the rear of the office.

The window here was dark. It was locked, too, but the sashes of unseasoned lumber had dried so that they were shaky in their frame. He pressed the lower pane inward, slipped the blade of his jackknife into the crack between the sashes, and eased back the catch. A moment later, he was inside.

He struck a match, found a candle, lighted it, and placed it on Mr. Alford's long work table.

The years he had spent keeping his ranch books had given him a pretty good idea of business records. Now he went through Alford's records systematically, with a fine toothed comb.

He first searched the table, found nothing, and moved to the wooden kitchen-type wall cupboards. He started at the upper corner of the end cupboard and worked down, carefully examining shelf after shelf, ledgers, papers, old correspondence. The first item of interest that he discovered was a sheaf of pink flimsies, bundled together, apart from other records. They were old cattle delivery receipts, and were signed in favor of Lazy U's southern neighbor, D-Bar-D. He took the receipts to the candle and riffled through them.

They puzzled him. They said that D-Bar-D had delivered to Alford in the last six years, at spaced intervals, a total of about four thousand cattle.

This was incredible. Four thousand cattle from that tiny, sorry, hardscrabbled spread, in shipments ranging from seven hundred to fourteen hundred cows per lot.

He was replacing the flimsies as he had found them, when he heard a faint hollow thump behind him, followed by another.

He wheeled. The room was empty.

If Alford had bought the cattle from D-Bar-D, they must have cost him something. Watts searched painstakingly, but could find no record of any monies paid out to D-Bar-D.

Now the thumping started again, rapidly, sounding as though someone was beating a barrelhead softly with a wet rope.

He glanced over his shoulder, and still saw nothing.

On a bottom shelf, back in a corner, was a canvas ledger stamped, *Special Accounts*. He opened it. Apparently it was devoted entirely to D-Bar-D.

In his own peculiar bookkeeping system, meticulous, fanatically detailed, Alford's entry noted the last shipment of D-Bar-D cattle delivered and below it, as a debit, he had written:

Charles Cranfield, Bear Paw Cattle Association, Nailhead Ford, pd $2000.

Watts restored the ledger to its shelf.

He had heard a great deal about Nailhead Ford. It was about sixty miles south of Folsbee, beyond the desolate Bear Paw Mountains, in the wilderness along the Missouri, between the Musselshell and the Judith rivers.

It was an outlaw hangout, exclusively, and, according to the talk in every barroom between Mexico and Canada, about the bloodiest of them all. This riverbank, for eight miles, was a country of horse thieves, wood hawks, rustlers, and drifting renegade killers.

There could be no cattle association at Nailhead. For that matter, in that wilderness, there were no cattle.

He knew then that this was it, the beginning of the end. Nailhead.

A faint muted whine trembled through the room. It seemed to come from the floor. Watts bent down. In the darkness under the table lay a huge dog, part mastiff, part Airedale. He was about the ugliest beast that Watts had ever seen. His great head was battle scarred from canine encounters and one eye was missing. About his neck was a cowhide collar studded with spikes. He was a watchdog.

For a long instant they stared at each other, in deep,

unexplainable friendship. *He's like I am,* thought Watts. *He fights who he wants to fight, and he likes who he wants to like.*

"Well, howdy, old timer," said Watts. He grinned, but he did not touch the dog.

Bang, bang, bang, went the bony tail against the floor.

Watts replaced the candle, snuffed it, and returned to town.

Main Street was deserted, dark, showing only a few feeble night lights behind shopfronts, three lighted windows on the upper floor of the court house, which was the jail, and a scattering of lighted panes, downstairs and up, at the Regina House. There was a light in Mr. Selden's room; and that was exactly where he would be at this hour, in his room, dozing his demijohn fever. Watts walked through the Regina doors, crossed the empty lobby, and climbed the stairs to the second floor.

The Underhill private suite was at the front of the hall, to the left of the stairhead. He hesitated, then tapped softly.

After a bit, the door opened and Ursula was standing before him. Her hair was in sleepy disarray, but her lavender eyes were awake and crystal hard. She wore a robe of green gossamer satin, which she clasped with one hand at the V of her throat. Her other hand, relaxed, hanging straight down at her side, held a Colt Army .45. It held it casually, almost unconsciously, as though she were simply carrying it from one place to another.

"Oh, it's you," she said.

"That's right."

"Well, I don't know what you want, but before we get into that, I'd like to give you a little advice. When a girl is alone in a room at night, especially a hotel room, you don't tap on her door. You hammer it good and loud. Understand?"

"Good and loud. Yes, ma'am."

Watts grinned, but got no smile in response.

She said, "Well, let's have it. What do you want?"

"It's about that new foreman of yours, McCracken. I had a little squabble with him some time back. He's a mighty hateful man. I came to register a complaint against him."

She looked unbelieving. "You mean you're afraid of him? You?"

"Well, I'm not exactly afraid of *him*. But I'm scared to death of those terrible faces he makes. Where did you get him anyhow?"

"When Brad Ives died, Mr. Alford sent him to me."

"You mean like a letter of condolence?"

"To take Brad's place."

"Mr. Alford always does the hiring for the Lazy U?"

"Of course not," she said, bridling. "He did it as a favor. He was a close friend of my father. He's been very helpful since my father passed away."

Watts stared at her in sympathy. He knew that he could never get into her mind and convince her that she walked in peril. She stood there before him incredibly lovely, defiant, aggressive. She was really hooked. She didn't know it but she was working for Mr. Alford now.

He said, "And I suppose he's a pretty good foreman."

"As good as Brad ever was. And that means he's perfect."

"Well, I'll be getting along," said Watts gravely. "This kind of talk breaks my heart."

He waited an instant for her face to soften, for her to make an answer, any answer at all.

When she didn't, he turned his back and left her.

The lobby was still empty as he passed through it to the street.

Outside, he crossed Main Street, took the brick walk around the court house, crossed the lot at its rear, and came out on Railroad Street. Here he turned left, past a parlor house and the high board fence of a lumber yard, and came to the Fort Kearny Saloon. Its white-washed sides glimmered in the moonless night. Its door was wide to the packed earth path which served the street as a sidewalk, and from within came the jingle of a banjo, a roar of bawdy, happy oaths, and a cacophony of quarrels and arguments. The Fort Kearny was doing a good business.

Watts made his way to the back door and entered the kitchen.

Hal Irwin came in, stood stock still, and gave his friend an owl-eyed, questioning look.

Watts brought him up to date on events.

"I'm going to Nailhead, Hal," he said.

"When?"

"Now. As soon as I can get my mare. I'll be back here in about fifteen minutes. Could you have some traveling supplies ready?"

"They'll be ready."

IX

By TEN NEXT morning, he had threaded his way into the outlying foothills, and through them, and by late afternoon he was in the fastnesses of the great mountains themselves. He followed an old Cheyenne-outlaw trail. Most respectable travelers added a few extra miles to their journey and skirted this wilderness.

That night he spent on a small high meadow, a little

marshy but rich in grazing for his mare, near a nest of springs which were the headwaters of a stream.

Next day the going was rocky and tough. In the morning, the trail dipped down and down, through gorges and crevasses, past huge polished boulders, and through a labyrinth of upstanding shards of limestone, knife sharp. Here, sometimes, stunted, twisted saplings fought for life in the splits and fissures of chasm walls. The rock was searing and the hot imprisoned air was lung-bursting, both to Watts and his mount. Then, when it had become almost unbearable, the trail began a steep ascent.

The harshness of the gorges fell away to sloping mountainsides of trees and outcrops, dotted with tangled brush and greasewood. By sunset, as he approached the crest, the greasewood had given way to spruce and tamarack. He slept that night on a lofty elbow in the ridge in a phantom, empty forest of jackpines.

When dawn showed like a copper wire in the East, he was already in his saddle. The olive gray of the early morning turned to rose and saffron among the tree boles. Soon, deep below him in the distance, he could see rolling plains to the south, covered with bunchgrass.

By nightfall, pushing his mare southward, he had crossed this grassland and was encamped in a thicket of willows on the bank of the Big Missouri. Somewhere to his west was the mouth of the Judith, to his east the mouth of the Musselshell. Here, in between, in the shadowy uninhabited riverbank country, hid the most bestial and dangerous of the outlaw world.

Watts examined his tough, lumpy old mare. She seemed as good as new. This far, it had been up to her; from now on, it was up to him.

He drank no coffee, and ate fireless, as though he

were in hostile Comanche country. These men were worse than Indians. For one thing, their spasms of blood-lust were unpredictable. For another, they were completely without loyalty, friendship, or humanity.

He slept soundly.

After a meager breakfast of cornmeal and water, he scouted a little, found the hidden trail—a narrow tunnel in the willows, scarcely the width of a saddle—and headed west.

Two hours later, the willows stopped abruptly, and he came into a bushy clearing.

A short distance away, a mounted man sat in his saddle lazily, eating dried apples from his hat on his saddlehorn. He said, "Friend, you got a noisy horse. Or is it a horse?"

He said it sociably enough, but this, Watts knew, could be trouble.

He examined Watts, and Watts examined him.

He was young, tough, competent looking, and mean. His shirt was calico, and his pants were dirty brown duck. The gun at his thigh was a .44 Smith & Wesson Russian, and Watts knew he favored it because its bullets carried an extra 41 grains of lead.

Coldly, but very carefully, Watts said, "What do you people want with me?"

"I could be a sheriff wanting your pelt," said the man. "But I ain't." He squinted, and added, "What do you mean, people?"

"You and the other one," said Watts.

There had to be another one, with a rifle on him.

"Come out, Shead," called the man, grinning. "Feller wants to make your acquaintance."

A second, older man rode up from around a salient of

brush. He was fancy in a shabby way, with a greasy green plush vest and matted bearskin chaps. His eyes were milky-blue, feral. His rifle was in its boot where it belonged, but his horsehide gauntlets, which should have been on his hands, were tucked into his belt. He had taken them off to aim that rifle.

Watts smiled tightly. It had been a close one.

"What do you think of it, Kimbro?" asked the older man, as though he were dressing a side of beef.

"All right, I guess. When you come right down to it, it's his worry, not ours."

"You can call me Santa Fe," said Watts. "I'm on my way to a place named Nailhead, to meet a friend called Cranfield."

"Your friend's dead," said Kimbro.

Watts paused a moment, then said, "I can hardly believe it."

"Well, that's the word, anyways," said Kimbro. "Two fellers killed him no-show up in Folsbee, they say. A barman and a hotel owner."

Shead said, "Let's move."

"We're headed for Nailhead ourselves," said Kimbro. "Maybe you better come along."

They rode out of the clearing together.

Watts had never seen either of them before.

They were pros, a long time gone on the gun, no doubt about that. But they didn't strike him as hired pistoleros. They were more the cow stealing type, or maybe horses. Whatever their trade, they were first-rate in it, they had to be. He knew top men when he saw them.

The hot noon sun was at its zenith when the trio reached Nailhead Ford. The creek itself, a tributary of the Missouri two miles to the south, was perhaps fifty yards wide, shallow and shaley. Across it was a high, undercut bank, crested with dead grass and snarled with exposed brush roots. Here, on the near side, was a flat sun-baked shelf of hard mud, and back a short distance from this surface, edging it, lay the village. Directly behind the village, looming high over it, were the giant cottonwoods which extended in a forest south to the river. Few places, Watts decided, could be more secluded, or difficult of access.

It was probably, too, the ugliest cluster of buildings that Watts had ever laid eyes on. Strung out in a row, with their back-ends to the woods and their doors facing the river, were about a dozen crude structures—huts, shacks, cabins, and one primitive store. Some were of unbarked horizontal logs, settler style; some were of short perpendicular logs, stockade style; and some were simply hive-shaped lumps of bent saplings, mud plastered. Almost all were squat and low, half-caves, built over pits, against the winter. Few had windows.

The store was an exception. It was built at ground level, a story and a half high, and across its front were three objects, a hitching rail, a watering trough, and an upright wagon tongue, like a flagpole, with a chalky bear's skull on it. The sides of the building had been weather proofed with stretched tarpaulins and patches of old canvas and rotting buffalo hides. Behind the store was a sizable feed barn, which would also be Nailhead's livery stable. Watts thought it was the most efficient looking building in sight. It would be; for these people lived not only by the gun but by the saddle.

Three mighty hard looking characters sat on their heels in the hot sun before a cabin. They sat here, Watts knew, because the inside of the windowless cabin was not only dark at mid-day, but probably stank to high heaven. Watts and his companions walked their mounts past them. The men ignored them.

There were no women in this place, or children, or even dogs. A gaudy fighting cock scratched in horse dung by the watering trough.

Watts, Shead, and Kimbro dismounted at the store and tied their mares to the rail. Without a word, Watts' two companions turned their backs and walked away. He was careful not to follow them with his eyes. Expressionless, he passed through the open doorway and entered the store.

He found himself in a long room floored with split cottonwoods. It was divided in half; the far half, to his left, was the eating and drinking section; the half he entered was the store. He was amazed at how well stocked it was. He saw on its shelves not only the customary items—the cans of salmon and peaches and tomatoes, and on the floor the barrels of brown sugar and flour and crackers, the baskets of onions and dried fruit, and, overhead, the hanging slabs of bacon, all these more or less favorites of traveling men—but other things, too, which surprised him. There was tapioca, and tinned jams, and rice, and raisins. Things which must have been carted up laboriously from some steamboat landing to the south. Visitors to Nailhead certainly came well furnished with money.

There was no one in sight. Watts called, "Hello." There was no response. He stepped out the front door, once more into the sunlight. Down the street, the three men who had been sitting in the dust were now standing and had been joined by Shead and Kimbro.

Watts circled the store to the rear. A chunky little man with a pink scalp and thin silvery hair was perched on the backstep, a gunny sack about his waist, weaving a turtle trap from willow withes. He nodded to Watts, and continued with his work.

"Am I talking to the right man?" said Watts.

"That's something one always wonders," said the man. "But I'd say yes. I'm Charley Goodhue."

"You own this store and barn?"

"The store, the barn, the town, and three deserted wives. What can I do for you?"

"To start off with, I'd like to stable my mare, eat some table food, and maybe spend the night. We'll see about that last, later."

"You said to start off with. What next?"

"I'd like a little information."

For the first time, the proprietor looked up.

"Come to think of it, so would I," he said. "I didn't catch your name?"

"Santa Fe."

"That's safe enough, I guess," said the proprietor, grinning. "In my life I've knowed about thirty-six Santa Fes."

"I'm a hungry, wandering cowboy," said Watts. "I was told by a friend named Cranfield that there might be a job here for me. With the Bear Paw Cattle Association."

"At Nailhead, we got turtles, not cows. You're miles south of the Bear Paw. Son, you're not only wandering, you're lost."

A voice behind Watts said harshly, "I never saw him before."

Watts turned slowly. There were five of them standing there, Shead, Kimbro, and the three others. They had come up like mountain cats.

Watts inspected the extras. One was a sandy haired boy, one was a drunken old man, cruel faced, sheathed in filthy rags, and the third was trouble if Watts had ever laid eyes on trouble. At first glance, he looked like an average, hard working, middle-aged rancher, any rancher; when you studied him a little, though, he looked different, smouldering and crazy. Back in '87, when the ice had taken the herds, ranchers had broken under the disaster, had collapsed. Most had recovered fully but a few had come out of it mentally maimed. Some of them were docile, some were frightful. This man, Watts decided, had suffered some disaster. He had become frightful. What had it been? An Indian massacre, a prairie fire?

This was the man who had spoken to him. Obviously he was the leader of the group.

"Everything's all right, Mogollon," said the storekeeper mildly.

Mogollon, thought Watts. There was as many Mogollons adrift as there were Santa Fes.

"You say you're a friend of Jimmie's," said Mogollon. "Well, I never saw you before." His voice was rasping and arrogant, but it was plummy and sly, too.

"I didn't say Jimmie, I said Cranfield," answered Watts. He remembered Cranfield across the bar in Paris, Texas. "I never heard his first name. That's what we called him down in Paris."

Everyone, including the store keeper, relaxed.

"If it ain't too personal," said Mogollon, suddenly amiable, "why was you supposed to meet him? Maybe I could help."

"I'd tell you if I could," said Watts helplessly. "He just said an outfit named the Bear Paw Cattle Association was looking for new hands. But Mr. Goodhue, here, says he's never heard of it."

"Neither have I," said Mogollon.

Watts wished he had a tintype of all of them. They were staring at him, frozen.

If this wasn't the Bear Paw Cattle Association itself, he would chop off his right arm.

He said, "Mr. Goodhue, can I stable my mare?"

The storekeeper nodded.

Only three had remained in the backyard, when Watts returned with Ivy: Mogollon, Shead, and the filthy old man in his stinking rags. They were standing around a beautiful bay mare, examining her, and as Watts passed they showed by their manner that they had partially accepted him. He took Ivy into the barn, fed her and made her comfortable, and rejoined them.

The big bay was a second string mount and belonged to Mogollon. As Watts stood a little back, and to one side, not to impose his presence on them, Shead led the bay back and forth across the dusty yard while Mogollon and the dirty old man watched. The bay was limping slightly.

Watts loved horses. Against his better judgment, he made a comment.

He said, "She's gone sick, eh? That's too bad."

In searching contempt, the old man said, "What kind of a cowboy are you? Sickness don't make a mare limp."

"She slipped on a flat rock crossing the creek some time back," said Mogollon. "And fell on her side. She's been limping ever since."

"She's in a bad way," said Watts.

The old man said, "It'll work out. She'll be all right in a little."

The bay had come to a halt. Watts bent over and studied its hoofs and lower legs. "Take a look here," he said.

They gathered 'round.

The hollow of her fetlock was swollen, and back and forth across the skin were tiny cracks. Watts touched it gently. It was hot.

"You know what that is, or should know," said Watts. "It's what horse doctors call 'the scratches.' Pus is rising under there. And if you don't do something, and quick, it will fetch off the whole hoof. She was lame, then, that's why she slipped."

"You're right," said Mogollon. "I seen it once before, when I was a boy. It is the scratches. I treasure that bay, and they ain't a horse doctor in a hundred miles."

The old man spat in disgust. "Don't tell me you're gonna listen to this big-mouth stranger? I forgot more about animals than he ever learned. I'm telling you the mare is already mending herself."

"Here's the cure my dad always used," said Watts. "Make some lye from wood ashes and boil some white-oak bark in it. It should be strong, both in the lye and bark ooze. Let it get cold. Wash off the leg with dish water, and put on the ooze with a swab. This will take off the hair. To bring on the hair again, make a salve by stewing sweet elder bark in old bacon."

"Thanks," said Mogollon stiffly. "Thanks, Santa Fe. We're heading out of here for a little trip tomorrow, but Goodhue will take care of it while we're gone."

"That's right, thank him," said the old man. "For mebbe killing a fine mare."

"I wouldn't put lye on no horse of mine," said Shead, suddenly entering the conversation.

"Did you ever see a hoof that had dropped off from pus?" said Watts.

"I'll fix up a little more of my A-number-one sprain liniment for her," siad the old man. "Like I said, it may take a little time."

Mogollon's face grew angry red. "You're the ignorant big-mouthed one, not Santa Fe. I shouldn't have let you mess with her in the first place."

The old man was a gnome of frozen hate.

Shead said, "Look at it this way. You go away, he goes away, and the mare dies. How are you going to hold him responsible. I wouldn't much want it that way, myself. I'd want him to pay the bill, and I don't think I'd take it in cash."

Very quietly, Watts said, "Mr. Shead, I hate to tell you this, but you're pressing in on me a little."

He waited. Nothing happened. He circled the store and entered its front door.

At one of Mr. Goodhue's tables, he had his first real meal since he had left Hal Irwin's kitchen at Folsbee. He had a beefsteak with three fried eggs on it, boiled onions, boiled green beans and salt pork, pones, and coffee; for dessert he had a can of peaches in thick syrup. Mr. Goodhue charged him five dollars, and grinned; Watts paid him, and grinned. No one traveled this route cheaply. Nailhead cost real money.

He decided to go whole hog, bought a five cent stogie for fifty cents, and relaxed on the bench, his elbow on the cluttered table, to think things over.

He hadn't gotten any proof, any real proof of anything, but it had certainly been worth the trip. He was utterly and completely convinced that Mogollon and his crew were topnotch rustlers, and that they were tied in closely with Alford and his feedingyards, and with D-Bar-D. And something was about to happen, for Mogollon had said he was preparing to set out on a little trip.

Over and over, Watts considered it, from this angle and that. The hours went by. He was left strictly alone.

Even Goodhue remained out of sight.

A little before sunset, he got the big idea. Could he join them, and go along with them, and find out himself what was what?

It might be difficult to bring off, but it wasn't impossible. They weren't too enthusiastic about him, but they weren't suspicious of him. Say, for instance, that Cranfield was supposed to have been in on this undertaking, whatever it was, and then had gotten himself killed. That would make them a man short. If he handled it right, maybe Mogollon would make him an offer to take Cranfield's place.

He smiled wryly. What would happen then? Would he find himself in their company, in Alford's office, facing Alford?

That would be lively while it lasted. And it would last about fourteen seconds.

He arose, left the coolness of the store, and stepped into the heat of the street. Across the creek, the brassy evening sun struck the faces of the shanties and cabins in full, blinding force. A short distance away, the three rustlers sat again on their heels in the dust, the ragged old man, the sandy-haired boy, and Mogollon. They sat in a huddle in the scorching sun, motionless. Such men as these seemed insensible to weather, wind or rain, cold or heat. They were not talking, just sitting. Each seemed alone.

Watts approached them. As they got stiffly to their feet there was the creak of leather, belts and chaps, and the clink of metal, buckles and hardware. Before Watts could speak, the old man said, "Why, it's the wonnerful horse doctor. Drag your tail, skunk, you ain't welcome here."

Watts ignored him.

The sandy-haired boy spoke to Mogollon. "That goes for me, too, boss. He turns my stummick ever' time I look at him."

"Take it easy, men," said Mogollon.

"What the hell goes on here?" said Watts mildly.

"To tell you the truth, friend, I never know," said Mogollon. "I'd say it was because you're an outsider. They don't care much for outsiders. I've had this happen before."

To Watts' surprise, he saw that Mogollon was enjoying it.

Shead and Kimbro appeared from behind a cabin and joined the group. They seemed to be enjoying it, also.

"I ain't agoin' to say it agin,'" said the old man viciously. "Turn around and walk away from here."

After the slightest pause, Watts said, "Sure."

"And when you speak to me, say 'sir.'" said the old man.

Now Mogollon did a brutal thing. He motioned the others back, leaving Watts and the old man facing each other alone, as though gunplay were inescapable. He was not only enjoying it, he was egging it on.

"I'd like to know a little about this," said Shead, his milky-blue eyes dull, blank.

"You seen and heered him!" said the sandy-haired kid. "He's fixin' to kill Dad!"

"I guess that's about his style," said Shead. "Why don't he kill me instead? I ain't busy."

As he spoke, he drew.

It was lightning fast, but a little muscle-bound, from working other folks cows, maybe. Watts knew instantly that he was the outfit's heavy-duty man.

Watts shot him twice in the heart, before his hammer hit its pin.

Shot him and wheeled. The kid had half-drawn, and Kimbro was staring, trying to make up his mind. Mogollon's face burned with delirious excitement.

To the kid, Watts said, "What's that you got in your hand?"

"Nothing," said the kid, and slipped his weapon back in its holster.

The old man was goggle-eyed. His age seemed doubled.

That was the trouble with men who were almost-good, thought Watts. They overrated themselves. And they spilled a lot of blood before it caught up with them.

To Mogollon, Watts said, "I was getting ready to ask you to take me on. But I guess there's not much chance now."

"No chance at all," said Mogollon reasonably. "But I'll tell you what. You done me a favor with the mare. I'll do you one. I'll give you fifteen long minutes to get out of town."

With Nailhead behind him, he retraced his way northward. He traveled hard and fast, camping light and quick, urging Ivy on, allowing her occasionally to stop and blow. By the second night, he was again in the southern Bear Paws and camped again at his old site, high on the ridge in the forest of jackpines, at the crest of the escarpment.

There, in his lofty lookout post, with the plains rolling away beneath him to the south, he waited.

Mogollon had said he was going to take a little trip. If this trip was to Folsbee, it could be highly significant.

He could, of course, be headed anywhere. But Watts' guess was Folsbee. Watts decided to wait here three days.

They appeared on the second day, showing up in the distance as four black specks in the grass, heading directly toward him, forming gradually into four riders, Mogollon, the old man, Kimbro, and the kid. They were moving at a slow, steady pace, in no hurry.

Watts watched them, far below him, as they stepped their mounts into the fan of rocky rubbish which was the entrance to the old Indian Trail.

He was deep in a thicket of tamarack, off the trail forty feet away, when they passed him.

He gave them an hour's lead and set himself on their track. They were careless with their sign, and he had no difficulty following them. He never allowed himself to draw in sight.

Down the mountain slope with its greasewood, they went, through the network of gorges and chasms, past the polished boulders, climbing, spending the night exactly as he had done, in the high marshy meadow.

He followed them in their final descent, through the outlying foothills, almost to Folsbee.

Six miles south of Folsbee, he lost them.

He lost them in an arid stretch of shale and no amount of circling and quartering would pick them up again.

He was certain that they hadn't spotted him, that they were being cautious for another reason, possibly because they were approaching a sizable town, but it came to the same thing.

All sign of them had vanished.

X

WHEN WATTS came into the Regina kitchen from the alley, Mr. Selden was standing by the butcher's clock with the cook, telling him how to cut up a side of beef. To Mr. Selden it was a mystery and a problem that had to be discussed at great length. The cook, who could cut up a side of beef in his sleep, pretended strict attention. He went through this rigmarole once a week, and was a patient man.

Watts expected Selden to fire him on sight for his absence, but Selden simply said, "Where have you been?"

"Away."

"You better go to your room and shave and bathe. This is the day you go on at noon."

"Where's Miss Ursula? I'd like to talk to her a minute."

"She's gone back to the Lazy U. What did you want to see her about?"

"To tell her I'm quitting, among other things."

Mr. Selden took this a funny way. It seemed to disturb him.

The cook began to cut up the meat. He was all ears.

Mr. Selden said, "But we need you here. Haven't you been satisfied? Haven't I treated you right?"

"You've treated me fine. You gave me my first taste of pickled oysters. I guess it's just that I'm a drifter."

Mr. Selden was suddenly, intensely interested. "You mean that you're moving on?"

"How do I know what I'm going to do?"

Mr. Selden walked hurriedly toward the door. It was almost as though he had to tell somebody about it. Watts watched him thoughtfully. This brought Mr. Selden, and a few other things, into a new light.

The cook, a thin man with a fat protruding stomach, said, "What in the hell are pickled oysters?"

"Search me," said Watts. "I never heard of them before."

The cook cut off a hunk of raw suet, the size of a walnut, sprinkled salt on it, spread it with mustard, and jammed it into his mouth and began to chew it. "I don't think I'd care for 'em," he said.

Rouse, when Watts talked to him in the barroom, was sorry to hear that he was leaving the Regina, but was careful not to ask him any prying questions.

"I've got to do it, Billy," Watts said. "I'm going to have my hands full. I've got to have it so I can move free."

"Well," said Rouse, looking at him, through him, into the old days, into the old loyalties. "If you need me, you know where to find me."

"You can give me some information," said Watts. He described Mogollon and his crew. "Can you place them?"

"No."

"They're rustlers, I'd stake my life on it. And I trailed them to six miles south of town and lost them. I know they're here on a job. And I got a feeling they've been here before. Have you heard of any big rustling raids hereabouts in the past?"

"No," said Rouse. "Not in the near past. These Montana ranchers are mighty well organized. Little stuff, of course, but nothing sizable."

Watts went to his room, washed and shaved, packed his gear and clothes.

If Rouse said there had been no sizable rustling, that was the truth, for Rouse would know. And Mogollan and his outfit wouldn't fool with anything that wasn't sizable.

Then why would they come to Folsbee, and where had they vanished?

Cattle had been stolen in sizable amounts, and had been marketed through Alford's feeding yards; Alford's records had showed that.

Where had these cattle come from? Could they have been driven up from the far South, Arizona, Texas, New Mexico? It was possible, of course, but unlikely. The distance was excessive. And between Texas, say, and northern Montana, a stolen herd could be disposed of dishonestly a hundred times.

And the men at Nailhead had had no cattle with them. Their raid was still ahead of them.

Another thing Alford's records had shown. They showed pretty conclusively that the D-Bar-D ranch was the funnel through which these stolen cattle came to the feedingyards.

The pressing thing now was to go to the D-Bar-D and have a little look around, and talk with Mr. Slatterly.

He might even find the Nailhead rustlers, holing up.

If the Regina was Folsbee's most elegant lodging house, the Star was its most squalid. But to a man with private business, it had big advantages. No one cared who you were, or when you came or went. Nobody talked about you. If you just laid down the thirty-five cents a night, and didn't much care where or how you slept, you had a home.

It was a dingy, ramshackle building, across the railroad tracks, just up the street from Hal Irwin's. Watts left his gear with the clerk and paid a week in advance. "I'm going on a little trip," he said. "I'll be back later." He left, and went down the street to the Fort Kearny Saloon.

It was noon. Irwin was alone, behind his bar, cutting and rolling lamp spills from an old newspaper. When Watts came in, he poured two whiskies and two beer chasers. "How did it go?"

Watts told him. Irwin listened intently. When Watts had finished, Irwin said, "Mogollon, eh? I can't say I recall either him or any of his crew by name or description. And you think they're here on a job?"

"I know they are. They said they had one coming up."

"And that they had been here before?"

"Yes."

Irwin shook his head. "You must be wrong. I agree with Billy Rouse. There's been no big scale rustling around here for a long, long time. You can't hide a thing like that."

"Alford's records say there has been. They say he's bought a total of six thousand cows over the past six years from D-Bar-D. D-Bar-D has to be his dummy. Those cattle have to be stolen."

Irwin said, "Do you think they could be train robbers?"

"Have there been any train robberies hereabouts?"

"None at all."

"They're rustlers," said Watts doggedly. "They're here to rustle. They've rustled here before. I don't know how they did it, or what happened, but that's the way it is."

When Irwin said nothing, Watts said, "I think I'll go up to D-Bar-D and see what's what."

A half an hour later, Watts, in the saddle again, came out of the Cloverleaf Stable, onto Main Street. Instead of turning north, toward D-Bar-D, he turned south on Union, to South Pike.

The old mill, in its forest of cottonwoods, looked lonesome and shadowy. He dismounted, entered the building, and climbed the timber stairs to the second floor.

As he had expected, there was nothing behind the mill-stones. Gone were the food, whiskey, and cigars—everything.

He saw no trace of embers where there had been any cooking, and expected none. Mogollon and his men, passing through, had had their banquet somewhere far out on the prairie.

It was the morning of the second day after, when Watts came onto D-Bar-D land. He came onto it from its barren southwest corner, instead of from the direct south as he had done before, in the hope he might run into something interesting. The land changed from medium good to miserable, abruptly. He passed through thin grass, through an area of tiny arid bushes, and across a chain of sun dried alkali pans, cracked into crusty little plates. After a bit, things got better again, but not much. The thin grass started again, but it was patchy and starved. It certainly wouldn't have fed six thousand market cattle.

The prairie here was flat as a pancake and without trees or swells or hollows. The sky was cloudless, the air was crystal clear, and, after a while, he could see the little ranch house and its out-buildings, sunwashed in the distance.

There were two horses tied at the rail by the barn and as he dismounted he recognized the Lazy U brand. He scanned the earth, looking for an excess of hoofprints, for the Nailhead men, but saw nothing suspicious. He walked to the cabin, and called, "Hello, anyone home?" and its door swung outward.

Slatterly, looking suave and contented, thrust out his head. "Mr. Denning," he said. "What can I do for you?"

"You can ask me inside," said Watts.

"It ain't convenient at the moment. I got company."

Watts wrenched wide the door, and jammed past him.

The room was small and dank, and its one window had been broken and was now boarded up on the outside. Though it was almost noon and bright sunlight outside, here it would have been dark but for a barn lantern which burned on a table. Clothes hung from pegs in the log walls, and riding tack. The clothes were work clothes, cheap, but the tack, while worn, was expensive stuff. There was a built-in bunk in a corner, with a rumpled blanket, two chairs, a cannonball stove, and a table. Ursula Underhill sat by the table; her foreman sat hunched on the rim of the bunk. It was no place for a woman, unless she was headstrong. They wouldn't harm her, but it was unladylike.

Slatterly, puffing, looking venomous at Watts' intrusion, said, "Well, now you're here. What do you want?"

"Well, I don't want strychnine," said Watts. "But maybe I'll take that up with you later."

Ursula had been talking to McCracken, and continued, ignoring Watts. McCracken, too, shot him a single glance, then seemed unaware of his presence.

The girl said, "It's might nice of Mr. Slatterly to offer to pay me for the use of the creek, if I want, but it's as much his as it is mine. It flows through his land, it's on his property, too."

"But it has its headwaters in them northern buttes on your ranch," said Slatterly, looking humble. "I want to be neighborly."

"You are," said McCracken, retorting as though he were reciting a part on a stage. "We know that at Lazy U. You're a wonderful neighbor."

Miss Underhill nodded solemnly.

They really had her tied and branded. She was overcome. They had won her trust completely. And with such monkey business as this, probably.

"Is that a usual thing around here?" said Watts. "For folks that use a stream to pay the ranch that has its headwaters? It seems unreasonable and foolish to me."

Ursula said, "Ever since my father died, Mr. Slatterly

has been doing his level best to be friendly. And I greatly appreciate it. That's why he made such a generous offer."

"You should have taken him up on it," said Watts. "And watched his face."

Slatterly said, "State your business and get out."

"I'm kind of looking for a man," Watts said. "A stranger in these parts, I think." He described Mogollon in detail, and waited.

Their faces told him nothing.

McCracken said, "I'll keep an eye out for him. Any message you'd like me to pass on?"

Watts said, "No."

"We don't see many strangers in this part of the country," said the girl. "We're too far north."

"That's right," said Slatterly.

"The only stranger I've seen since I've been back at Lazy U," said Ursula, "was that dirty old man."

"That doesn't sound like the fellow I'm looking for," said Watts, poker faced. "What did he look like?"

She described Dad.

"That's not him," said Watts. "You make him sound pitiful to look at."

"He was," said Ursula. "He was in the ranchyard, talking to Mr. McCracken when I came up. I sent him to the cookhouse for a good meal."

"Just a drifter, I guess," said Watts.

"It was sad, really," said Ursula. "He was a crazy old prospector, looking for gold. He didn't even know he was in Montana. He thought he was in Wyoming."

"Is that a fact?" said Watts. "That is sad. I hope you set him straight?"

"Mr. McCracken did. I didn't get a chance to talk to him. He walked away as I came up. I sent Mr.

McCracken after him to offer him food. Mr. McCracken told me all about it later."

"I'd better be getting back to town," said Watts politely. "I want to thank you all for your warm hospitality."

XI

ABOUT TWENTY townsmen, shopkeepers, citizens, and loafers were standing in the hot sun in the middle of Main Street before the courthouse, blocking the street, when Watts returned. In the center of the gawking group was the sheriff's delapidated buggy, and on the front seat sat Sheriff Finch and a boy. The boy wore handcuffs and leg irons. He was scarcely more than fourteen, with untidy mouse-colored hair and pale blue eyes. He was dressed like a farmer in coarse butternut homespun.

Pulling his mare to a stop, Watts spoke to one of the by-standers. "Who is he?"

"Name's Sully Weedin," said the man. "Comes from a big tribe of homesteaders just south of town. They're all fine people, all but Sully. He's always been a bloodthirsty breed to himself."

"What's he done?"

"Strangled his father-in-law and cut out his tongue in an argument over a farrow of pigs."

"Father-in-law?" said Watts. "He don't seem scarcely old enough to be weaned."

"He's weaned, all right."

The boy was glorying in the spotlight. He was turning his head from side to side, speaking to people, some he knew, some whom he didn't know. When he saw Watts, he said, "Take a good look, friend. I'm a bad one."

You would have been, thought Watts, with about ten

years on you. But your days are numbered now.

Expressionlessly, he pressed his mare with his knee, and moved her slowly down the street, toward the Star Hotel.

How many times he'd looked into eyes like those, he didn't care to remember.

The Star had been built as a dance hall, and, because of repeated difficulties with the law, had been crudely remodelled into a rat-nest lodging house. It was a one story frame structure, long and narrow, extending back from the packed earth sidewalk into a clump of sumac bushes. Watts entered its front door, and went into its tiny lobby, with packing-box desk, register, and night-bell. To the left of the desk was the open corridor to the midget rooms at the rear, which paraded back, one after another, in a series of partitions—pigeonholes with no doors.

The clerk and owner, a wispy little man with tattooed hands, greeted him placidly, showed him to his room, Number Four, and returned to the lobby with him.

He wanted to talk about the sheriff's prisoner. "I tell you, Mr. Denning, I've had that boy in here now and again, to spend the night, and I shivered until he was off the premises."

"What did he do? Barricade himself and wait for the law to come?"

"No. He run. But Sheriff Finch out-thought him. As soon as he got the word, he figured he was heading for Birdsong Ravine and Canada—which he was, which he later admitted—and cut him off before he even got started."

"What's Birdsong Ravine? I don't believe I ever heard of it."

"It's that old outlaw pass up north. It ain't used much

anymore. And Mr. Denning, I almost forgot. Mr. Alford was in the other day, asking for you. He says he'd like to see you."

"Thank you," said Watts, and went out onto the street.

There were three or four hardcase punchers and a pair of blackleg gamblers at the bar when Watts came into the Fort Kearny Saloon. The punchers were drinking expensive whiskey which meant that they were over the edge, as they had probably started on cheap stuff. The gamblers, hunched, whispering to each other, were watching them, waiting. It was a picture Watts had seen many times before. Irwin, disliking it, but knowing he was helpless, slammed down his bar-rag and walked with Watts outside to the doorstep.

Watts said, "I picked up Mogollon's trail. One of his crew, an old man they call Dad, stopped at the Lazy U."

"Is that so?" said Irwin. "What for?"

"I wish I knew. He talked to McCracken, but wouldn't face Miss Ursula."

"Well, they're not after Lazy U cattle," said Irwin decisively. "Because Lazy U only has a token herd, and this is a big operation."

Watts looked stony and mean.

"What about this?" said Irwin. "Do you think maybe they could be train robbers, hiding out on Lazy U land?"

"No, Hal, I don't," said Watts doggedly. "Those boys are rustlers, and from the way they talked down at Nailhead, I'd stake my life on it that they're on a rustling job right now. And that they've been here before on other rustling jobs."

"It can't be," said Irwin. "You can't rustle a big herd in secret. And I haven't heard the slightest rumor. I've told you that a dozen times."

Watts mentioned the boy prisoner, at court square.

"Yeah, I know," said Irwin, the best informed man in town. "And I'm mighty glad he's out of circulation. How did Finch catch him?"

"He was headed for Canada, and Birdsong Ravine," said Watts. "Hal, what's Birdsong Ravine?"

"It's a big canyon in those buttes up on the northern boundary of what's now the Underhill place. It used to be an outlaw trail, a famous one. But it's too famous now, and isn't used anymore."

"Why was it so famous?"

"They used to run stolen cattle through it, Montana cattle, up to Canadian ranchers."

After a bleak moment, Watts said, "But they're not doing it now?"

"Of course not, how could they? When there haven't been any cattle stolen."

Watts looked moody. Irwin said, "Come in and have a drink on the house."

"Later," said Watts. "Right now I've got to see Mr. Alford. I hear he's been asking around for me."

"What's he want?"

"Who knows?" Watts grinned wrily.

He returned to the Star Hotel, got Ivy from her rack, and took her to the Cloverleaf. When he walked again down Main Street, the crowd before court square had dispersed. Birdsong Ravine, he thought, and sat down on the church pew beneath the scraggly little tree.

Birdsong Ravine, he felt with a chill, was the answer to everything. It had to be. Mogollon and his men, working for Alford, were running stolen herds up through the notorious canyon again, up into Canada. It didn't seem possible, but it had to be a fact. It would explain the presence of the rustlers in this part of the country, everything. It was so obvious, it simply had to be true. The problem was, of course, what cattle? Where did they come from?

Where did they come from?

They weren't local cattle, but they came from somewhere. And how did they get here?

Why couldn't they have come in on the railroad? Why couldn't they have been stolen in the far South, say, and been shipped to Alford and his feedingyards, and transferred, say, to the D-Bar-D, a staging point where Mogollon took over and moved them up out of the country through Birdsong Ravine?

You didn't need a bill of sale to ship a stolen cow on the railroad. And shipping them eight or nine hundred miles, up here to northern Montana, was a lot quicker and safer than trailing them.

Aford could have been using this trick for years.

Watts sat forward on his seat, and went over it again, analyzing it. The cows would be picked up, perhaps, in Colorado and shipped to Alford. From Folsbee, some dark rainy night, they would be moved to D-Bar-D, and then to Canada.

But between D-Bar-D and Canada lay the Lazy U.

In the past there had been no Lazy U, just emptiness. Then, Mr. Underhill had come and bought the land and built his ranch house, and laid a block in Alford's path.

So Mr. Underhill had been killed.

And Miss Ursula, with an Alford man as her foreman, was being manipulated.

Alford, apparently all set, was about to do business again, as usual.

There was only one difficulty in this whole line of reasoning. It was a difficulty that bothered Watts seriously. It was the part about moving a big herd, sight unseen, from the feedingyards on the first stage of their journey, to the D-Bar-D. It would be almost impossible to do it, even if you would throw in a black night and a thunderstorm, even if you did it at three in the morning, without somehow attracting attention.

But Alford had certainly worked it out somehow.

The day was Monday, and Monday, as the whole town knew, was Alford's day away from his office. Not Saturday, because Saturday was Folsbee's big business day. Anyone who wanted Alford on Monday could find him at home. But it had better be important, because Mr. Alford, on his day at home, didn't like to be disturbed.

In type with the character he painstakingly presented to the town, he lived in a humble brown cottage on the rutted road which was the tail end of Plum Street. The yard was treeless, grassless, eroded, and the cottage itself, with a rusty tin roof, was hardly larger than a henhouse. When Watts came into the yard, he found Mr. Alford on a ladder at the rear, picking snap beans which he had trained to grown on a trellis up the clapboards of the kitchin siding. It was a very domestic, homey sight. He came down the ladder, laid his basket on the ground, and said, "Good of you to come, Mr. Denning. Shall we go into the parlor, out of the sun?"

"I believe not," said Watts. "This shouldn't take long. I didn't come because you asked me to. I came out of curiosity."

"I relied on that," said Mr. Alford, dispassionately.

"Well, what?"

"You've moved from the Regina to the Star."

"Right."

"Why?"

Watts grinned and shook his head.

Alford said, "You've just come back to town. Where have you been? Up to Lazy U, visiting Miss Underhill?"

"No," said Watts. "I was up to D-Bar-D."

"Why?" The man was good. He seemed hardly interested in his question.

Watts took a chance. He said, "I was looking for out of state cattle. Say from Colorado, or Utah, or Arizona."

Alford's complacent mask slipped. He seemed genuinely confused. Watts became suddenly worried. Could he be wrong about the whole thing?

Alford said, "And what did you find at D-Bar-D?"

"Well, I found Slatterly and McCracken and Miss Underhill, sitting around and calling each other wonderful neighbors."

This bothered Mr. Alford. He said, "Miss Underhill, was she in good health?"

"Oh, sure."

"We've discussed this point before. Let's keep her that way."

"I used to be worried about her," said Watts. "But I'm not any longer. I've changed my mind. I've finally decided Mr. Slatterly and Mr. McCracken will see that nothing harms her."

"What do you mean by that?"

"I mean they won't let her ride a fractious horse, for instance," said Watts.

He turned his back and walked away.

XII

CHERRY STREET, squalid and ramshackle, was coated with liquid gold in the afterglow of the setting sun when Watts came up to the old burnt out freight office. He stepped through the charred doorframe, passed through the black, tumbled wreckage, and entered the fire scarred door at the rear. Mr. Pennyman, the wolfer, alone in the shipping room, was having his supper. Sitting on his heels by an oil can stove, he was eating a bowl of grits and hog jowl. He picked up a second bowl, prepared to fill it, but Watts shook his head. If you wanted a word with a Montana man, Watts knew, any Montana man, get him at meal time. The code of hospitality would force him to be courteous. "Evening," said Pennyman. "Sit."

Watts sat crosslegged on the floor in front of him, as though they were out on the prairie. He offered Pennyman papers and tobacco; Pennyman rolled a cigarette, nodding his thanks.

Neither of them spoke.

Watts again took invoice of him, his brown withered cheeks, his ragged hair, his frayed and greasy clothes, and decided again that here was a man who could be as cunning and savage and hostile as one of his perpetual wolf enemies.

When Pennyman had half finished the cigarette, he extinguished it, unrolled the paper and rubbed the remainder back into his mouth, on his lower gum, like snuff.

He then took off his jacket, which he wore despite the heat, and his shirt. He turned the shirt inside out and began searching its seams for lice. And finding quite a few, Watts observed.

"Of all God's creatures," Pennyman said. "Least of all I understand a louse. When you hate *him* so much, how can he love *you* so much?"

Watts released his breath, slowly, in relief. Pennyman had decided to be sociable.

Carefully, Watts felt his way. "Mr. Pennyman," he said. "Why, the last time I talked to you, did you say you didn't like me?"

"I was having one of my bad days. I didn't like nobody."

"And this is a good day, when you like everybody?"

"I never have no days like that."

They lapsed again into tomblike silence.

"Mr. Pennyman," said Watts. "Being a wolfer, you must have crisscrossed this county more ways than a porcupine has quills. It can't have any secrets from you."

"It don't have no secrets from me, but I sure as hell have some secrets from it."

"That I don't doubt. Mr. Pennyman, I want to hire you to take me to Birdsong Ravine. I want to go so I don't pass any people, at D-Bar-D, or Lazy U, or anywhere else. I'll pay you twenty dollars in gold."

"You on the dodge, son?" asked Pennyman solicitously. "That ain't the place to hit for. It's too well knowed. If you live by your gun, and I'm damn sure you do, no matter what your other trade might be, I'd head for the Owyhee desert in Idaho."

"I want to look for cattle tracks."

Pennyman looked suddenly unhappy. "Don't tell me I just offered a bowl of delicious hog jowl and grits to a lowdown cattle detective?"

"I'm no cattle detective," said Watts.

"Well, you won't find no cattle tracks in Birdsong Ravine. It got too bad a reputation some time back."

"How long has it been since you've been there?"

"Eight years. They ain't no wolves there neither."

"Just the same, I want to go."

Pennyman held out his hand. After a second, Watts got the idea and handed him tobacco and papers. The wolfer smoked and meditated.

At last, he said, "Who gathers the firewood?"

"You do," said Watts, not to make it too easy.

"That'll be an extra thirty cents. Who does the cookin?"

"I'll do the cooking," said Watts. "If you insist."

"I insist you don't," said Pennyman. "That firewood question was just to throw you off guard. When do we leave?"

"Tomorrow morning," said Watts, getting up. "You be out in front of the Star Hotel at three. And if you have my mare with you, saddled, from the Cloverleaf, there'll be an extra dime in it for you. What about the grub?"

"You get your mind off the grub. I don't want you messin' with it. I'll bring the grub and the pack horse."

"Pack horse? We're traveling faster than that."

"See you tomorrow morning," said Mr. Pennyman.

Sheriff Finch was in his office when Watts came in. He was sitting behind his desk and standing in front of it was a farm couple, a skinny little five-foot woman in patched calico and a big, brutal looking man, obviously her husband, in a denim shirt and baggy canvas pants. They were glowering at each other. The woman had a black eye which spread down her cheek, about the size of Watts' hand. The sheriff was scolding them, in a deep bass voice.

"I'm not going to throw nobody in a cell," he said. "Though God knows I should. You've put me through this too many times before. You better listen to me. The home is no place to fight. Now get out of here."

When they had gone, Watts said, "If there's one thing I can't abide, it's a wife-beater."

"In this case, it's a husband-beater," said Sheriff Finch. "She got that black eye chasing him through the woods at night, with an ax handle. Well, how are things going?"

Watts told him. First he gave him a quick summary of newly discovered facts, then he gave him his theory.

Stolen cattle were being brought into Alford's feeding-yards by rail, from a distance. Maybe from the South, maybe from the Dakotas. Then, somehow, they were jumped to the D-Bar-D. At D-Bar-D, they were moved by professional rustlers up through Lazy U, up through Birdsong Ravine, to the large ranches in Canada, probably for big prices. That explained Mr. Underhill's murder; he was an obstacle to them.

"I don't believe it," said the Sheriff, appalled. "I don't much care for Mr. Alford, but nothing like that could happen under my nose. My county's just one big happy family."

"One big father-in-law strangling, husband-beating family."

"Them's minor details," said the sheriff with dignity.

"I might have missed out on some little fact along the way," said Watts emphatically. "But I'm sure the picture I just gave you is right, when you take it all in all. Is there any way you could get into the railroad's shipping records?"

"I might," said the sheriff doubtfully. "My wife's cousin is the shipping clerk. I might, on the quiet, through him. I wouldn't want to do it officially, on the strength of my badge. Because if you're wrong, and you have to be, it could hurt Mr. Alford bad. I take it you want me to look up old records of cattle shipped into him in the past?"

"If you would. For me?"

Sheriff Finch sighed.

When Watts walked into the barroom of the Regina, the big Seth Thomas clock on the wall said twelve minutes after six; Billy Rouse wouldn't show up until six-thirty. He went to the bar and drank a vanilla cream soda, waiting restlessly. The bartender, the new man who had taken his place, was dumpy, middle-aged, and full of exuberance. He pounded his way into Watts' consciousness with a torrent of small talk about race-horses, the weather, and city girls he had known. Finally, Watts said mildly, "Where did you work before you came here?"

"Well," said the barkeep. "It might surprise you to hear that until last week I was a drummer, sold windmill lubricating oil. I gave it up. The profits are too uncertain, and the life's too hard."

"And this is easy," said Watts.

"Nothing to it. You just fill a glass from a bottle. When I was on the road, I was always getting into trouble. Now I'm safe."

"I never thought of it that way," said Watts. "You just stand back there, behind the mahogany, and keep filling glasses from bottles, and trouble can't touch you?"

"Right," said the barkeep, beaming.

Rouse appeared behind the bar, saw Watts, lifted the counter-flap, and stepped out into the room. Together, they went out through the door onto the sidewalk, where they could talk in private.

Watts said, "Billy, I've got twenty-six hundred dollars saved up in the Ranchers' Commercial Bank down at Globe. If you don't see me by the middle of next week, I want you and Hal Irwin to split it fifty-fifty."

Woodenly, Rouse said, "Why?"

"They're going to cancel me out. They've been playing with the idea, yes and no, but they've been afraid to because of Finch. Now they're panicked and have to take the chance."

When Rouse, looking ugly, made no answer, Watts said, "The banker's name is Eads. Just write him and say you're my Apache half brother. Those are the words that will release it to you. Mr. Eads is an old-timer, with his own ideas, and worked out the key himself."

"Listen," said Rouse, in a hoarse, forced whisper. "You're a friend of mine. You know what that means, friend? I couldn't touch a penny of your damned money."

Watts smiled.

"On second thought," said Rouse. "I'll do it. Hal and me will bring up twenty-six hundred dollars worth of Huntsville boys and really wash out this town."

"Then maybe I'd better stay alive," said Watts.

"Maybe you'd better."

After a light supper at the Railroad Cafe, Watts returned to the Star Hotel. He was physically exhausted. As he passed the corner of the deak, headed for pigeonhole Number Four, and bed, the clerk handed him a tan colored envelope. "This was left for you, by Sheriff Finch," said the clerk.

Watts tore it open, drew out a folded sheet of notepaper, and held it to the lamp. It said:

> *Dear Watts, I have checked the railroad shipping records, like you asked me to. The feedingyard hasn't received no in-shipments of any size at all. From Arizona or the Dakotas, or nowheres else. It has to be just what it's supposed to be, an outlet for honest local cattle. So you are all wrong. Anybody can be wrong. I'm sorry. Sheriff Lucian Finch. P. S. These records has to be correct.*

"Anything wrong?" said the clerk solicitously.

"Why should there be?"

"Well, your face says you sure didn't like it, and it's from the sheriff."

Changing the subject, Watts said, "I may leave sometime during the night."

"Naturally," said the clerk sympathetically. "Well, you won't be the first one."

The pigeonhole which was bedroom Number Four had unplaned boardwalls and a dirty mattress on the floor, in a corner. That was it; that was all. No washstand or bowl; you would shave on the backporch. No slop jar; the privy would be out back. There was an inch long candle stub in a broken saucer, but as faint light came in from a lamp in the hall, Watts ignored it. He stretched out on the mattress, clothes and all, but with boots off, and was instantly dead asleep. He slept rangewar style, with his gunbelt under his knee.

He woke up with a start, took his watch to the open doorway, and looked at it in the lamplight from the hall. It was a quarter of three. He put on his boots, his gunbelt, and went down the hall through the empty lobby to the sidewalk.

Shortly after, Pennyman came down the road, riding his stumpy horse, and leading Watts' mare and a loaded pack horse.

"Morning," said Pennyman. "I took your advice and brought us along a pack horse."

XIII

BY NOON the third day, Watts began to believe—as he had suspected all along—that Mr. Pennyman was half wolf himself. He began to understand the need for the pack horse, too, for the trip was becoming interminable. They had gone north, east, west, even south, at a slow, wary walk. In a land that was flat and treeless and arid, they seemed to be traveling constantly behind a rise, or through a clump of alders, or deep in a sage hollow. He had told Pennyman he didn't want to be seen; and though it took a little extra time, Pennyman was delivering. Never talkative, he grew more silent. He was like a man with a painstaking job to do, concentrating ceaselessly on the best way to do it.

The fourth night, as they made camp in a brake of red cedars, Pennyman said, "Remember this morning, in the first quarter, when we scared up that flock of birds out of the grass?"

They had been riding through a shallow dip of land. Watts nodded.

"Well, it wasn't us that scared 'em. My guess is that it was some triflin' goings on at Lazy U. We was just over the rise from the Lazy U ranchyard."

"I don't even remember D-Bar-D."

"You wasn't supposed to."

"When do we reach Birdsong Ravine?"

"About this time tomorrow, or maybe a little earlier."

"Time is important," said Watts. "From here on, Mr. Pennyman, let's make a little better time."

Mr. Pennyman looked hurt. "If you say so, boss. You're the boss, boss."

Next morning they entered the area of the great buttes, the sombre monoliths of shale and sandstone. Some were as lofty as small mountains, and some, more diminutive, were split and partially shattered, like ancient rocky tombs. Under foot were weathered shale and rotting sandstone rubble. Between the buttes, great and small, some close together, some at a distance from each other, was a web of helter-skelter aisles and avenues and passages, veining them, seeming to hold this enormous rocky mass together, honeycombing it. Pennyman took the lead. Watts followed him, looking intently for signs, and seing nothing of interest.

All at once, they were in a deep canyonlike ravine, perhaps forty feet across, its channeled walls looming high on either side and lipped overhead with tangled brush.

"How do you like it?" asked Watts.

"I don't," said Mr. Pennyman. "You can't see the scenery for the scenery. This is the southern mouth of Birdsong. We're about a quarter of a mile from Canada."

The ravine widened into a cavernous, bulbous, open-topped chamber of stone, narrowing again on the far side. To the left the wall rose sheerly in smooth rock. To the right it was undercut, from the groundline up for perhaps twelve feet, eroded by centuries, forming a long narrow cave, open on one side and roofed by shale.

Roofed by shale, and floored with clay.

An here in the clay, as they reached it, Watts saw cattle tracks.

"Here we are," he said, and swung to the ground. Leaving Pennyman in his saddle, he walked beneath the ledge, and dropped to his hands and knees.

Then it happened. From a crevice in the lefthand wall, hardly six yards in front of them, burst Slatterly, shooting wildly. Man and horse, they erupted from the side-ravine in a frenzy, as though they had been shot from a cannon, the horse at full gallop, legs thrashing, hooves flying.

Watts turned, and slipped. He saw the crazed horse run Pennyman down, knock him from his saddle, and pass him.

He saw Pennyman arise, take his rifle from its boot, and shoot the disappearing Slatterly through the back of the head. He saw Slatterly's hat go flying, saw Slatterly slide from his saddle, his spur became entangled in his stirrup, and the horse drag him to a stop.

Watts got to his feet.

"It's never necessary to shoot a man in the back," he said coldly. "Any man."

Mr. Pennyman's flaky jet eyes were unmoved, unexcited. "You live by your rules, I'll live by mine," he said.

Watts disentangled Slatterly's spur from his stirrup. Using his own picket rope as a lead rope, he tied Slatterly's mount to the pack horse.

"Look here a minute, Mr. Pennyman," he said.

Pennyman followed him beneath the overhang of rock.

Here, protected from the weather, were old cow tracks, hundreds of them, track upon track, where great herds passing through the ravine, swelling it from side to side, had churned and molded the thin, clayey soil. And all of them pointed south.

Not north *to* Canada, but south *from* Canada.

"They've been rustling them in," said Watts. "Not taking them out!"

"They sure have," said Pennyman, interested despite himself.

Watts scarcely heard him. This was the answer to everything. Everything.

"And why not?" said Mr. Pennyman. "You ever been up there. Some of their ranches is small kingdoms. Their beef is topnotch, mighty well fed. Fact is, we all got about the very same strains. The only real difference between a Montana cow and a Canadian cow is that they hold their forks different when they eat."

"All right," said Watts briskly. "Let's go."

"Ain't we going to bury the gentleman who got hisself

shot? Though I admit, with this stoney earth and all, I don't much look forward to the prospect."

"We're taking him with us."

"Clear to Folsbee? In this hot sun? I wouldn't recommend it. He'll ferment."

"To Lazy U. We'll make McCracken bury him."

"That's better," said Mr. Pennyman. "Now ain't you glad we brought the pack horse?"

XIV

WHEN WATTS and Pennyman came up to the Lazy U ranch house, they approached it on its blind side, the north. "My!" said Mr. Pennyman, when they caught first sight of its rambling roofs, and bay windows, and snowy white paint. "It reminds me of the beautiful mansion my papa had down in the Mississippi delta. Only when you come right down to it, he didn't exactly have it. It had him, you might say. He sharecropped for it." They passed a few outbuildings, the barn, some sheds, and came into the side yard. Their horses moving at a slow walk, they circled the corner of the house and pulled to a stop at its front. Four horses; three men, one dead.

The house was built facing the east, so that its deep veranda, colonnaded with fluted pillars hung with honeysuckle, would be in pleasant afternoon shade. McCracken lolled on a porch step. He was in his town finery, not his work clothes. He did very little work these days, Watts decided. Above him, on the veranda in a fan-backed wicker chair, was Ursula Underhill. She was in a frothy frock of icy blue, and looked unbearably exquisite and lovely to Watts. The whole scene was that of a courting cowboy, and suddenly, in alarm, Watts wondered if that was precisely what he was looking at.

If McCracken wasn't working on a little side project on his own.

As the little cavalcade hove into view, horror showed on Ursula's face. Alarm and anger showed on McCracken's.

Pennyman said, "Could I bother you folks for a drink of water? It's dusty travellin'."

He dismounted, stiffly, amiable, and walked to the well.

He drank noisily, with gasps of deep satisfaction, while the two on the porch stared at the pack horse and its grisly burden.

"It's Slatterly," said McCracken, getting up. "He's been shot. Who did it?"

"Me," said Mr. Pennyman, from the well.

McCracken examined the body. "In the back of the head," he said, in fury. "In the back!"

Mr. Pennyman rejoined them. "He shot at me four times, and then run," he said sociably. "I shot at him just once. One from four leaves three. He still owed me three shots but seeing he was dead I was gentleman not to take them."

On the porch, Miss Ursula looked confused.

"You feel a special interest in him?" said Watts.

"No," said McCracken, crawfishing. "Why should I?"

"How did it happen?" said Ursula. "And why?"

"He was up in Birdsong Ravine," said Watts. "On a scouting trip, I should say. To be sure everything was okay. We surprised him, and he got scared, and tried to kill us."

"I don't seem to get any of this," said McCracken.

"Neither do I," said Ursula.

Patiently, Watts explained. "Mr. Alford, back in Folsbee, is the head of a cattle stealing ring. The cattle are stolen in Canada, brought down through Birdsong Ravine, staged at D-Bar-D, and then moved into his feedingyards, where he ships them, probably under D-Bar-D bills of sale."

"That's utter nonsense," said Ursula.

"Right now," said Watts. "Right this very minute, he's got a crew of rustlers up there headed by a man named Mogollon."

"And our wonderful neighbor, Mr. Slatterly, was working with them?" said McCracken. "A thing like this is easy to say. I don't believe it."

"Of course not," said Ursula scornfully. "Mr. Denning, I don't understand you and never have. What are you after? What's in all this for you?"

"So they've got this nice little business going," said Watts. "Running herds down from Canada. I'm talking now about back before your days around here. This is lonesome, uninhabited country. There's just Birdsong, and a strip of poor land, which is now the Lazy U, if you'll excuse me, the D-Bar-D. At D-Bar-D, they're safe."

"Well, what do you know about that!" said Mr. Pennyman, fascinated.

"Look how Alford has cut down his risk," said Watts. "He brings his rustlers up from the South, his cattle down from the North. And after the job, cows and rustlers vanish. There's no local trace anywhere around."

"Everything vanishes," said McCracken dryly. "Except your imagination."

"Then what happens?" said Watts. "Mr. Underhill comes here, and builds his house, and sets up a little token ranch—and blocks the way. Some of these Canadian herds are mighty big, and Alford knows it's going to be impossible from now on to move them across this land without discovery. So what did he do?"

"You tell me," said Ursula tolerantly.

"He removed the obstacles. He had your father killed. And then Brad Ives, your fine, honest old foreman."

"You know this for a fact, I guess," said McCracken. "You were there when these two men died?"

"No, I wasn't," said Watts. "But I sure wish I was."

"There's a point you overlook," said Ursula. "There would be one obstacle left. Me."

"If you'll pardon my saying so," said Watts politely. "I don't think they consider you much of an obstacle."

She looked stunned. Watts watched her face. She was beginning to show doubt.

Mr. Pennyman, as though he were discussing an impersonal historical matter, such as Custer's massacre, said, "Who do you reckon killed Mr. Underhill, anyway?"

"Cranfield was hired for the job," said Watts. "But he missed out. It could have been McCracken here."

McCracken, his eyes suddenly wild, said, "When Mr. Underhill was killed, I was up in the Wind River Mountains."

"I said it as a guess," said Watts. "We'll know for sure when Mr. Alford confesses."

"Confesses?" said Ursula, shocked.

Watts told her about the cattle tracks in the ravine. This didn't seem to impress her. She looked unconvinced.

Mr. Pennyman cleared his throat.

"The gentleman on the pack horse," he said innocently. "This Mr. Slatterly, died with his head in my lap, poor soul. He told us all about it before he died, made a full confession about all of them. And a dying statement is legal tender in any court of law."

McCracken went for his gun, and Watts shot him. Something, maybe his natural malignancy, maybe the desperation of Ursula's presence, goaded McCracken into a professional mistake. Not in his draw, which was smooth as silk, one of the best Watts had ever seen, but in his expression. He made a terrible, savage face. That would have been all right, Watts reflected later, if he hadn't started the face a little before he started the draw. Even then his gun sight cleared leather.

He went down in a spin, and was dead before he hit the ground.

Ursula put her hands over her face.

After an interval of silence, Mr. Pennyman said approvingly, "My, that was nice."

When Ursula could speak, she said, "Is it true? Was that why my father was killed?"

"Yes," said Watts.

"And you've been trying to help me all along."

"I guess you could say that."

He could hardly believe it. All at once, she trusted him completely. She hardly seemed like the same girl.

"Go in and put on some traveling clothes," he said. "We're on our way to Folsbee, and Sheriff Finch. All of us."

When she had gone inside, he said, "I'll go to the work shed and see if I can find some shovels."

"But where are we going to put 'em?" said Mr. Pennyman. "Lazy U is brand new. It ain't got no burying ground."

"We'll start one," said Watts. "Where would you suggest?"

Mr. Pennyman looked about him, pursing his lips in thought. "How about over yonder, behind the barn? Where their spirits will be sheltered from the cold winds out of the North, and where it looks like easy digging."

He took off his coat and rolled up his sleeves.

"This is the hardest twenty dollars and thirty cents I ever earnt," he said. "And the busiest."

XV

THEY ARRIVED at Folsbee two days later, in the early afternoon. Watts paid off Mr. Pennyman at court square, and the wolfer headed for his den in the back of the burned-out freight office on Cherry Street. As he left them, he said cautiously, "It's been tolerably nice knowing you both." They stabled the horses at the Cloverleaf, and went together toward the Regina House.

During the long trip in, the affair had been carefully left unmentioned. Now, as they walked along Main Street, Ursula said, "If I told you I'm miserable about the way I've treated you, would you believe me?"

"You don't have to apologize to me," said Watts angrily. "Ever."

"I treated you like a dog."

"When you come right down to it, I am a dog. And a mean one."

"Do you know anything about cows?"

"A little."

"Lazy U needs a new foreman. Will you take the job?"

"No."

"Why not?"

"For one thing, there's a chance I won't live that long. This business isn't finished."

"When it's finished?"

"Still, no. It wouldn't work. I'm a rambler."

"That can be changed."

"It hasn't been yet."

She looked to see if he were joking, but he was dead serious.

Watts left her at the door of the Regina, telling her that he would probably see her later, and crossed the street. He walked through court square, around the corner of the court house, and entered the building by its back door. Sheriff Finch was not in his office. Watts mounted the staircase, and found him in his undershirt, still working on his financial report for the county commissioners. The papers, bills and ledgers were now on Mrs. Sheriff Finch's parlor table. The sheriff looked haggard, a nervous wreck. Watts nodded, and sat down.

"How are you making out?" said Watts. The sheriff was apparently still sweating over the jail food bill.

"I'm down to beef stew," said Sheriff Finch. "Twice a week, that's a hundred and four times a year, Sophronsia feeds 'em a big bowl of beef stew. She makes awful good beef stew. Them nosey county commissioners want to know the cost of everything. Who can figure out the cost of a bowl of beef stew? It's so mushy and mixed up."

"I just got back from Birdsong Ravine," said Watts. "Mr. Pennyman, the wolfer, had to kill Slatterly of D-Bar-D. We stopped at Lazy U coming in, and I had to kill McCracken, their foreman."

The sheriff, gaping slightly, said, "Forevermore!" He laid down his pen very carefully, leaned back in his chair, and loaded up his pipe.

Watts told him about the cow tracks in the ravine.

"So that's what's been happening," said Sheriff Finch. "You were nearer right than you knew."

"Oh, sure," said Watts. "I was exactly right. Except I couldn't tell South from North."

Now he told the sheriff about Nailhead, and Mogollon. This time he said, "They were moving north on a schedule, on a time plan. One of their stops was just south of town here, at Sterrett's Branch, at the old mill. Next, probably, was D-Bar-D. Next, still further north, was Lazy U, where the old man called Dad showed up and talked to McCracken. This tells us two important things."

The sheriff asked, "What?"

"First, Mr. Underhill had to be killed in advance, to clear the way."

"And second?"

"They think they're safe. They'll be back."

"I never met a fellow I liked better than you," said Sheriff Finch. "But I never met nobody that brought me more grief."

"What are you going to do?"

"How do I know? I got to think it over."

"And what about Alford in the meantime?"

"We got no real proof agin Mr. Alford."

Angrily, Watts started for the door.

He was halfway there when the sheriff spoke behind him. "Watts?"

Watts turned. The sheriff's eyes were twinkling. "My you get mad easy. Well, I've thought it over. Be at the Regina tonight at eight-thirty."

Watts had his supper that night with Hal Irwin in the kitchen of the Fort Kearny Saloon. He was in a state of tension, because he knew that, when you come right down to it, Sheriff Finch was right. There wasn't a shred of real evidence against Alford, or anybody else, for that matter. It was touch and go. Say a warning had somehow got up into Canada to Mogollon that Slatterly and McCracken were dead? The tracks in the canyon were just tracks, and incriminated no one in particular. He had seen men as bad as Alford get out of snares a good deal worse. A year from now, say, he, Watts, could very well be tending a bar in Texas, or New Mexico, and Mr. Alford could still be running his prosperous feedingyards here in Folsbee, and walking the town's streets, and having people salute him with respect and maybe even with sympathy. A court trial could accomplish magic things. For that matter, it might not even come to court.

Hal Irwin, a look of understanding on his scarred face, studied him sympathetically as they ate. He said, "The world's terrible, isn't it? You've worked like a dog, and got nowhere. Right?"

Watts glanced at him, surprised.

"I've been that way myself, lots of times," said Irwin. "You're half dead. You've been going too hard. And I got better sense than try to cheer you up. I tried to cheer up one fellow once, and he put it all on me, and did his best to bite off my ear."

In spite of himself, Watts smiled. He felt a little better, but not much.

It was at that moment, when he was in his deepest despondency, that he suddenly thought of something. It was a little thing, trivial, but little things, if you gave them enough attention, could become big things.

He got to his feet, and said, "Thanks for the meal, Hal."

Irwin said, "What now?"

"I was just wondering about Billy Rouse."

"Billy Rouse?" said Irwin fiercely. "He hasn't got anything to do with all this. You leave him alone. He's as good a man as you are."

"Better," said Watts. "I didn't mean it that way. I was

just wondering what he did with the bar money three weeks ago?"

Watts came into the Regina bar from the street door, and sat himself at a table in the corner. Behind the mahogany, Rouse and his new assistant, the windmill-oil drummer, were medium busy. When Rouse saw him, he lifted the flap at the end of the bar, came across the room, and sank heavily in a chair beside him. "I hear there was a bit of a fracas up at Lazy U," he said. "And you outlived it. Well, there goes my twenty-six hundred dollar inheritance. But most of all, I'm going to miss Mr. McCracken. The world won't be the same without him."

When Watts, wrapped in thought, simply nodded, Rouse said, "And I hear Mr. Pennyman, the wolfer, got his jackrabbit, too. Slatterly."

"Shot him in the back," said Watts in distaste.

"Glad to hear it. Right and proper," said Rouse. "I've often had the urge to shoot him in the back myself."

"Billy," said Watts. "Put your mind back to the days before I came. What did you do with the bar money then? At night, when you closed up?"

"Sometimes I gave it to Mr. Underhill, sometimes to Mr. Selden."

When Watts waited, Rouse said, "And whoever I gave it to would put it in the safe, naturally."

"Because they both had keys."

"Yes," said Rouse. "At first."

"At first?" said Watts. "What do you mean?"

"Couple of weeks before you showed up, Mr. Selden lost his key."

"How?"

"He couldn't remember for the life of him. When you lose a key to an important door, the careful thing is to change the door's lock. But a safe key's different. You'd have to throw away the safe, and get a new one, and that's too expensive. So they took a chance, and went on using it. When Mr. Underhill was in town, he carried the key. When he went out to Lazy U, he passed it over to Mr. Selden. They shuttled it back and forth that way."

"It's not that key I'm interested in," said Watts. "It's the one that disappeared."

The bar clock said five minutes after eight. Watts went through the arch which led to the lobby, picked a comfortable chair against the back wall where he could watch the street through the big front windows, and tried to relax. His bones ached with weariness.

Outside, dusk darkened into night. Mr. Selden came through the lobby, lighting the lamps in a proprietorial sort of way, making quite an official business of it. When he saw Watts, he mumbled something unintelligible which Watts took as a startled, but polite, greeting.

At twenty-five minutes after eight, Ursula came down the stairs. Across the lobby, Watts got to his feet, but she simply nodded to him, turned left, and entered the seclusion of the ladies' waitingroom. She closed the door behind her. Mr. Selden, behind his desk, watched her intently.

At exactly eight-thirty, Sheriff Finch and Mr. Alford came along the sidewalk outside the window. Mr. Alford was chatting amiably. Sheriff Finch looked frozen and unhappy.

As they came into the lobby, Watts arose and joined them.

Alford said affably, "Good evening, Mr. Denning."

They walked to the ladies' waitingroom, and Mr. Alford entered.

The sheriff touched Watts' arm and slowed him to a stop.

"What's going on?" said Watts in a low voice.

"Plenty," said Sheriff Finch in a rough whisper. "After you left, I went to the railroad shipping office and checked on their out-recods. Over the past years, D-Bar-D has been sending out big shipments. This was all I needed, I thought. I was all set to hunt up Mr. Alford for questioning, and what do you think happened. He come to the courthouse himself, and looked me up."

"Why?"

"He told me his story and asked my help. He said you put it into his head that maybe D-Bar-D had been shipping stolen cattle through his feedingyards. He didn't want to get into any trouble over it. He thought it was his duty as a decent, upstanding citizen to report it to me."

"And Slatterly is dead, and nobody can contradict him."

"I told him Slatterly was dead. He said this was news to him."

They stared at each other.

Finch said, "We got no case against him whatever. I'm an old-timer in the sheriff trade, and I know what I'm talking about."

"Then why did you bring him here just now?"

"I didn't bring him. I guess you could say he brought me. He said he wanted to get us all together and tell us about it. He says he admits it looks bad for him, if you don't know how innocent he is."

When Watts could speak, he said, "If he wants to tell us all about it, we'll let him."

They stepped into the ladies' waitingroom.

XVI

MR. ALFORD sat on the horsehair couch, beside Ursula, his bony hands on his scrawny knees. The stained-glass lamp on the small table threw his shadow onto the wallpaper behind him, a hunched, black crow. He was explaining to her the situation in which he had, unfortunately, and innocently, found himself. She was listening intently, entirely unconvinced. This wasn't the same Miss Underhill at all, Watts realized. As Watts and the sheriff took chairs, Alford said, "So we're all back again to where we were before the unpleasantness began, good firm friends."

"I never was a friend of yours," said Watts.

"You are now," said Alford generously. "I'm a forgiving sort of man."

Watts said, "Did you ever have any dealings with an outfit down at Nailhead which calls itself the Bear Paw Cattle Association?"

"Never heard of it," said Alford, graciously.

"If you'd had business with it, your records would show it, wouldn't they?"

"They certainly would."

"May we look at them?"

"You certainly may."

So he had altered his ledgers. There was nothing here, either.

Sheriff Finch said uneasily, "Better drop the subject, Mr. Denning. Mr. Alford could take it into his head to sue you."

"Not me," said Alford. "I wouldn't sue anyone. He means no harm."

The door opened and Mr. Selden came in with an extra lamp. His face was twitching with curiosity. He placed the lamp on the table beside the other, said, "I thought you might like a little more light," and loitered at the doorway. When Ursula said, "Thank you," he left.

Same old Mr. Selden, Watts thought, yearning to eavesdrop.

From his chair, Watts appraised Alford. He was completely unbothered, genuinely at ease. It just didn't seem possible.

Watts said, "Mr. Alford, I'd like to ask you a couple of questions about McCracken. I understand you produced him for Miss Underhill."

"That's right. McCracken came into the feedingyards, out of a job. I talked to him and decided he was a good cowman. Miss Ursula badly needed a foreman."

"McCracken was a professional gunman."

"That's your opinion," said Mr. Alford. "My opinion is that he was just a good-natured, clumsy cowboy. Though I'm not criticizing you, of course. I understand he drew first."

Sheriff Finch sat up and blinked. If Alford was so well posted on the fight at Lazy U, he must also have heard of Slatterly's death when he denied it.

Before the Sheriff could speak, Alford said, "I heard about that *after* I spoke with you, Sheriff.

Once more Mr. Selden came into the room. This time he had a tray with a coffeepot, cups, and saucers. The pressure of not knowing what was happening had turned him haggard. "Coffee?" he said. His smile was ghastly. He was ashen gray.

When no one answered him, and as he reached for the doorknob, Watts addressed him. "That key. The one you say you lost. Did you give it to Cranfield, or Mr.

Alford? You know the one I mean. The one they framed me with, out at Knuckle Springs."

Selden gaped.

Alford said quietly, "You may go now, Selden. This is a private conversation."

"I'd like to hear the answer." said Sheriff Finch with a lazy drawl.

"Why?" said Selden hollowly, stalling, desperately trying to ward off inevitable disaster.

"I gave it to Mr. Alford," he said dully. "He said he wanted to play a joke on his good friend Mr. Underhill."

The silence was ghastly.

"He paid me twenty dollars for it," said Selden miserably. "But then he had me in his trap."

"And later," said Watts. "He used it and forced you to kill Mr. Underhill."

"I didn't kill Mr. Underhill," said Selden. "That night, I was trembling so that I could hardly even hold a gun."

"So Alford killed him himself," said Watts.

"That's right," said Selden. "He got exasperated and did it himself."

Sheriff Finch said calmly, "Mr. Alford, I place you under arrest for murder. And I enjoy doing it."

"On the word of a drunk?" said Alford. "I'll ruin you."

"I doubt it," said Watts. "Now I get the whole picture."

When no one answered, he said, "Just before supper tonight, Mr. Alford heard about McCracken and Slattery; Mr. Pennyman probably spread the story. He knew he was finished."

"Why finished?" said Alford.

"Because one of these days Mogollon and his gang will be driving in that Canadian herd of stolen cattle. And when they do, and when they're caught, because Sheriff Finch will be waiting for them, they'll have some testimony themselves on this thing. They won't want any part of Mr. Underhill's murder."

"Then why didn't he stay clean away from me?" said Sheriff Finch. "Why did he look me up at the courthouse this evening and—"

"He was playing for precious time," said Watts. "When Mogollon showed up, he was going to be a dead duck. So he tried to pacify you in the interval. Or even part of the interval."

"How would that help him in the long run?" said Ursula.

"It would be the difference between freedom and jail, maybe hanging. You see he was going to leave Folsbee, and in a hurry. But he didn't want to leave a poor man. It was late in the day, and the banks were closed. It's my guess that in the morning he was going to draw out his entire cash deposit, and make tracks."

"What about my assets in property?" said Alford, sneering. "What about my feedingyard?"

"Who wants a feedingyard in prison," said Watts. "You wanted to be long gone, and I mean now."

"But he's an important man," said the sheriff. "The bankers here respect him. They'd come down and open up for him, even at night—"

"That would be a disaster," said Watts. "Too sensational. That would be cutting his own throat."

Mr. Alford stood in the light of the two lamps, frozen. He bared his teeth, but said nothing.

"He almost got away from us," said Watts.

"But not quite," said Sheriff Finch.

Mr. Selden went to the coffeepot. "I think I'll have a cup of coffee," he said quietly.

After they had all gone from the room, Sheriff Finch with his prisoner, Selden back behind his wicket in the lobby, Ursula said, "What about that job with me, as foreman at Lazy U? Will you take it?"

"Why not?" said Watts. "I'm going to tell you something I've never told anyone else. I'm lonely when I'm not around cows. This may be my last chance. I'll never have a ranch of my own again."

"Life is full of surprises," she said contentedly.